# NOBODY'S FOOL

# NOBODY'S FOOL

## Marten Claridge

Walker and Company
New York

First published in the United States of America in 1991
by Walker Publishing Company, Inc.

Published simultaneously in Canada by Thomas Allen & Son
Canada, Limited, Markham, Ontario

Library of Congress Cataloging-in-Publication Data

Claridge, Marten.
Nobody's fool / Marten Claridge.
p.   cm.
ISBN 0-8027-5793-6
I. Title
PR6053.L288N6   1991
823'.914--dc20                           91-6631
CIP
Printed in the United States of America

2   4   6   8   10   9   7   5   3   1

With love and thanks to Liz
and all my friends who have made
the hard times such good times.

# NOBODY'S FOOL

# Prologue

Odd that.

How it was always the feet that captured his attention. Mesmerised him almost. Not the white hairless thighs or curveless hips or the stretched ribcage and dangling arms. Nor even the hairless mound or young breasts, nipples pointing like sightless eyes at the ceiling. Neither was it the twisted neck in the grip of the noose or the bulging, comical eyes that drew his gaze. And never the grotesque mask, the slack mouth and lolling tongue or the blue-grey pallor of the skin. No. It was always the feet that riveted his attention, held him spellbound.

Why, he neither knew nor cared.

Tiny feet, even for a girl of her tender years. Like dolls' feet. Now lifeless, they turned inwards, big toes touching, sheathed in cotton socks.

He wondered why he hadn't removed the socks. Perhaps a momentary impulse – he couldn't remember. The motives behind his actions had become so obscure recently they no longer merited contemplation. Leave the final analysis to the psychologists – it would be their problem, not his.

He stood before the girl, her dead eyes level with his.

1

He saw nothing new. He ran his hands over her skin, cold and bloodless beneath the pads of his fingers.

A globule of dried blood clung to her left breast. He smeared it off with his forefinger, saw the small break in the skin where he'd bitten too hard. Forced to stir her from apathy, he'd become angry in the process. Too bad. For her.

He removed an ivory-backed razor from his pocket and with a single slash, cut her down. She sprawled to the ground in an untidy heap, face in the dirt floor, buttocks in the air.

So ungainly.

He donned gloves and set to work. In ten minutes he had her wrapped and tied in bin-liners. It was the fashion, after all.

He left her by the door, removed his gloves, and stepped out into the evening. He climbed the garden path, humming tunelessly, the July sky pinkening like a spreading, watery bloodstain. He entered the house and went upstairs to his study. He could hear the tinny orchestrations of Mother-dear's television downstairs, but the sounds retreated when he shut the door.

If rooms reflect personalities, then he was not only unpretentious, but his life was sparse. In the corner behind the door stood an old oak desk which had belonged to his father. It had lions' mouths for handles. Three folders lay open on its top, along with a sheaf of black and white photographs. The walls were white and unadorned; the mantelpiece, a dusty ledge. The varnished pine floorboards bare except for a white mohair rug, in the centre of which stood a tall leather-backed armchair commanding a broad view of the garden through the dormer window.

To anyone else, a cold characterless room. To him, retreat.

He sank into the armchair and stared out at the twilight, his thoughts turned inward. They careered down well-worn paths as he waited for darkness to fall.

Darkness, because in darkness there is anonymity.

It was time.

He was already packed. The suitcase was on his bed, primed. Camera-case in the darkroom, also primed. Janice Young in a bag, ready for the car. Then deal with the Mother-dear.

He carried his suitcase out to the car and positioned it carefully on the back seat. Then he opened the boot and unfolded a transparent plastic sheet which he spread carefully across the floor. He was a man who recognized the value of traces.

The sky was metallic-blue and starlit. Light slashed across the lawn from the downstairs window. He made his way cautiously back down the garden path. A goods train rumbled by, clattering over the points beyond the line of trees. He could feel the vibration through the soles of his shoes.

He carried the packaged body to the car. The girl seemed heavier now, as though congealed blood and stiffening tissues exerted more strain on gravity. Janice fitted neatly into the boot. *How* considerate.

Mother-dear was a shrivelled-up prune. Folds of

sagging flesh had transformed her cheeks into jowls, and her dark eyes had sunk into lined craters. She had a hairline mouth with pursed lips which puckered when, like now, she was without her dentures. Her hair was white and greasy beneath the hairnet. She wore a grey pleated skirt, cream blouse, navy-blue cardigan and fluffy pink slippers. Sometimes she revolted him. She did so now.

'Good evening, Mother-dear.' He picked up the remote-control for the television from the small table by her chair and lowered the volume.

Mother-dear glared. 'I was listening to that.'

'And so was half the neighbourhood.' He walked to the window, checked the lock.

'You know my hearing's bad.'

'Not so bad you can't monitor every move I make in this house.'

He replaced the remote-control console and adjusted a pack of cigarettes on her table so that it lay aligned to all four corners.

'I'm going away for a few days,' he said. 'There's plenty of food, so you won't starve. The exercise should do you good.' He touched the walking-stick which hung over the back of her chair and smirked. 'You should get about more, see the world.'

'I've seen all I want to see.' Her voice was flat and toneless as always. She grabbed the remote-control the way a junkie grabs a packet from a dealer. But she didn't turn the volume up.

'That's a different world out there,' he said, crossing to the window and drawing the curtains. 'It's not like television.'

'I happen to prefer television.'

'Cut the self-pity, Mother-dear. No-one cares.'

'I care.' She was watching the screen again. She'd been pretty once, he recalled. But she'd been in love then – and not with his father.

'I'll be back Monday,' he told her. 'You be good, okay?'

'You're always going away. You never spend any time with me anymore.'

'Things to do, places to go.'

'We used to do so much together,' she said wistfully. 'Now you spend your time getting drunk or down in the barn. What on earth do you do in there?'

'Clearing up. You know, looking after the boys.'

'You and your damn snakes. I think you prefer their company to mine.'

'Don't be silly, Mother-dear. They need looking after, just like you. You know me – try to keep everyone happy.'

'Mm.'

He planted a kiss delicately on her hairnet. 'Goodbye, Mother-dear,' he said, wiping his mouth on the back of his hand. She didn't move, she didn't speak. He closed the door behind him and the television began to blare again.

The car started immediately. In two minutes he was on Morningside Road. He passed the clock, on up Comiston Road. The roads were busy with Saturday night traffic. People coming in from Oxgangs and Comiston for a night on the town. Poison for their minds, flesh for their flesh.

At the top of the hill he turned into Greenbank Drive, leaving the traffic behind. He drove slowly to where the road divided, pulled in and waited five minutes, saw nobody. Okay. He turned and drove back, stopping by a padlocked gate in the fence which ran the length of the drive. He donned gloves and left the motor running.

The chain on the gate could have been a daisy-chain the way it snapped in the teeth of his pliers. He dropped both in the boot of the Escort, dropped his camera in his pocket, scooped out the neatly packaged Janice and carried her through the gate. He pushed through dense undergrowth and thorny bushes. Through a line of trees to a low stone wall beyond which lay the dried-up bed of a small stream. He tossed the body over the wall, took out his camera and shot off five exposures on automatic, the flashes bright explosions in the quiet dark. His heart pumped faster as adrenalin coursed his veins. He returned briskly to the car. As he pulled out, he had time to notice again the sign just inside the gate that read: NO TIPPING. He allowed himself a smile.

Traffic flowed like a sluggish metal river down through Tollcross onto Lothian Road. It took him longer than usual to reach the Glasgow road, but once there, the traffic thinned and all but disappeared. It wasn't long before he joined the M9, mild cross-winds tugging gently at the wheel beneath his fingers. He maintained a steady speed of fifty-five, taking pleasure in the dark passing countryside.

Ninety minutes later he passed through Callander. On the outskirts of town he left the A84 and took a small B-road west. He slowed as the road narrowed, then

6

twisted and turned through leafy tunnels, the glint of moonlit river to his left, the steep forested slopes to his right. Then, past the surging black mass of the falls, the more tranquil expanse of Loch Cruik came into view through gaps in the shoreline trees. Then the village came up on him fast, fast as it always did.

Ballaig.

White stone cottages, set back from the road by a wide pavement where cars were parked. Signs in windows offering 'Bed & Breakfast'. A small craft shop. On the left, a group of wooden chalets, just this side of the river. A garage, ever the way he remembered it, with its solitary pump out front and ramshackle building behind. Further on, where the road began to bend out of the village, Bovellie the Grocers and opposite, the Ballaig Hotel. The only sign of life, the lights and shadows that moved behind drawn curtains.

He pulled over onto the pavement and parked outside a guest-house. Vacancies, said the card in the window.

He collected his bags, locked the car and knocked at the door, noticing the new coat of paint and the wooden tub of flowers by the door before it opened.

'Cathy,' he said.

'Dominic. Come in.'

She was in her late thirties, with long dark hair tied back. She wore baggy jeans and a yellow granddad-shirt unbuttoned low enough to see that she wore no bra. She used no make-up apart from the shadow of blue around her eyes. He walked past her into the narrow hall.

'Good drive?' she asked, closing the door.

The hall was low and narrow, she had to squeeze by.

7

He caught the familiar scent of her body as she passed.

A man's angry voice came from a room off the hall. 'Who is it?'

'It's Dominic, Joe,' Cathy called. 'I told you he was coming for a few days.'

'You tell me nothing, woman,' the voice growled. 'I might as well be dead.'

'Don't start that again. I've enough on my hands already. I'll show Dominic his room.'

'He should know where it is by now. And ask him what bloody time is this to arrive.'

Cathy led Dominic up the stairs to a small room at the back of the house. Of course he knew the way: eleven years was long enough to learn your way around any house.

The room overlooked the courtyard, the garden, and the heath beyond. It had been his room once.

'He's getting worse every day. I don't know how much more I can take,' Cathy said, switching on the light, walking across to draw the curtains. 'I suppose it's what you get if you marry an older man. You end up with a patient.'

Dominic dropped his cases on the bed. 'I don't understand why you married him in the first place.'

'You wouldn't, Dominic, would you? You left, remember. You moved to the city. You don't know what it was like.'

'I could have known.'

'So you always say. But you always go back.' She hadn't moved from the window, was watching him unpack. The bitterness in her voice did not escape him.

He went over, closed her in his arms. She pushed him gently away.

'Don't, please.' Weariness replaced the bitterness.

Dominic laughed. 'He won't last long, Cathy. He's on his last legs. You'll soon be free of the old sod.'

'Don't talk like that!'

'And then you'll be able to live, do what you like. Think of it . . .'

'I do. That's what's so damned . . .' Her voice trailed off in frustration. She came over, took his arm. 'I'm sorry, Dominic. Not much of a welcome, I'm afraid.'

Joe Gillespie's hoary voice drifted up the stairs. 'What's taking so long, woman? Think I don't know what's going on up there?'

Cathy made a rueful face. 'I'd better go. See you tomorrow. Breakfast's at eight.'

He locked the door behind her and went over to the wash-basin where he stood for a long time studying his reflection in the mirror.

Forty-one years old, with an almost boyish face that belied his age. Delicate curves, large brown eyes. Straight nose, if a little small. Fair hair, cropped short, ears flat against his skull. A generous mouth with full-blooded lips.

There was a change in his reflected image. He could feel it. Something strange about his eyes. Nothing he could define – just that they were different. Alien.

He laughed, a short bark.

He finished unpacking, then stripped off, washed and dried with the towel provided. There'd been no wash-basin in his day, no light green wallpaper, no dressing-table, no 'Highland Scene' prints on the wall. It had been a child's room then. A strange child's room.

He brushed his teeth, counting each stroke of the stiff brush. Memories collected on the borders of his consciousness like stormclouds gathering on the horizon. He pulled back the covers of the bed, checked for snakes. None. Patted the pillows, then crawled naked between the cool white sheets. He lay back, arms by his sides, legs straight, like a corpse embalmed.

For a while he stared at the ceiling, letting the day's events filter through his mind with slow precision as night-sounds came to him through the open window.

Home again, was his final thought.

# Chapter One

No missing it.

Beneath a steady drizzle from grey skies, Greenbank Drive was a mess of badly parked cars and flashing blue lights. Men and women, uniform and plainclothed, stood around in small groups awaiting instruction. Dogs pulled handlers through the long grass where men in overalls on hands and knees collected anything that wasn't grass in plastic bags for evidence. Ribbons marked out perimeters and beyond them the kind of people who can smell a murder ten miles off and like to make a day of it. The scene was familiar.

I parked badly, pulled up my collar and pushed through the crowd. The air was full of static from Personal Radios and the subdued buzz of speculation. The constable at the gate nodded me through.

I was on a strip of untidy wasteland that runs the length of Greenbank Drive. A minefield of dogshit and used condoms beneath unhappy trees, tangled vines, weeds and overgrown bushes. The strip slopes down to a low stone wall, a ditch, and beyond, the tidy gardens of houses where bodies are never found.

Harry was down by the wall. I made my way down,

ducking branches and keeping to the plastic sheeting laid down to protect any clues along the established path of entry to the locus.

Harry did a double-take. 'Frank! What the hell are you doing here?'

'I'm not sure,' I told him. Twenty minutes ago, I'd received a call from the Procurator-fiscal's office. Report to the man himself at the locus on Greenbank Drive. End of message. End of two weeks sitting on my arse.

We shook hands.

'You must be tired of living,' Harry said. 'If Kettle finds you here, he'll crucify you.'

'And on the third day, McMorran shall rise again and smite that ugly Irish bastard in the teeth,' I said. 'Let him try.'

Detective Sergeant Harold Todd smiled a nervous smile and looked anxiously about. He's a big man, Harry – stands six-two in his boots and about the same around his chest. With his red, acned face, thick neck and tufts of sandy hair over his ears, he sometimes looks more like a farmer than a cop. His restless eyes are stone-grey sponges that absorb every little detail, and his mouth is that of a man who takes himself seriously and expects the rest of the world to do the same. Today he wore his usual shapeless grey suit and belted raincoat and looked every inch the plod he is.

'Where's the fiscal?' I asked. I knew he was around somewhere because ID Branch were already at work. Harry shrugged.

'About. Somewhere.'

'Who's the pathologist?'

'Parrish.' Harry indicated the screens set up beyond the wall. 'He's with the body now.'

I nodded. Parrish was good, one of the best. Some pathologists didn't like coming to the locus; he did. Said it helped in the post-mortem examination and recon-struction of the case.

'And Kettle?' I asked.

'On his way.'

'It's not the end of the world, Harry.' I couldn't help the smile. It was good to be back – however temporary.

'It might be when he gets here,' Harry said, shuffling his feet, watching them shuffle. He didn't look up as he asked: 'When's the inquiry?'

'No date yet. I think they want to let the press cool off.'

'And you? How do you feel?'

'I'm all right, Harry.'

'Then why the drinking?'

I couldn't answer that. Not in a way that Harry would understand. We stood and looked at this and that until the silence had finished speaking for itself.

'You were right,' he said eventually, when our eyes met across the space of our thoughts. 'It's The Hangman again. Same MO. A man out with his dog found the body. A young girl, fourteen, fifteen, wrapped in bin-liners.'

'So I was right,' I said harshly. 'Is that supposed to make me feel good?'

Harry looked hurt. 'If they'd listened——'

'The girl might still be alive? Rubbish, Harry, and you know it. Where's the guy who found her?'

'Over with the Heavy Mob.'

13

'Is he sound?' I asked.

'They're checking him out now.'

The Audio-visual team had set up their equipment ten yards from the wall in a small clearing that commanded a wide view of the locus. I caught the eye of one of the men and beckoned him over.

I pointed to the line of rubbernecks beyond the cordon. 'Get some close-ups of the sightseers over there. Video and stills, if you can. I want all their faces.'

The photographer shrugged like he thought I was crazy. 'If that's what you want, sir,' he said, and wandered off.

'You think he could be there?' Harry asked, scanning the crowd beyond the cordon. I didn't answer.

'Coming?' I said.

Harry's face screwed into a mask of disgust. 'I've seen enough,' he said.

'Okay. Then see what you can find out about the guy with the dog.' He stalked off as I climbed the wall and pushed inside the screens.

Jack Parrish was kneeling by the body writing copiously in a loose-leaf pad. He greeted me with a raising of his head and an airy wave of his long arm. I tossed him a compressed smile and looked at the girl.

She lay like a piece of twisted cod on a fishmonger's slab, stiffened in an almost foetal position on the bin-liners which had been carefully cut away to allow access to photographers and pathologist. She was naked but for white ankle-socks. Her face was small and triangular with a pert nose and pointed teeth, framed by hair the colour of golden sand.

14

I squatted down for closer scrutiny. I noted the lividity along the side of her body where the red blood cells had obeyed the laws of gravity and settled in the lower vessels. I looked for damage to her arms, but there were no bruises, cuts, or scratches – the usual signs of struggle. I noted the bruises on the side of her neck and just below her left nipple and tried to suppress the bile that rose in my throat.

I looked into her eyes, seeking some kind of expression. If I saw anything, it was resignation.

Parrish finished writing and put away his pad. He was a tall, gangly man in his early forties with a face that was drawn and thoughtful. His nose was a pinched blob of flesh and his pale skin was pulled tight across angular bones, like parchment stretched to dry. His hair was thick and wild and dark and kept falling across eyes that were deep and ponderous. A brown tweed jacket and rust-coloured jersey hung from his coathanger bones and black flannels flapped like wind-socks around his legs.

'Back on the beat?' he asked, with a tight smile.

'Could be,' I said.

'You're off-limits you know, Frank. Everyone's been warned off. You can hear the sound of sharpening knives every time someone mentions your name.'

'So ignore me then.'

He stood up and lowered his dark eyes onto mine.

'I'm not everyone.' He took a long thermometer from his bag and inserted it carefully into the girl's rectum.

'Glad to hear it,' I said. 'When did she die?'

'You want the precise minute?' The sarcasm was not unfriendly. He pulled out the thermometer, took the reading and made a note in his pad. Then wiped the

15

thermometer on a rag, returned it to his bag and peeled off his plastic gloves. 'You know the score, Frank. I can only give you a guesstimate. I might be able to be more specific after the autopsy but . . .'

'A guesstimate, then.'

'Sometime between midday and six o'clock yesterday afternoon.'

'I thought the presence of lividity narrows down the time . . .'

'Not in this case. All it means is the body's been lying here at least eight hours. That's how long it takes for the lividity to become fixed.'

Parrish took some white plastic bags from his case and handed several to me. We worked in silence, slipping them over her extremities – head, hands and feet – then taping them in place. When we had finished, I asked him how she died.

'Well,' he said, 'the rope was still around her neck when I got here – embedded about a quarter of an inch. My initial impression was she died by asphyxiation, but when I cut away the rope, I found bruises on each side of the voice-box – *below* the impression of the rope. So I can't say for definite yet whether she died of the strangulation or the subsequent suspension.'

'Any indication of assault?'

'Attempted, maybe. But again, I can't say for sure until after the autopsy. There's no external damage – except the bruises on her thighs there – and she's still *virgo intacta*. However, I did find traces of semen in her umbilical but you'll have to check with Forensic if you want more on that.'

16

'At least she was spared something.'

'Yeah?' Parrish said with heavy sarcasm. 'Lucky girl.'

'You know what I mean, Jack.'

'Sure. Don't worry. You notice anything strange about the girl?'

'How d'you mean?'

'Her pubic hair's been shaved. Recently, I think. Wouldn't you say that was rather odd for a girl of her age?'

'Did she do it herself?' I asked.

He shook his head. 'Can't really tell. Not now. Maybe later.'

We lapsed into what could have been a two-minute silence, both staring at the body of the girl.

Parrish eventually broke the spell. 'Know what this is?' he said. 'An act against humanity. Revenge, frustration, whatever. The man who throttled her was throttling all of us. You, me, everyone. The whole damn world in the shape of a wee lassie. That's a sick and dangerous man out there.'

'You're telling me?' I said.

'Anybody who'll listen,' he said, and picked up his bag. 'Will you be at the autopsy?'

'When will it be?'

'Soon as she's been identified.'

'I don't know,' I told him. 'I'm not even sure what I'm supposed to be doing here.'

'Like that, eh? Well, I'll see you around.' He dipped his head to go through the screens and I was alone with the girl.

I stood there in the sea of timelessness that is the home

of the dead, and thought about a young girl, probably untouched by the hand of a lover and who now, in the space of twenty-odd hours, had been touched by the vicious hands of her killer, the impartial hands of a pathologist, and the tentative hands of a detective. And still to come, mortuary porters, technicians, under-takers . . .

And I thought about . . . Hell, I don't recall the exact substance of my thoughts or how long I stood there. Only the direction in which they were set by the forces which were the sum of my life.

I heard the voice, placed it, ignored it.

'McMorran!'

We met in a tangle of briar.

'What the fuck are you doing here, Inspector?' he demanded, in a voice that could invoke rutting fever in a Canadian moose. You had a choice. You could call him Kettle, Chief Inspector or sir. I shrugged and called him nothing.

'You got a professional death-wish, McMorran?' He was a huge block of a man who might have been hewn from Castle Rock if it hadn't been so soft. He had a torch of red hair that met in a V on the crags of his forehead and his features were wide and flat and smooth as polished stone. His eyes were slitted chips of quartz and even his eyelashes looked aggressive.

'I was bored,' I said.

'Whatsamatter?' he snapped. 'Pubs run dry? You're out of order, pal. Go get bored somewhere else.'

I brushed past him without a word. He called me back.

'How'd you hear about this?' he demanded.

I sighed, let him hear it. 'The fiscal called me, told me to come out here.'

'Barrie? What's he want with you?' He jerked the cigarette from his mouth, exhaling the way you would if a train hit your solar-plexus.

'Where is the little shit? I'll soon sort——' He broke off, glaring over my shoulder.

I turned to watch the small, neatly-dressed figure of George Barrie pick his way through the undergrowth. Manoeuvring his umbrella and placing his patent leather shoes carefully, he looked more like Mary Poppins than the Procurator-fiscal. Although half the size of Kettle and twenty times as pretty, there was nothing extraordinary about his face – but he always left me with an impression of slicked-back hair, clear clear eyes and perfect teeth.

'Morning, Harlan,' he said to Kettle, then dipped his sleek head in my direction. 'Frank.' He was on first-name terms with the whole human race.

Kettle jerked his thumb at me. 'What's *he* doing here? He's supposed to be suspended.'

I made to walk away but Barrie put a hand on my arm. 'Stick around, Frank,' he said. 'I'd like a word.'

Kettle dropped his cigarette, ground it into the mud with his boot and killed me not-so-softly with his eyes. 'This is a blatant breach of regulations,' he said, through clenched teeth. 'I'll have to see the Chief Constable.'

Barrie was unruffled. 'I already did. We both agree that the priority right now is to find the killer. Anything else can wait.'

Kettle's face strained to match the colour of his hair,

the buttons on his waistcoat threatening to burst all over the place. I bent down and picked up the fag-end he had discarded and put it carefully in my pocket. I like to live dangerously.

Kettle snorted and pushed past without a word. He did not look pleased. George Barrie and I looked at each other and we both held onto our thoughts like they were the copyrights of our lives.

'Well, Frank,' he said, finally. 'What do you reckon? Are we dealing with a serial killer?'

'No doubt about it. Identical MO. Same kind of rope. No apparent signs of assault. Same bin-liners.'

'But this time it's a girl . . .'

'Dead is dead,' I said.

'I heard you expected a repeat.'

'The murder of the Watson boy was too much of a ritual to be a one-off,' I told him. 'Why hang him up after he was already dead? It made no sense unless it was part of some kind of ritual. And rites are for repeating.'

'But so soon?'

'Two, three weeks can be a long time to any desperate man.'

'And all we've got to show for it is one more body. When did she die?'

'Parrish reckons sometime between midday and six o'clock yesterday afternoon. She was probably left hanging a couple of hours and then dumped here after dark. That would make it any time after nine. We'll need to appeal for witnesses.'

'Mm . . .' Barrie pinched his nose, sniffed, and surveyed the locus as Harry came plodding over.

'Any ID on the girl yet?' I asked him.

'They're still checking.'

'What about the guy who found her?'

'Ex-Army. No form. Seems okay.'

'Tell me more.'

'Name's Ronald Brown. He says he walks his dog along here every morning – only this morning, the dog disappeared and he had to go look for it. Found it tearing at the bin-bags the girl was in. He checked the girl was dead and then phoned from one of the houses across the road. That's about it.'

'Where is he now?'

'In my car.'

'Okay. Take him in. Get his statement and prints, then take him home. See what you can dig up.'

Harry glanced at the fiscal.

Barrie nodded. 'Do it, Sergeant,' he said. Harry grunted and plodded back to his car.

By now, the whole locus looked like a lesson in chaos. The mortuary van and ambulance had arrived, the crowd beyond the cordon had doubled and swelling ranks of the press were jostling for position. A tailback of traffic had formed in both directions while Kettle raged back and forth, cursing everything that moved. I returned my attention to the fiscal.

He said, 'Lucky someone found the body so soon. It could have lain there for weeks, and no-one ever known.'

'Yeah. Lucky.'

They were removing the body now, Jack Parrish escorting the stretcher like it was his own daughter in the

21

body-bag. He was possessive that way; no-one would touch the body until he'd finished the autopsy. As he passed, I caught his arm.

'Jack,' I said. 'You'll be checking for drugs?'

He regarded me steadily for a moment. 'You noticed?' he said, brushing a tangle of hair from his eyes. 'Aye, I'll test for drugs. Anything else?'

I shook my head, glanced at the fiscal.

'I'd appreciate your report as soon as possible, Jack,' Barrie said. 'There'll be a case conference tomorrow, if you could.'

'I'll be there,' Parrish said, and rushed after the stretcher now being loaded into the mortuary van.

'What was that about drugs?' Barrie asked.

'There were no cuts or bruises on her arms – the usual signs of a defensive struggle. You don't normally let someone kill you without a fight. Unless, perhaps, you've been drugged.'

He thought about that. We both thought about it. When I got fed up thinking about it, I asked him what the hell I was doing there anyway, what my position was.

He picked a hair from the sleeve of his light-grey suit, watched it float to the ground, then settled his guileless eyes on mine. 'Your position, Frank?'

'My position is this, sir,' I said. 'Officially, I'm suspended, pending the fatal accident inquiry into the death of Ruben Maxwell. Okay, that's mandatory, no problem. I've got nothing to hide. But it's hanging over me, you understand, and I'd like to get it over with, my name cleared.'

'I can see your point, Frank, but these things take

time. It's up to me to fix a date for the inquiry with the Sheriff, but you can see the way things are – I've just got too much on my plate at the moment. Now with these murders, and the press screaming for action, well . . .'

'So where do I stand?'

'I spoke to the Chairman of the Committee of Chief Constables before I came out here. Your name came up, and it seems he was well impressed by your handling of the Maxwell inquiry – so much so, that he wants you back on this case.'

'Impressed? Last I heard, he wanted my head on a platter. Why the sudden change of mind?'

'Ours not to reason, Frank. Maybe you're just flavour of the month. Anyway, he feels the way I do, that everything must be done to find this madman. We decided on this: you'll be temporarily assigned to my department as an Advisory Investigative Officer. You'll report direct to me and nobody else. You'll have full access to all files and incoming data and I'll assign someone to liaise between you and the Murder Squad. Anyone in mind?'

'Harry will do,' I told him.

'Very well. I'll arrange it with Chief Inspector Kettle. Anything else?'

'What *exactly* do you want me to do?'

'Find that psychopath – and find him quick.' He almost looked worried for a moment. A trick of the light, perhaps.

'What the hell can I do,' I asked, 'that the whole Murder Squad can't?' Something smelled, and I didn't like it.

'Don't put yourself down, Frank. You've got a flair for detection. A little unorthodox in your methods perhaps, but your talent is natural. You get results – and that's what we desperately need.'

Flattery now.

'And the inquiry?'

'Forget it for the moment. Concentrate on finding this killer.'

'And then, come the inquiry, I'll be tossed to press and public as a sacrificial offering. Isn't that the way it goes?'

'Sometimes, maybe. But I don't think——'

I snorted my disbelief.

Barrie pinched his nose again, and sniffed. 'Don't forget, Frank, it's my duty to reassure the public of police accountability.'

Glib. Too glib. Like a smug politician.

'Yeah. At my expense,' I said, angrily.

Barrie merely grinned. He had the most perfect teeth. No wonder he smiled so much. 'Don't give me that shit,' he said. 'It's the process of law. We both know people get mangled in the machine, but it's the only system we've got. Until such time——'

'Maxwell was a psychopathic little runt!'

'Shut it!' Barrie hissed, his smile vanishing like a fart in a hurricane. His index finger punctuated each word. 'You don't want to say *anything*. You want to keep your damn mouth *shut*. Understand?'

Our eyes locked and held. 'Sure,' I said, not caring if the sarcasm was too heavy. 'McMorran the Martyr. He'll go to the wall with his face firmly shut. Honourable to the very end.'

The smile was back on his face. 'Good. Everyone loves

a martyr. Now,' he glanced at his watch, a big solid Seiko, 'was there anything else?'

'How do I contact you? When do I report? What about Kettle? What authority have I got? Where do I work from?'

He took a card from his wallet, gave it to me. 'Contact me through this number,' he said. 'If I'm unavailable, leave a number and I'll call you back. You report only when you have something I can give the Murder Squad. I'll appraise Chief Inspector Kettle of the situation. Just stay out of his way. I want you to keep your profile low enough for ants to shit on your head, okay? Your authority is that of your rank, but don't force it. Work from wherever you like and keep a record of all expenses. Clear?'

'As milk,' I said.

'Phone me tomorrow. I don't want you at the case conference but I'll try to set something else up. Okay?'

I nodded and we parted company on mutually wary terms. I watched his diminutive form pick its careful way through the undergrowth, back to the main road. If there was one fact in my life I knew with complete conviction, it was that I needed a drink. Fast.

I found Harry outside the ID van. He detached himself from the group of white-coated officers and came across. The drizzle had eased off a bit but the sky was bruising to the north and the wind picking up.

'What did you say to Kettle?' Harry asked. 'He's going mental.'

I suddenly felt better. 'Barrie gave me the go-ahead to

work the case,' I said. 'Kettle didn't like it.'

Harry frowned. 'Why do you do it? Why couldn't you just stay at home and enjoy your holiday like any sane person would?'

'Because it is not a holiday. It is not fun. I have nothing else to do except watch television and that's not the kind of suicide I would choose anyway. Okay?'

He held up his hands. 'Okay, Frank. I'm not deaf. I only asked.'

I muttered an apology. Gracious to a fault.

'You back on the squad, then?' Harry asked.

I filled him in on my conversation with George Barrie. He listened, eyes fixed on his boot as it scuffed at the ground. When I finished, he shook his head slowly.

'The whole set-up stinks,' he said. 'If I were you, I'd——'

He was interrupted by a shout from the ID van. A PC stood waving a sheet of paper. Kettle hurried across.

'Looks like news.'

'Where's Ronald Brown, Harry?'

'Still in the car. Why?'

'Do me a favour, take him home like I said. You're not going to miss anything here. I'll leave a message with Marcie, meet up with you later. Okay?'

Harry trudged reluctantly back to his car. By the time I joined the knot of steaming bodies by the ID van, the PC was saying:

'Janice Young, reported missing last night at 23.45, D Division. Last seen yesterday afternoon when she went to the Commonwealth Pool. She was due to attend a party last night but never turned up. Her mother got worried an hour after Janice should have been home and rang the girl having the party. She was told her daughter had never arrived. She then phoned us.'

'Description?' Kettle snapped.

'Age fourteen, reddish hair cut short, five foot one, slim with no distinguishing marks. There's a list here of the clothes she was wearing, including white cotton ankle socks. D Division are trying to get hold of a photo.'

'Get back onto D Division,' Kettle ordered. 'Have them send someone round to pick up the parents. I want that body identified immediately. Then have them taken down to Fettes and I'll see them there.'

Kettle snatched the paper from the PC and shooed him away. He noticed me standing there and dropped his eyes on mine like a hod of bricks. When I gave no sign of buckling, he pulled me aside, lit a cigarette and snorted the smoke from his nostrils like a frustrated bull.

'If Barrie wants you on this case,' he said, 'then that's his problem. Don't make it mine. I don't even want to see you. You can have your tame Sergeant, and if he's got half the sense of a peanut he'll keep you out of my way. If he hasn't, he can expect to join you on the dole. Okay?'

What could I say? I said nothing.

'Good,' he continued. 'Now fuck off.'

# Chapter Two

Cowgate is Old Town.

It is a dank, lightless gorge where the road burrows beneath the George IV and South Bridges, joining Grass-market to Holyrood Road. The walls of the gorge are tall, grey and anonymous: windowless buildings, the backs of buildings, deserted buildings.

This morning, Cowgate was a dripping tunnel through the bank of fog rolling in off the Firth of Forth. Where buildings rose disappearing into the mist, lights hung eerily, shimmering. Small tributaries flowed into the road from steep High Street closes.

Cowgate is Slab City.

In 1975 they moved the old mortuary from the mauso-leum behind St Mary's to its new premises across the road. It's as anonymous now as it ever was – probably as any mortuary ever will be. The lead-grey brick façade has been carefully designed to blend in with the sooted grey surroundings and the windows are the kind you can look in only if you walk around on stilts. A small brass plaque engraved with the words 'City Mortuary' hangs on the wall and a card over the doorbell tells you to ring for attention. I did so.

The man who came to the door looked as though he had just climbed from one of the cold-room drawers. His skin had the pallor of death and hung like sacking over the bones of his face. He was short and squat and dressed in grey, with a light-blue shirt and narrow black tie. His eyes peered out from tired sockets, like someone looking up from the bottom of a well. He spent a minute or ten trying to find the right key. Another minute trying to fit it in the lock, and then I was out of the rain, shaking myself down like a dog out of water.

'Mornin', Charlie,' I said. 'Jack Parrish around?'

'Aye.' He led me along the carpeted corridor, past anonymous doors and pictureless walls to a small glass-walled office overlooking the unloading-bay. 'He expecting you?'

'Yes and no. Thought I might pick something up on the girl.'

'You'll be lucky. Her father's in there now, giving it the ID.'

'How'd he get here?'

'Couple of uniforms brought him in.'

While Charlie filled my name into his duty register, I sat on the edge of his desk thinking I wouldn't wait around for the autopsy – I hadn't had breakfast yet and anyway, the room gets pretty crowded. Apart from the two pathologists, there are usually a couple of production officers, a mortician, two forensic scientists, an ID Branch photographer and a representative from the Procurator-fiscal's department. Too crowded, too morbid, and too close to lunchtime.

So I waited till they all piled out of the cold-room, then

like a lion picking out the weakest in the herd, I went for the girl's father. He wasn't hard to single out. He was the one between the two uniforms, with the directionless shuffle, the sagging shoulders and the ravaged face. His eyes still reflected the body of his daughter, and saw nothing more.

'Mr Young?'

He turned towards me.

'Detective Inspector McMorran,' I told him. 'I'll have to ask you a few questions.'

He stared at me angrily.

'Have you no decency, man?' He tried to sound indignant but failed to raise the power. His eyes were bloodshot, rubbed red.

The older of the two uniforms stepped between us.

'I've orders to bring Mr Young direct to Fettes, sir,' he said.

'I know your orders, constable, but I'm here on the Procurator-fiscal's authority. You want to check, I'll give you his number and you can speak to him personally. But the time it takes you to do that, I could be finished and gone – and you on your way.'

The PC thought fast on his feet. 'Five minutes, sir?'

'Ten.'

'We'll wait here.'

I found Jack Parrish in the postmortem room. The girl was already on the table and the ID Branch photographer was clicking away while a gypsy in the corner was busy sharpening knives. My weird sense of humour.

'Jack,' I said, choking on formaldehyde. 'Okay if I use your office for a few minutes?'

31

He nodded his shaggy head irritably and waved me from the room.

The pathologist's office was a shoebox with a high window and a door. A black-topped desk took up half the space, two chairs and a grey metal filing-cabinet the rest. On the desk, a confusion of folders and reference books, a telephone, and a glass jar containing a cross-sectioned larynx suspended in some kind of formalin solution. There was a small hand-basin in the corner and, on the wall above it, a poster which read: *Histological Patterns of Adenocarcinoma of the Prostrate by the Gleason System 1–5*. Now you know.

Mr Young was in his early forties, with a fleshy face and the build of a businessman with a large expense account. His dark-grey trousers were flared, his shoes black and his tie a turquoise fishtail with a large knot. Not a dedicated follower of fashion. His sausage-like fingers were clasped across his belly to stop it spilling out of his crisp white shirt.

I opened by offering condolences, followed by the usual reassurances that it was only a matter of time before we arrested the killer of his daughter. I asked what he did for a living.

'Assistant Manager with the Bank of Scotland,' he replied, in an automatic tone that demanded my respect and got none. I made interested noises in the back of my throat, and then asked:

'What can you tell me about your daughter?'

'She's . . . she was . . .' His face collapsed and he couldn't tell me very much at all. I searched through the drawers of the desk, then the filing-cabinet, and found the bottle of Grouse whisky in the bottom of the latter. I rinsed out the two glasses in the basin and filled them both liberally.

'Drink, Mr Young,' I said, pushing a glass across to him. 'It'll do you good.' Though I knew who would benefit most.

He drank, spluttered, and drank. Colour came to his cheeks. A sort of bluey-whiteness, like the new biological soap powders advertised on TV. He made the basin – just. I found some paper towels and when he had finished he wiped his face clean and stammered his thanks and apologies and, still clutching a couple of the towels, regained his seat.

'I lost a daughter, too, Mr Young,' I told him. 'She was seven. She was coming home from school one afternoon and never even saw the car that killed her.' I had his attention now. He was listening to my voice, not the sound of his own grief. That was a start. I went on lying through my teeth. 'It's not easy, Mr Young. We never expect to outlive our children, we are never prepared. I know how you feel because I've been through it all myself. You've got a long way to go, and for a while it's going to be hell. You've got to be strong, and patient. Your wife is going to need all the support you can give her. You must work together, find——'

He began shouting. 'I told her not to let Janice go to the party. She didn't listen. She always knows better, said it was normal these days for kids to stay out so late. She wouldn't listen.'

'Were you close to your daughter?'

He'd stopped shouting but the anger and bitterness

were still there, twisting his face as much as his words. 'Close? She was my only child, man!'

'Then you'd know what she was doing on the day she died?'

'She was . . . with friends.'

'Which friends?'

'I don't know their names. Ask my wife.'

'You knew she was going swimming?'

'Yes. She goes most Saturdays.'

'Did she ever go alone?'

'Maybe, I don't know.'

'Did she ever mention meeting someone there?'

'Not to me.'

'Perhaps you weren't that close . . .'

He threw me a look that shrivelled my bones. 'What are you trying to say, Inspector?'

I wasn't too sure. 'Did you give Janice pocket-money?' I asked. 'Or an allowance?'

'She got the same as any girl her age. She wasn't spoilt, if that's what you mean. She had an account at my branch and I paid her pocket-money straight into that.'

'Did she visit you at the bank?'

'She drew her money out from the machine.' A trace of resentment in his voice.

'She never actually came into the bank?'

'I didn't say that. She came in once or twice. But I'm a busy man, I couldn't give her much time. The manager didn't like it.'

'Anyone in the bank who might have reason to . . .'

'Don't be silly, man!'

34

I made a few scrawls in my notebook, and then asked:
'Which school did she go to?'

'Watson's.'

'Did she like it there?'

'I suppose so. She seemed happy enough.'

'Were you happy with her reports?'

Young shrugged. 'She could have worked harder. She was intelligent but . . .'

'Could have done better?'

'Yes.'

'Did she ever complain of harassment at school? Bullying, or suchlike?'

'Not to me.'

'Did she work during her school holidays?'

'She didn't need to.'

'Any hobbies?'

'Not really, no.'

'Belong to any clubs?'

'You'll have to ask my wife.'

'When did you last see her?'

'Breakfast-time, yesterday.'

'How did she seem to you?'

'Same as usual.' His tone was petulant.

'No moods? Not happy or sad or angry . . . just the same as usual?'

'That's what I said.'

'Did your daughter have a boyfriend?'

His head snapped up. 'No. Most definitely not. Out of the question. Christ, man – she was only *fourteen*.'

I said nothing, resigning myself again to the fact that the closer you are to someone, the less you can see.

Intimacy breeds blinkers. I asked him where his wife was, why she hadn't come.

'Why do you think? It's not exactly pleasant seeing your only daughter lying dead on a slab.'

'I'll need to ask her a few questions.'

'She's at home with a friend. But you won't get to see her – no-one will.'

'Fair enough,' I said, and left it at that. Then took out the old favourite, dusted it off. 'Do you know anyone who might have wished your daughter harm?'

Young looked at me as though I'd just asked him for an unconditional loan at zero-rate interest. He planted his hands palm down on the desktop and pushed himself to his feet. The chair creaked. 'I don't think I wish to answer any more of your questions, Inspector.'

'Was your daughter using drugs, Mr Young?'

'No!' Blood suffused his face and rubbery neck.

'Would you know if she was? Would she tell you?'

'Don't be ridiculous! Of course she would.'

'Does your wife take drugs? Tranquillisers, that kind of thing? Or you, perhaps?'

'Such a suggestion is slanderous!' He rounded the desk, reached for the door. I was already there.

'Was your daughter mature for her age, Mr Young?'

He spluttered, stopped in his tracks.

'What kind of question is that? Have you no decency?'

'Decency won't find your daughter's killer, Mr Young,' I said harshly. 'Only the truth will.'

I didn't exactly believe that . . . and neither did he. He jerked the door open and pushed past me into the corridor. He was wearing Brut aftershave. Definitely out of touch with reality, I thought.

'Thank you for your help, sir,' I called, but he didn't acknowledge me and stormed from the building followed by the two hurrying uniforms. I let him go – just one more Assistant Bank Manager who wouldn't want to see my face again.

Charlie was still behind his desk. 'Any luck?' he asked.

I grimaced, shook my head.

'Looks pretty posh – what's he do?'

'He's a banker, Charlie,' I said. 'And that's with a capital W.'

I put a call through to Harry, told him to meet me in a bar on the Grassmarket, then broke out the front door like a fugitive, glad to escape the stench of formaldehyde.

The fog had rolled in and the buildings were dark smears behind the thin veil of feathery rain. I turned up the collar of my jacket, and with fists thrust in pockets, headed back along Cowgate.

Grassmarket cowered beneath the squat bulk of Castle Rock and the Esplanade. Today, the castle was blurred and indistinct, like a smudged sketch. The rock below glistened like smoked glass.

The bar was full of Sunday hangovers, most of the men looking like they needed the whole fur of the dog rather than just a hair. Harry arrived halfway through my second pint and I didn't leave it on the table.

'Where to?' he asked as we climbed in his car.

'Did you get the Young's address?'

'Aye, no problem.'

'Let's go, then.'

'After Mrs Young – what?' Harry asked.

I wasn't sure. 'We need direction, Harry. We've been running around with our heads up our arses for the last

37

couple of weeks and getting nowhere. Kettle's not going to be any help, so we'll have to break out of the mainstream investigation and look at the facts from a different angle, try long-shots, go with hunches. That's why they got me in on the case, I'm sure. If I succeed in finding the killer, everyone gains. If I don't, I'm the only loser. The perfect scapegoat.'

'I lose, too, remember.' Harry corrected, morosely. 'It was you dragged me into this. I would have been happy enough just shuffling files and letting Kettle walk all over me. I'm not cut out for this kind of fiasco. It's okay for you. You're young, single, and carefree – and bloody irresponsible. I'm looking at retirement next year and have a family that relies on my income. And now what? I'm out on a limb, trying to cover my arse and praying that you won't do something that'll get us both on a disciplinary.'

'I didn't realise . . .' I said, lamely. 'You should have said.'

'You see nothing but yourself, Frank. You don't listen.'

'Sorry?'


Babylon Drive is a cosy little cul-de-sac hidden away in a quiet, secluded area off the main Morningside Road. Nearby streets go under the names of Jordan, Nile and Canaan. Evenly-spaced trees sprout from the pavements, and in the gardens of the four houses that line each side, there are more trees . . . cherry, beech and cypress being the only ones I recognised. The houses are all sandstone, tucked away behind rose-bushes, flower-beds, rockeries and garden-paths. Manicured hedges and black iron gates. Netted windows.

Harry mumbled something I didn't hear. I said, 'What?'

'It's an old saying about the people of Morningside. "Lace at the windows but no sheets for the bed". Something like that, I can't remember exactly.'

The rain, heavier now, ran down the back of my neck as we approached the house, and fallen leaves formed a soggy carpet beneath our feet. Somewhere in the distance a dog barked incessantly and, in a house nearby, someone was practising scales on a piano. It seemed that a sense of timeless calm and exclusivity hung over Babylon Drive – like a gentlemen's club or a backwater pool where ageing trout wait around to die.

Today however, the pool was full of barracuda. They must have been sitting in their cars to keep out of the rain. As we approached the Youngs' house they were already focusing cameras and switching on tape-machines.

I was hit by a deluge of questions as microphones were jostled under my nose. I shouldered my way through the snapping pack, tossing 'no comments' to left and right. Harry fought a rearguard action while I gained the front door and rang the bell.

A lace curtain twitched in a window to the left of the door so I took out my warrant card and pressed it to the glass. A minute later, the door opened a couple of inches and a minute after that, we were inside.

'Mrs Young?' I asked.

She nodded, and dabbed a small, lace handkerchief at her eyes. Her right eye was puffy and swollen and she had the dazed, vacant look of someone who had not slept in days. She turned and led us into what was obviously the living-room.

It was oppressively hot. A stacked coal-fire glowed in the wide stone hearth. Delicate Chinese figurines in soft pastel colours lined the dark mahogany mantelpiece. In the centre, a large, ornate clock ticked sleepily on towards eternity.

'I spoke to your husband a short while ago,' I said. 'He mentioned you had a friend here with you.'

'She'll be back shortly. I thought that was her at the door. When will those horrid reporters go away and leave us alone? Can't you do something? Isn't there a law——'

'Not if they stay off your property, I'm sorry.'

She waved us into a deep sky-blue sofa with embroidered lace antimacassars. She clung to her hand-kerchief as though it was her last vestige of hope. While Harry almost disappeared into the cushions, I sat on the arm and took in the rest of the room.

It was the kind of room where you had to be careful not to speak too loud or breathe too hard in case something cracked. The smell of polish and air-freshener hung faintly in the stuffy air. Woodwork gleamed, glass sparkled and I couldn't see a speck of dust anywhere. The ceiling was high, the cornices elaborate and the walls papered in pastel yellow. Watercolours of rivers and mountains and trees and trawlers clung to various parts of the wall; dried ferns and flowers shot from porcelain vases like frozen rockets. Most of the framed photographs on top of the oak writing-bureau by the bay-windows were of Janice; one of them, I noticed, was obviously Mr and

Mrs the day they married. She was smiling then, pretty in a coquettish sort of way, life just beginning.

Not so now. Smiles were a long way from her face. The coquettishness was still apparent, but it is not easy to look pretty with a black eye poorly concealed by make-up. Her eyes were dull, her mouth a trembling crease, the corners pulled down by emotional gravity. Her permed dark hair was untidy, as though she'd just tumbled from bed.

She perched on the edge of her armchair, her clothes hanging haphazardly from her listless bones.

'I'd like to talk about Janice . . .' I said. 'I know this must be painful, but——'

'Questions, questions, questions!' she snapped. 'Will they never stop? My daughter is murdered and you treat me as though I killed her. Like I'm a suspect or something. And all the time there's a maniac out there and . . . and . . .'

'I'm sorry,' I told her, 'but I'm afraid it's standard procedure. Not just to establish your innocence but also to ensure that nothing gets overlooked.'

'Overlooked? What more can be said? I've spent all morning answering questions. Questions won't bring Janice back.' She shrank back in the chair and stared at the fire, as though it offered retreat from a world intent on smashing her life into a billion smithereens.

'As you said, her killer is still out there – and there are other mothers who love their daughters just as much as you. We have to find him before he kills again.'

Her eyes seemed to turn in on themselves as she thought this over. It seemed to take a long time. I wondered what tortured images she was witnessing. She suddenly leant forward.

'I brought her up as well as any mother can do,' she said. 'There wasn't anything I denied her. Maybe that was wrong, perhaps I spoiled her, allowed her too much freedom. But she is - was - a sensible girl. Always did as she was told, never talked to strangers, always called me if she was going to be home late. She was so considerate, so thoughtful. Nothing was ever too much to do. We were close, you know, very close. Everyone remarked how close we were, how alike . . .' She trailed off. I don't think she even realised we were there. I said nothing - what was there to say? What can you say to a mother whose life's work and selfless devotion has been suddenly flushed down the drain by one senseless brutal act.

Harry got up and strolled around the room. Examining pictures, picking up souvenirs, studying photographs, noting this, noting that, with eyes that never missed a sodding trick. Mrs Young went on, her voice a drone on the air. I listened to the words - rather, I heard the words, filed them away somewhere in my subconscious for later. Meanwhile, I was trying to subdue the compulsive desire for a drink.

What was the woman saying? She'd been rambling on for minutes, reliving old memories, recreating days of familial bliss. And the memories were all she had left, like an old chest in the attic, full of days gone by. In my profession you can only feel so much pity. Then life must go on.

Harry sniffed loudly. 'Something's burning,' he said.

Mrs Young sprang to her feet. 'Oh my God!' she

exclaimed. 'Eddie's lunch. He'll kill me!' She made for the door.

'Looks like he's already tried,' I said.

She turned and dabbed at her eye with her hanky. 'What do you mean?'

'I suppose you walked into a door,' I said.

Harry touched my arm. 'Easy on, Frank,' he said.

Mrs Young burst into tears and ran from the room. Harry threw me a venomous glare and went out after her.

I moved around the room examining this and that, much as Harry had done, trying to formulate a picture in my mind of how the Youngs had lived. I worked quickly and quietly, my fingers like ghosts through the drawers of the desk by the window. I rummaged through the cubbyholes, the letter-rack, the postcards and photographs, the bills, the demands, the marriage papers, birth certificates – everything that ties a family down, together and up. I was just closing the bottom drawer when I heard footsteps in the hall. I was looking studiously out the window when Harry came in.

'I've persuaded her to eat,' he said. 'She's calmed down a bit but she's scared out of her wits. Says her husband blames her for Janice's death and won't even speak to her anymore.'

'Sounds like him,' I agreed.

'Go easy on her, Frank,' he murmured. 'She's on the point of collapse.'

I followed him through to the kitchen.

Mrs Young was stirring a pot of thick, dark gravy. Harry watched with hungry eyes. She must have read his mind. 'Will you join me? There's plenty . . . and I hate to eat alone.'

Harry, reluctantly, assented. Mrs Young wouldn't look at me, but repeated her invitation.

I told her no thanks. 'Smells great, though,' I said, and sat down.

Mrs Young picked at her food, moved it around her plate, mashed the potatoes to pulp, then repositioned them to form a dyke between the peas, the gravy and the slice of chicken-and-mushroom pie. She ate the peas one by one, spearing them like an eskimo at a fishing-hole. Harry talked as he ate, his sympathetic voice smoothing the edges of the woman sitting next to him.

'Jeanette was just saying how much her husband adored Janice.'

'Only as a projection of himself,' Mrs Young broke in, the bitterness evident in her cracked voice.

'Were they close?' I asked. 'As close as you and your daughter?'

'He didn't understand her at all. He's lost in his own self-importance. To him, she was just another possession – like this house, the car, me. He wanted to control every bit of her life, the way he's controlled mine. But I wasn't having it. I didn't want her brought up like some cosseted museum-piece. Me and Janice, well, we worked things out.'

'Did Janice have many friends?'

She took a long time to reply, perhaps chewing on her thoughts with the same deliberation she used on her peas. 'She had several close friends whom she saw quite often. But no-one who would . . .'

44

'Did she go out a lot? At night?'

'I never let her out later than ten. She always had to be back here by then because that's the earliest Eddie ever gets back from the Club.'

'What about her interests? Did *she* belong to any clubs or go to any night classes?' I asked. 'Or have any hobbies that might bring her into contact with adults?'

'She went to dance classes at The Studio every Thursday and she was in the school Dramatic Society. But she didn't really have any hobbies, as such.'

'Which studio?'

'That's what it's called, The Studio. Down on the Royal Circus.'

'You mentioned earlier that she was supposed to go to a party last night,' Harry said, wiping his plate clean with a corner of bread.

'It was Sue Hemple's birthday. They've been friends ever since . . . oh, I don't know. They did everything together. The party was due to start at five. Janice was going to meet Sue there earlier and help out with the food and stuff.'

'But she never arrived . . .'

Her voice was very small. 'No.'

'Yet she went swimming as usual?'

'Yes. A couple of the girls at the party saw her at the pool, but they didn't see her leave.'

'Do you know their names?'

'I think one of the girls was called Helen. But I told all this to the officer who came round earlier. He said he'd look into it.'

'What about a boyfriend, Mrs Young? Did Janice . . .'

45

'There was a boy called Philip she used to talk about. But I don't think there was anything serious between them. She would have told me otherwise.'

Harry was making notes between mouthfuls.

'The next question is rather personal, Mrs Young,' I said. 'If you don't want to answer, please don't feel you have to. I'd like you to tell me if your daughter was mature – physically.'

She stared at her plate of mush, didn't raise her head to answer. 'Her periods had started, if that's what you mean.'

'Did she have any, shall we say, unusual sanitary habits for a girl of her age?'

She glanced up from her plate. 'What exactly are you getting at?' Her voice had cooled by several hundred degrees.

'Did you know your daughter had recently shaved her pubic hair.'

'She what? What do you mean? How . . .'

'The pathologist thinks——'

'Never! Not Janice. Why the hell should she? She was only fourteen. She wasn't old enough to . . . to . . .'

'So, to your knowledge——' Again I was unable to finish.

Mrs Young looked me deep in the eye. 'You may take my word, Inspector, that if Janice had done anything of the sort, I would have known about it. I told you, we were close. We didn't hide anything from each other.'

'Thank you,' I said, and veered sharply away from the subject. 'The last time you saw her, what sort of mood was she in?'

'She was quite excited. Looking forward to the party, I think.'

'So she wasn't depressed?'

'No, not at all.'

'And you gave a list of the clothes she was wearing to the other officers?' She nodded.

'Have you thought of anything since then that you might have forgotten at the time?' She shook her head, dropped it into her hands.

Harry frowned across the table at me. I rose.

'Would you mind if I took a look at Janice's room, Mrs Young. It won't take a moment.'

'Do whatever you like. It's the first door at the top of the stairs.'

It was a small room, walls cluttered with posters, mostly Bros and Tiffany. A bed with a patchwork quilt squeezed between the window and a wardrobe. A glass-topped dressing-table with photos tucked beneath the glass was littered with a large variety of cosmetics. The photos were mostly holiday snaps taken somewhere where the sun was shining.

Mrs Young had not been lying when she said that Janice wanted for nothing. Evidence was the wardrobe packed with dresses and coats and jackets and bags and shoes and blouses and trousers, all expensive, all still fashionable. An oak chest of drawers beneath the hirsute chest of George Michael revealed more of the same, all neatly folded. I rummaged through her underwear – a favourite hiding-place – but turned up nothing. When I left the room and closed the door I was convinced that Janice Young had been like any other spoilt middle-class

47

girl of that age. I paid a visit to the bathroom and then went downstairs.

Harry was folding up the dishcloth when I entered. Jeanette Young still sat at the table, chin cupped in her hands, eyes seeing far beyond the limits of the close horizon.

'Mrs Young,' I said. 'Yesterday afternoon, when Janice left to go swimming, was she wearing make-up?'

'I think so,' she said quietly, her face puckered in a frown. 'No, I'm sure of it. I remember noticing her eyeliner wasn't quite straight. I didn't mention it, though.'

'Thank you, Mrs Young. You've been very helpful. If there's anything we can do . . .'

'Get rid of those damn reporters,' she said, her voice completely drained.

'I can't do that,' I told her. 'But I'll arrange for a PC to watch your door. That, at least, will stop them hounding you.'

She smiled weakly and murmured her thanks. Then began to cry again.

That's how we left her: sobbing quietly alone amidst the wreckage of her shattered dreams.

# Chapter Three

Sinking fast like a ship ablaze, the cool afternoon sun sent vague shadows scuttling across the clearing and a soft breeze, almost warm, rippled through the long grass, tugging gently at the smaller branches of the silver birch, beech and Scottish pine that bordered three sides of the open space. The fourth side sloped leisurely down to moss-covered rocks and the silver slash of river.

At the back of the clearing stood an old log cabin, and behind it, a cliff rose sheer and menacing, its face rugged and black.

Dominic Bain emerged from the darkness of the cabin and stood framed in the doorway, feet set apart, fists thrust deep in the pockets of his combat trousers. He gazed down at the leap of river at the foot of the slope, eyes squinting against the glare of the sun. His face registered no emotion, exhibited no trace of what he felt within.

The only sounds, the cry of a kingfisher and the laughing, tumbling, dashing course of the river.

*His river.*

The laughing waters mocking – scornful of him and his city ways.

The trace of a smile tugged at the corners of his mouth.

'Like old times . . .' he murmured, and re-entered the cabin.

Three minutes later he padded naked down to the river. The river was in shadow, the air no longer warm. He ploughed into the water until his thighs parted the falling current. For several minutes he stood there motionless, allowing the icy mountain water to chill his bones. He looked about him, taking in the once intimate scenery with fresh new eyes.

Whose eyes? he wondered, not for the first time.

It was a small gorge cut out of the hillside, deep inside the forest. It had taken him almost an hour to reach from the village, following old trails, now overgrown. Few people strayed this far, not even forestry officials and workmen.

Opposite the cliff the wall of the gorge was a steep, tree-speckled scree which shallowed out as it dipped towards the river. Here it was stubbled with bushes of wild gorse and briar, myriad shades of fern and bracken and the softer, purple hue of thistles. Untidy huddles of vine-choked trees, bent and crooked like arthritic pensioners leaned out towards the darting tongue of river and, further down by the water's edge, two willows hunched wearily, their long thin fingers trailing in the current. Of the huge boulders that had once adorned the heights, some were now dark islands scattered amidst the tangled undergrowth, others amidst the clear headlong rush of water.

Like a negative this secluded gorge, this timeless retreat, had absorbed scenes from his past. Here, all around him. Almost tangible, the very essence of his childhood. The love, hate, happiness and pain; the desire, disgust and fear. And, as the gorge had once born witness to the birth of his childhood dreams, it now witnessed his rebirth. Watching with cold impartial eyes as he lowered himself abruptly into the driving stream of water.

The piercing cold forced the breath from his lungs and he shivered uncontrollably. He ducked his head. When he surfaced even his brain tingled. He began to wash.

He washed with intense care, like a cat. His muscletone was good and firm and there was little fat on his body. He exercised regularly, swimming several times a week at the Commonwealth Pool; one day a week, a gruelling session at the weights in the Fitness Centre. There was a certain relief, satisfaction almost, in pushing himself to the limit. See how far he could go, and then go further.

A fine antique. It was true – his body was comparable to a fine piece of mahogany. Like one of his father's sculptures. Smooth curves, as soft as any woman's skin. He recalled as a child running his hands tentatively, almost awesomely, over the polished busts. So smooth. So lifelike. To a young boy, it had seemed like magic, the way the sculptures emerged from beneath the skilled hands of his father. So coarse a man, so blunt the hands, yet . . .

He despised hair. It revolted him. Ugly, dirty, carrier of disease. Apart from his head – and there his scalp was almost cropped – there was no other hair on his body. His genitals cowered strangely in the crutch of his legs, denied the protection of pubic hair, recently shaved.

The Renaissance artists had had the right idea. They had seen the beauty, the true aesthetic quality of the human body. Soft curves and contours, subtle shadows. No sprout or bush of dark curly hair to vulgarise their paintings. No hairy armpits or fuzzy loins. Nothing to conceal or confuse, to distract and draw the eye from perfect lines.

He thought of Janice. The disappointment. The wispy hairs, first sign of maturity. He had hated her for that. It had meant shaving her. And she had succumbed to that with the same indifference with which she had succumbed to death. Little cow.

He had been twelve years old when Mother-dear was forced to sell up the cottage in the village – now the Gillespies' guest house – and drag him away to live in the city. By then, his father was already eight months into his life sentence.

The first months in the city had been a constant nightmare from which he could not escape. He thought he would wake to find himself back in Ballaig, warm as a cat in front of the cosy glowing hearth, safe in the knowledge that he was home. But the day never came. New horrors greeted him with every relentless twist of his new life.

The dirt, the grime, the noise and confusion . . . all had served to instil in him a profound disgust, an unrelenting hatred for the city, his new home.

But the stench of the city penetrated deep. It had soon crawled beneath his skin. He felt its progress – squirming like maggots beneath the surface of his skin. He had learnt to survive in the alien environment and the anonymity had been his unwitting ally. He had wrapped it like a cloak around his body, a veil around his mind. He had no friends, but what did he need friends for . . .

And always there, crouched and snarling like a malevolent beast straining at a flimsy leash, the undiluted anger that poisoned his mind.

It crouched still.

A bright dart of colour flew past his head and he turned in time to watch the kingfisher as it dipped and swerved downstream until out of sight.

He noticed again the faint, forgotten scars across his wrists, more like folds now. He'd slashed them on his fourteenth birthday, with Mother-dear's razor – the one she had used to shave her legs. By then she had given up trying to look good and the razor was blunt and rusty. As it sliced through his skin it left dual tracks of red dust on either side. Then the blood had washed them away.

He had sneaked home from school early. No-one missed him. Mother-dear was out. A brief note on the kitchen table. *Make your own tea.*

He ran the bath, steam soon clouding the room, shutting out the cold. He studied himself in the mirror over the basin, had to keep wiping it.

Strange eyes, even then.

The razor was there on the shelf beneath the mirror where it had lain for the last six months. He had fingered it absently, then studied it. If ideas had formed in his mind, he had been unaware of them. He had undressed and stepped into the scalding water. It hurt at first, but his skin soon got used to it, always did. There was subtle pleasure in the pain. The razor lay between the taps. His thingy, a small fish nudging the surface.

And then he was drawing the blade across his wrist. No pain. Warmth. Lightheadedness. Water turning pink, then red. Soft, easy flow. His bladder emptied unconsciously. He lay back, suddenly tired. Images swimming in a sluggish mind. Fading into warmth, back to the comforting darkness of womb. Sleep. Edging into slumber. Warmth. Nothing.

Later, much later, he had surfaced into a cold, white room. Nurses. Concerned faces. Questions, questions, questions. People peering into his mind, extracting things, private things. Never alone. Talk, talk, talk.

Mother-dear, crying over spilt blood. *There, there – silly boy. You won't be so silly again, will you, Dominic? It was just a prank, wasn't it? Wasn't it?*

He finished washing and dived deep into the middle course of the river, pushing for the river-bed. Surfacing twenty yards downstream he ploughed his way to the bank. His whole body tingled and glowed, flushed red. He felt alive again, the cobwebs washed away. Globules of mountain water clung to his skin like glistening rivulets of molten silver. He felt like a snake, shimmering. Having shed his skin, he would slide off into the grass, a new being.

He towelled himself dry with the same precision with which he had washed. Satisfied, he stood for a long time gazing downstream, following the course of the river until it disappeared behind the willows on its tumbling journey to the lower reaches.

The sun had slipped below the dark curtain of pine and now shadows crawled across the long grass towards the cabin. The sky was a blue crystal ball, crinkled white, shapeless forms . . . the air, strangely calm. Before the storm? he wondered.

He made his way back up to the cabin, his thoughts turning to Cathy. He and Cathy had been friends since so high – platonic or whatever the word was. But that didn't mean shit on a shovel. Time was the great leg-opener. Well, it was obviously going to take a little more time, and tomorrow he had to get back to the city, back to work. Better to wait till the old sod was out of the way for good – then make the big push. Play it cool.

Slick and cool, aye – like nobody's fool.

# Chapter Four

By Monday morning the rain had passed and a hesitant sun edged from one bit of cover to the next, never showing its face long enough to give an impression of warmth. Harry picked me up early and we drove down to the Squad headquarters situated on a narrow, seldom-used backstreet not far from the Tollcross intersection.

It is an anonymous, three-storey dark-brick building, separated from the street by high walls and a small, cluttered yard. Over the arched gateway, a faded wooden sign still displays the logo, *G Mackenzie, Building Merchant*, a legacy from the previous owner and good enough cover to explain the unmarked vans and cars continually using the yard. Perhaps the only flaw in the otherwise innocent façade is the twenty-five foot aerial on the roof, powerful enough to transmit and receive radio calls to and from anywhere in Scotland.

Marcie, in reception, looked pleased to see me. Her main purpose is to discourage people coming in off the street. No-one has got past her yet.

A big woman in her early thirties, with short blond hair and, behind the most innocent blue eyes I have ever seen, bubbles the filthiest sense of humour. She is highly efficient – which might have something to do with the slimming pills prescribed by her doctor – and her infectious laugh can usually be heard all over the building.

'Come here, darling,' she grinned. 'Give Marcie a kiss.' She proffered her cheek and I had to lean over the counter to kiss it. 'That's better,' she said. 'You don't know how frustrated I get waiting for a real man to come walking through that door. All I get is the likes of old Harry here. As much fun as a rubber truncheon! Did you miss me, darling?'

'Sure,' I told her, 'My lovelife has never been the same. Can you spare ten minutes? I'll meet you in the cupboard under the stairs.'

She boomed with laughter. 'Ten minutes, Frank? Don't be so modest. This is Marcie you're talking to, remember?'

I smiled what I thought was a bashful smile, said I would see her later, and followed Harry up the stairs.

We spent a couple of hours sorting through the mountain of files and reports on Harry's desk, splitting them into two piles. One pile for the first victim, Craig Watson, the other for Janice Young – though there wasn't much in on her yet. That done, we sat and read through every sheet of paper, Harry working on Watson, me on Young, until each of us had another two piles in front of us; one for information we considered relevant, the other for garbage. That took us another couple of hours. When we had finished, the piles were not visibly smaller, but the stack of discarded files on the floor told another story. We packed the two relevant piles into boxes, carried them down to the car, drove them across the Meadows and deposited them in my flat.

'What now?' Harry asked as we climbed back into his car.

'Queensferry Street – the fiscal wants to see me. You can drop me off, then get to work on Records.'

'Records?'

'How many times do I have to tell you, Harry? I want all the files on murder by hanging going back as far as you can. Scottish and English – but Scottish first. Also, have a word with the collation officer, try and get a list of all relevant Missing Persons Reports.'

'Is that all? Why not shine your shoes while I'm at it? Christ.'

'Harry?'

'What?'

'Just do it, okay?'

'Yes, *sir*.'


George Barrie was 'in conference and not to be disturbed', so I sat in the small waiting-room off the reception hall and counted the ugly paintings on the wall. When I got to fifteen, I gave up and tried to fathom the complexity of my situation.

I thought about internal politics and the sudden scramble for power in the upper ranks of the Scottish Special Crimes Squad where I had been assigned for the last ten months.

I thought about the Committee of Chief Constables set up in 1969 to control and direct the operations of the Squad – which consists of the eight Chief Constables responsible for the regional forces and is chaired by the present Chief Constable of the Strathclyde region.

And I thought about the Commander of the Squad, Detective Chief Superintendent Aitken, whose grip at the helm had always been a tenuous one. Aitken was a man who owed allegiance to nobody and gave none. He disliked the power struggles, the backstabbing, and the influence of politics on his career. He was a copper who wanted to do his job – a perfectionist who did not hesitate to sanction unorthodox methods to conclude an investigation to his own high standard. A copper after my own heart.

It was thanks to Aitken that I was finally able to nail Ruben Maxwell. No other officer would have given me the leeway and support I needed during the last few days of the inquiry. He took risks and got results. Similarly, he accepted responsibility when something went wrong – like it did when Maxwell died. It followed, therefore, that if I was disciplined for Maxwell's death, Aitken would be looking at a transfer to the Outer Hebrides. And that would leave the door open for Detective Chief Inspector Kettle, ambitious to a fault and with friends on the Committee widely rumoured to prefer a Commander with a less radical approach to the politics of crime detection. Personally, I needed Kettle as Commander as much as I needed cancer to live.

Now someone else had thrown his hat in the ring – George Barrie, the Procurator-fiscal. But to what end? Where did he fit in and what did he stand to gain? Promotion? It didn't make sense.

My deliberations were choked mid-thought as the man himself came smiling into the room, hand outstretched.

'Thanks for coming, Frank,' he said, as we shook.

'Sorry to keep you waiting.' He led me up the stairs to his second-floor office, where the watery sun seeped through tall windows, splashing the book-lined room in shallows of warmth. He left me alone for a few moments and returned with two cups of coffee. Then he came to the point.

'Have you seen the papers yet?'

'I could hardly miss them.'

'Someone, somewhere, has been talking,' Barrie said. 'Chief Inspector Kettle's ordered an enquiry, but what's the use in that - the damage is done. We can now expect a host of copy-cats and hoaxes, and even more wasted manpower.'

'Maybe now the public know, they'll take more care, not let their kids out unattended.'

'Hell, Frank - you know better than that.' He pulled out a copy of the morning's paper. 'I mean, look at that: "Capital Hangman claims second victim". Now we're going to have the nation's press hounding every step we take, putting on the pressure. They want to print the truth, sure - but at what cost?'

'Business is business,' I said. 'The life of a child costs them nothing.'

'Yeah, yeah. What a great world we live in.' Barrie lit a fresh cigarette off his old one. 'Okay. I've had my grumble. So we've lost an edge on the Hangman - see, I'm even calling him that - and now we've got public indignation to put up with as well. Okay. All in a day's work. So, tell me, what's new?'

'You've seen the Path. Report?'

'Yup. Parrish was at the conference this morning.

From the digestion of the food still in her stomach, the girl died sometime between six and seven on Saturday evening. Question is, where was she between the time she was last seen at the Commonwealth Pool – about 1.30 – and the time her body was thrown over the wall. Answer that, and we're halfway there.'

'No witnesses come forward yet?'

'Thousands of them. Seems like half the city saw her that afternoon – all over the place.'

'Makes a change,' I said, then asked, 'Forensic come up with anything yet?'

'I thought your sergeant was keeping you abreast of the situation.'

'Harry's busy.'

Barrie leaned back in his chair and regarded me shrewdly over steepled fingers before answering my question. 'So far nothing. No fibres, traces, hairs, blood – nothing, that is, except the semen. What do you make of that?'

'Guy's clever. No prints, either.'

'Parrish reckons the killer washed the girl down after she was dead. But that still doesn't explain the semen found in her belly-button.'

'I think the guy's playing with us, getting cocky.'

'Good. Let's hope he makes a mistake.'

'He already did. The Commonwealth Pool. Both victims went there the day they died. Janice with friends and Craig Watson with his father. The Watsons went every Saturday morning, had lunch in the cafeteria afterwards and then parted company. That day, the father went to the match at Tynecastle and the boy met a couple of mates and went to a matineé at the Odeon. After that, they all went different ways and no-one saw Craig again till they found his body on the railway line. Same applies to Janice. After she left the pool, she disappeared. It looks like the killer saw them there, followed them out, then waited till they were alone – and took them.'

'But where?' There was a note of helplessness, frustration – or both – in his voice.

'He has a car, that's obvious. Cars drive into garages, and garages often have taps for hosepipes and doors you can pull down so your neighbours can't see you killing young kids.'

'You have a point.'

We sat in silence a while as the sun slipped behind cloud.

'Both crimes were committed on a Saturday,' Barrie observed.

'Maybe he works Monday to Friday. Or he's a travelling salesman or long-distance lorry-driver and only returns home at weekends. Or maybe he's on the dole and kills to add a little excitement to his life. Or it could just be a coincidence.'

'What do *you* think?'

'I think everything about these murders is premeditated. The guy's methodical, you can tell by his MO. You commit a murder on the spur of the moment and you're going to leave traces all over the place, have witnesses by the score. This guy leaves nothing and is seen by no-one. I think Kettle had better put the pool under maximum surveillance on Saturday. Saturate the place, in and out of the pool. Photographers in the gallery and cafeteria.

Two men on the security cameras, two more in a van outside to capture every face as it comes out, and a couple of men down in the changing-rooms. Also, someone positioned at each of the underground windows.'

'Too late. He's already organised a reconstruction to take place at the pool on Saturday. With so much police presence there's no way The Hangman's going to show his face.'

'But he might,' I argued. 'You've got to take that chance. Maybe he's feeling so confident, you know, high on his luck, that he'll come to gloat. Easy. You let anyone in who wants in, and stop everyone coming out and get names and addresses, descriptions, the lot. Then at least if he is there, we'll have him on file. Kettle can then put all the data through HOLMES and see what he comes up with.'

'HOLMES?'

'Home Office Large Major Enquiries System. He's got a terminal at the West End Station.'

'Ah, that beast. Mmm, yes.'

'He'll be checking all the staff at the pool?'

'I bloody hope so.'

There was a knock on the door and we both looked up as his secretary entered. She was a severe woman in her mid-forties, dressed in shapeless tweed, with grey hair scraped back from her wide forehead and tied in a harsh knot on top of her head. She deposited a bundle of manila files on the desk, and was about to leave again when Barrie called her back.

'Find Chief Inspector Kettle, will you please, Martha? If you can't raise him, leave a message to contact me immediately. Oh, and bring in a copy of the case conference minutes, and a spare radio-pager.'

Martha stretched her lips over her teeth and marched out of the room. Barrie lifted the top file, glanced at the writing on the cover, tossed it back, and sighed. Lit another cigarette, used it to draw patterns in the ashtray.

'While Kettle is busy with all that,' he asked, 'what will you be doing?'

'Trying to find an angle. You know, approach it from a different direction. I've got Harry checking up on all crimes of a similar nature, going back as far as he can. We're also digging out all outstanding Missing Person Reports over the last few years to see if any similarities come to light.'

'Won't the Murder Squad be doing that?'

'Could be, but no harm in double-checking.'

Martha returned and handed me a stapled sheaf of papers and a pager.

'The Chief Inspector's at the STV Studios,' she said to Barrie. Her voice was flat, toneless and annoyingly efficient. 'I left a message.' She glanced pointedly at her watch. 'You have a meeting with the Chief Constable in fifteen minutes – shall I arrange the car?'

'Yes, go on,' he said, irritably stubbing out his cigarette as Martha retreated in dignified haste. He put his smile on automatic, said: 'Sorry, Frank. You know how it is.'

'Sure, no problem.' We shook hands again and promised to keep in touch. As I left the building, I wondered why I'd been asked to come and what the hell Barrie was playing at.

I had a liquid lunch in a bar on Rose Street, and when

that failed to still my troubled mind, I phoned a friend, then weaved my way down to Easter Road. I could have taken a bus or a taxi but I had time on my hands and furthermore needed the exercise.

Every time I visit Dave Nicholl, I walk away feeling insignificant. Whether he realises it or not, he is a meter against which I measure myself. In the light of his disabilities, my normal everyday problems are like candles to the sun.

Dave is an ex-colleague. We were partners once, when we were both detective-sergeants working out of Central CID. We were young, hard and over-enthusiastic. Fancied ourselves as a kind of Starsky and Hutch or Bodie and Doyle. One day we got in a chase, speeding around the city, me at the wheel, Dave shitting himself in the passenger seat. The guys we were after were a couple of wide-boys who had been doing turns on OAPs, getting heavy when there was no need. We wanted them. And we had them, too – until I took a corner too fast, had to swerve to miss a pedestrian and put the car through a lamp-post. End of story. End of Dave's career. He came out paralysed from the waist down, me without a scratch.

He now lives with his common-law wife in one of three new bungalows built amidst a jungle of tiny allotments, between the Hibernian football ground and Lochend Park. He buzzed the door when I rang, and I walked through to find him in the front room behind his desk. The patio doors were open, looking out over the back of Arthur's Seat and Salisbury Crags. He grasped my hand warmly.

'How's the world's greatest criminologist?' I asked.

'Doing away. Christ, where have you been, Frank? I thought maybe you'd lost my address.'

'I've been busy, Dave. Sorry.'

'Poor excuse,' he said, letting a smile split his boyish face. 'Anyway, how's it been?'

I shrugged, the best explanation.

'Like that, eh?' He wheeled himself round the desk, waved me to sit. 'Still, you're looking good. Fancy a wee goldy?'

'Twist my arm.'

'You were born with a twist in your arm.' He poured generous measures in large glasses, saying, 'Bring them over.' I did. We contemplated MacAllans twelve year old for a while before Dave asked, 'You still suspended?'

I nodded. He ran his fingers through his dark curly hair and regarded me askance. 'Taking their time, aren't they?'

I told him why, adding, 'There's something funny going on.'

'You always were a suspicious bastard. Not just suspicious, but definitely paranoid. The way I see it, they're giving you a chance to prove yourself. A lot of people respect you, Frank, you're a good cop. They don't want to see you go down just because you can't handle your guilt. On top of that, it looks like they need someone with a working knowledge of the case, someone with a good nose, who's prepared to back his hunches all the way – and that's you.'

'I always thought my nose was too big . . .'

'Shit, you never listen. Always putting yourself down, always so hard done by. Chrissakes, Frank, will you grow up?'

'Hey, c'mon——'

'Okay. I had my say and you had it coming. Now will you tell me what really happened on that roof?'

A lot of people had asked me that recently, and not so pleasantly, either. The roof in question was on a high-rise block in Little France, where me and Ruben Maxwell had a little chat before he fell to his death. Dear sweet Ruben who could never hurt a fly but roasted his family for the insurance.

'He tried to kill me,' I said.

'I saw a copy of the Path. Report, Frank. Maxwell's face was ripped to shreds. Eyes hanging out, nose torn, ear almost bitten off . . .'

'I told you. He tried to kill me.'

'Mmm . . .' He sounded doubtful.

I let it go. 'How come you saw the Path. Report?'

'Friends,' he said, smiling vaguely, then dismissing the subject with a wave of his hand. 'Ach, forget it. Tell me about The Hangman instead. How's the enquiry going?'

I gave him a copy of the case conference minutes and studied him as he read. Thirty-three years old, he had a broad open face, deep brown eyes widely spaced above a flattened nose, and a lopsided mouth with full lips. His whole complexion exuded health. He finished reading and tossed the papers back.

'There's precious little to go on.'

'You're telling me?'

'The guy's a psycho – that much is obvious.'

'What else is obvious?' I asked.

'Well, he's not politically motivated.'

'Not this guy. We've already got a Prime Minister.'

'You know what I mean. Anyway, he could be the self-assertive type, who kills so the world will stand up and take notice. To prove he exists, that sort of thing.'

'You mean like Ryan, the Hungerford sharpshooter?'

Nicholl shrugged, shook his curls. 'Who knows what went on inside his head. No, I think we're dealing with a cold and callous psycho here – in my mind, the most dangerous of all. He's totally loveless, compassionless and merciless in the gratification of his desires. The perfect serial killer.'

'Could he be schizo?' I asked.

'It's possible, but you'd be surprised how small a proportion of violent crimes are actually committed by schizophrenics.'

'What about these split-personalities we keep hearing about?'

'You'll only find that in the critical stages of the disease, where he'll create an imaginary world to give his anger direction. It's usually the innocent who get hurt in an imaginary world.'

'In any world. You mentioned anger . . . why?'

'It's motive enough. Most psychos are social, sexual and emotional failures. They blame their inadequacies on everyone but themselves. So someone has to pay the price. Doesn't matter who, so long as that chosen unfortunate recognizes *his* power, *his* greatness, before he takes their life.'

'That's all very well,' I said, 'but how does it help me find him? He's probably a model citizen, respected by his family and friends, works hard, goes to church, takes the dog for a walk. Normal in every way except that once in a

69

while he goes out and strangles some kid to satisfy his twisted mind.'

'You think he's married? Could be. Studies into paedophilia suggest it's an outlet for incestual desires.'

'But he doesn't assault them. He merely throttles and hangs them. Okay, he might achieve a certain sexual gratification from the act of killing, but——'

'Sex is not always the primary motivation, Frank. This guy's killed a girl and a boy. That suggests some other motivation, perhaps some trauma he suffered as a kid, recently aggravated – that kind of thing.'

I shook my head. 'More like he's just into power,' I said. 'You know, pick on the weakest——' I broke off suddenly as my pager bleeped.

'Help yourself,' Dave said, indicating the cordless telephone on his desk. I dialled the fiscal's number and listened to Martha's efficient monotone as she told me Harry had called, and to contact him at the Squad's Incident Room. I thanked her, cut the connection, dialled and asked for Harry. He came on immediately.

'Central Vice have just brought some guy in,' he told me. 'Kettle thinks he's our man.'

'Have you seen him yet?'

'Not a chance. Kettle's got him stashed away somewhere and is not letting on. I asked if we could interview the suspect but he wouldn't reply. He's looking pretty damn pleased with himself though.'

'Nothing in on the guy yet?'

'All I know is he's got a previous on child-molesting, was at the Commonwealth Pool last Saturday.'

'Okay, Harry. I'll get onto the fiscal, have him push

Kettle into letting us see the guy. Meanwhile, try to find out where they're keeping him.'

'Sounds like action,' Nicholl said.

I told him the score.

'Looks like you might be out of a job,' he said when I'd finished.

'Don't remind me. Sounds like Kettle's gloating already. If he pulls this off . . .'

I called the fiscal's office again, told Martha I had to speak to Barrie as soon as possible, if not sooner. She said she didn't know where he was or when he'd be back. I swore and slammed down the phone. Then I rang back to apologise and leave Nicholl's number.

'Stay for tea, Frank,' Nicholl suggested. 'Dorothy should be back soon.'

'Sod the tea, Dave. I need another drink.'

It was evening before Barrie called.

# Chapter Five

Some people perspire. Me, I sweat.

I was sweating in the small observation room behind the two-way mirror and Harry was perspiring next to me. The radiator on the wall was one of those typically British heaters that won't switch off in the summer and never work in the winter. We had been breathing the same air for almost two hours now. The headphones were painful on my ears and my legs ached for mobility. My throat croaked for liquid but I couldn't bear the thought of another cup of piss-coloured coffee from the dispenser. So I suffered in silence.

Kettle was enjoying his little power games – we had been waiting for hours. It was now 1.34 am and the scene through the mirror hadn't changed much in the time we had been sitting there. The interview room was the same as most: sparse and uninviting, anonymous and unfriendly. The actions of the three men in the room came across as though in slow-motion.

Chief Inspector Kettle was enjoying himself. He strutted about the room, employing long silences and sudden bursts of anger like an amateur dramatist, his bullish torso threatening to burst from his shirt at any given moment.

The other detective was new to me: about thirty-five, with a lean hungry look, suspicious brown eyes and snarling lips. Vice Squad, I thought.

The third man was dwarfed in the presence of his two inquisitors. In his middle-forties, he was small and fragile with a white face and pink tips to his nose and ears. His ash-blond hair, parted at the side, swooped across his forehead and almost obscured the small pebble eyes that rolled nervously in bland sockets. His voice came across as a continuous whine. Vile habits apart, there was something about the man that made me cringe, want to smash his teeth down his throat. But The Hangman? I found that hard to imagine.

I heard Kettle say, 'And after that, what did you do?'

'Went home.'

'Straight home? You didn't stop off anywhere on the way?'

'No, I told you. I stayed in all night.'

The Vice Squad detective stepped forward. 'And watched television, eh?' he said with vicious sarcasm. 'Sure. We believe you. Just like we believe all your other lies.' He slammed his fist on the table, sending plastic cups sprawling. 'What do you take us for, Moxton? Do you think we're stupid or something?'

Kettle laid a restraining hand on the detective's arm. 'Hey, take it easy, Bob,' he said, playing Mr Nice. Lucky Moxton.

Bob backed off. 'The bastard's lying, I know it.'

'So?' Kettle said. 'It's natural. He's frightened.' Turning to Moxton, 'Aren't you, Horace?'

'I'm telling you the truth!'

'Now, now . . .'

Harry nudged me and I took off my headphones. He motioned me out of the stuffy cubicle. A PC was sitting on a chair further along the hall. He nodded, then ignored us.

'The guy's right. Moxton's lying,' Harry said.

'Through his rotten yellow teeth,' I agreed. I leant against the wall, sucked in fresh stale air and waited for the blood to find my legs again. 'But do you think he did it?'

Harry didn't answer immediately. He removed his glasses and rubbed the bridge of his nose. 'Mmm. Kettle seems to think so.'

'Only because Moxton is lying.'

'And he wants it to be Moxton. He wants a quick result.'

'If he wants to stitch Horace up, he can,' I said. 'Same blood group, no alibi or witnesses for either day or night of the murders and a history of child-molesting. What else does Kettle need?'

'Proof,' Harry murmured.

I could have laughed.

'Too easy, Harry,' I told him. 'The man's scared shitless. He's hiding something, sure, but I don't think it's a confession to murder. Maybe a little hocus-pocus on the side, but . . .'

'He was seen at the pool that afternoon,' Harry reminded me. We had been present earlier when one of the locker-room orderlies at the pool confirmed that Moxton was the man he had seen. Asked how he could be sure, he said he had had trouble with Moxton before –

complaints from boys, stuff like that – though nothing that could be proved. So the staff had been warned to keep their eyes on him. He was definitely there that Saturday afternoon because they had seen him looking on when a kid slipped and broke his ankle and had to be taken to hospital – though no-one was sure what time he came and left, Saturday being the busiest day of the week and all that.

Still, I wasn't convinced.

Harry said, 'You still see a lot of Nicholl?'

'He's a friend, Harry.'

'You sure it's not your guilt drives you down there?'

'What would you know about that? I went down to see if he could give me a profile on The Hangman, nothing more.'

'He give you anything?'

Before I could answer, Kettle and Bob from Vice emerged from a door along the corridor. We met like duellists at dawn.

'So the vultures have come to pick the bones,' Kettle sneered. Bob from Vice giggled.

'Have you charged him yet?' I asked.

'Have you charged him yet, *sir*,' Kettle corrected.

'Have you charged him yet, *sir*,' I said. It didn't hurt – much.

'We're holding him on a minor.'

'Has he had legal representation?'

'You going soft or something, McMorran?'

'It wouldn't look so good if he got off on a technicality.'

'You let me worry about that. You start looking for another job.'

76

'Ha-ha.'

Kettle scowled. 'Careful, Inspector.'

I asked what the arrangements were for watching the Commonwealth Pool on Saturday.

'Maybe we don't need them anymore. Moxton was there the afternoon the girl got hers. I reckon he's our man.'

'Are you serious?'

'He'll crack, given time.' Kettle glanced at his watch. 'You can have him for twenty minutes, not a second more.' He thrust the folder at me, adding, 'That's his sheet. Read it. You might change your mind.'

I took the proffered file. Kettle took a few steps, beckoned Harry with a jerk of his head.

'Sergeant – a word, if you please.' They moved off down the corridor. I felt currents moving underwater. Was it just paranoia, like Nicholl had said?

'So you're the famous McMorran,' Bob from Vice said.

'Yeah. And who are you?'

'DI Pitts,' he said. 'Licensing.'

'How nice.' Thinking, what the hell was going on between Harry and Kettle?

Then Harry came plodding back down the corridor. He told Pitts to meet Kettle downstairs and the DI loped off like a faithful puppy, the kind Kettle prefers. Was he being groomed as my replacement, I wondered. Paranoia, funny the way the word kept coming back.

Silence is the great inquisitor. It offers you no defence. You cannot silence the voice of your thoughts, nor shut out the soundless screams of your fears. You are forced to hear them out. Leave a man alone with his fears and they will gnaw at him until he is little more than one big gaping wound. Then add salt and stir a little.

Horace Moxton had had time to gnaw at his wounds, and when we entered the room and dismissed the PC, we could see the relief on his face that the silence was over, the waiting was over. So we waited in silence a little longer.

I sat in the only available chair across the table from him and studied him coldly. His eyes looked hopefully into mine. A sneer crossed my lips, I couldn't help it. I felt no compassion for this piece of garbage. It would have been a matter of great enjoyment to slowly beat the shit out of him. I'm that kind of bully.

He squirmed beneath my unfeeling eyes. Harry had moved round behind him, was standing silent, unnerving Moxton with his quiet immobility. We played this game for a few minutes, then I asked, 'Why did you kill her, Horace?'

'I didn't! How many times do I——'

'Till you tell the truth.'

'I've told the truth.'

'The whole truth?' I asked.

'Yes!'

I leaned forward across the table. 'Your first lie, Horace.' Then I leant back in my chair and waited. Always give them silence after they tell a lie. It gets them thinking about the weaknesses behind the lie and soon they start trying to shore the initial lie up with secondary lies. Knock out secondary lies and more often than not, the initial lie goes with them. Horace, however, was not playing. He was saying nothing, perhaps wondering how much we knew. I let him wonder, watching him all the time. Eventually he spoke.

'So I was a little economical with the truth,' he admitted.

'That's fine,' I said, 'but you're no Cabinet Secretary, Horace. You won't get away lying through your teeth. The rest of your life will be decided here, now, by the answers you give. So let's move on. Your first offence – when was it?'

'1963.'

'How old were you?'

'Twenty-three.'

'The offence?'

'Rape,' he said, softly. 'I was . . . drunk.'

'So?'

'I didn't know what I was doing.'

'So you did it again two weeks later, just to make sure.'

'It wasn't like that!'

'You mean you were sober the second time?'

'No! I mean, yes! I mean . . .'

'You work for the Council?'

'Yes.'

'Do your colleagues know about your perversions?'

In a small voice, 'No.'

'You mean it's not on your personnel file?'

'I don't know.'

'So you got the job under false pretences.'

Moxton dropped his head, said nothing.

'How long have you worked there?'

'Seven years.'

'You enjoy sex with children?' Harry asked. His large

hands rested on the back of the prisoner's chair so that Moxton had to turn his head awkwardly.

'No . . .'

'You do it because you hate it, then?'

'No. It's not like that! It's something I can't control . . . a feeling. I can't help it.'

'Is that how it was when you killed Craig Watson? Did you get that feeling when you murdered Janice Young?'

'But I didn't——'

'Why did you kill them, Moxton?'

'I tell you, I didn't! I wasn't there when——'

'Weren't where, Moxton?'

'Wherever they were killed. I don't know . . . I told you I wasn't there.'

'Where were you?'

'Out. Walking. I go out every Saturday afternoon.'

'Where did you walk last Saturday?'

'Around . . . I can't remember exactly where.'

'Did you see anyone you knew, anyone who could vouch for you?'

Moxton shook his head.

'You were seen at the Commonwealth Pool.'

'I often go there. There's no law against it.'

'To pick your next victim? To watch the little boys in the showers? Is that it?'

'No! I go to swim.'

Harry sighed, went and straightened his tie in front of the mirror. Moxton's gaze was fixed on the pack of Embassy Regal on the table.

'You smoke, Horace?' I asked.

He nodded.

'Bad habit,' I said. 'It can cause fatal diseases. But so can long-term prison sentences. You know what prisons are like at the moment . . . overcrowded, three or more to a cell. No cells left to isolate sex-offenders from fellow inmates. They hate people like you, have kids of their own. You wouldn't last long. If the inmates didn't get you, AIDS probably would. No escape from that, not you, with your slim figure and pretty blond hair. You'd attract all the big butch bastards like flies to shit. Though maybe you'd like that?'

Moxton seemed to retreat within himself. I pressed on.

'Of course, there's a difference between assault and murder. If you didn't kill the two kids, why are you lying? Perhaps you were doing something else, Horace? Something you don't want to admit to. If that's the case, then you'd better ask yourself if your silence is worth it. Your life is already in ruins. Don't think you will walk out of here and everything will be back to normal. If you can't prove what you were doing at the times of the murders then you'll go down for them. There's enough evidence already to convict you. With your record you'd never see the outside world again'

Harry came back across from the mirror. 'Do you live alone?' he asked.

'Yes.'

'Flat, house, bedsit . . . what?'

'Bedsit.'

'What about your landlord – can he vouch for your presence at home?'

'He's out boozing most nights. I never see him anyway, he lives on the top floor.'

'So you watched television all night?'

'That's what I said.'

'On the nights of both murders?'

'I told you. I'm a man of routine. I do the same every Saturday.'

'So does The Hangman, Horace,' I said.

He looked around helplessly, like a cornered rat.

'Where did you kill her, Moxton?'

'Why did you hang her?'

'Did she laugh at you? Did she insult you? Is that why you strangled her?'

'She recognised you, so you had to kill her . . .'

Moxton's head fell to his arms on the table. He banged his fists in time to the words. 'No . . . no . . . no . . . no!'

'It wasn't like that then? Okay, tell us how it was,' Harry retorted.

Moxton's head rose with angry, tear-filled eyes. 'Why don't you leave me alone! I didn't kill them. I'm tired. I want my lawyer, I've got a right to a lawyer. I want to sleep. You're torturing me, you know that?'

'You'll see your lawyer in the morning,' I told him. 'You can sleep when you've told the truth. And if you think this is torture, let me tell you we haven't even started yet. We're just warming you up for the next shift.'

He suddenly began sobbing; a moment later, he was bawling, tears splish-splashing all over the table.

This is it, I thought. We've bloody cracked it.

# Chapter Six

Dominic Bain walked into the city beneath an overcast sky. It had been raining steadily since midday, a light drizzle in a clammy atmosphere that dampened clothes from inside and out. Days like this and Edinburgh seemed to close in on itself like a flower contracting when the sun goes in. Moods turned introspective.

The afternoon yawned and stretched before him with all the languor of a satisfied beast. In a way he was glad to be back. In the village he had only memories; here he had substance, for this was the seat of his power. Today he wanted to taste that power.

He walked to the subtle rhythm of the streets. He dodged and ducked, dummied and swerved his way through Morningside, down into Tollcross. He touched no-one and was touched by no-one, arriving at the Tollcross Clock untainted.

He descended West Port into the Grassmarket.

But here also, memories.

The Middle Ages seemed to loom over him. The sense of huddled poverty still pervaded, despite the fashionable store-fronts, the wide pavements, the split-level bars. Forget the hostels for the down-and-outs, forget the characterless, grey façade: look at the trees, the cobbles, the burrowing sunless streets and closes, the steps, the narrow stairs; and the shuffling dossers in their balaclavas and fingerless gloves, sandals in the snow and lives in Jenners bags. The poor at heart and the poor at life, they all meet on the Grassmarket.

He glided up Victoria Street and on to George IV Bridge. Packed traffic, stalled at the High Street lights. Buses trundling up The Mound. Lunchtime hordes in and out of pubs and queuing in take-aways. The two main libraries dribbling students onto the polished pavements, clutching books and scornful of the rain. Soberly-dressed clerks and typists, stotting along in high-heeled shoes and umbrellas. Medallion-men in pinstriped suits darting from cover to cover with newspapers over their trendy perms. Dour, dripping faces standing in line at bus-stops. And tourists. Tourists everywhere, with their tartan Tam o' Shanters, sensible shoes and Burberrys. Wearing away the High Street, up and down, from the Castle to Palace, the Palace to the Castle.

Down to the Royal Mile. Here, he could not help but admire the mad beauty, the incestuous fornication, the coupling of old and new. It was not hard to imagine the High Street then, back in the Middle Ages, with its towering tenements and open sewers. Or the gay and gaudy colours of folk who liked to dress beyond their means at a time when only appearance could hide their stinking lives from the critical gaze of their peers. Had anything changed in the passage of years? The smoke-stained skies of Auld Reekie, perhaps. But even now, dull leaden sky.

He turned on impulse down a sidestreet, away from

the shopping crowds. When he came to a narrow lane, off to the right, he followed it, through scarce light and heavier rain. Felt himself drawn, compelled.

*What if he was there?*

He heard the music above the steady patter of rain on cobbles and cars. As he approached, two men spilled onto the street, pulled at jacket collars, dashed to their car. Dominic tasted the musty smell of the bar, knew he was going in, father or no bloody father.

He was hit by a wall of heat and smoke. Men stood holding pints, talking soft or laughing loud; some in suits, some in overalls, some in need of a job. Dominic shouldered his way to the bar, ordered a pint, the barman serving him as though he were some kind of pervert.

It was a low-ceilinged room with subdued lighting and small windows. He found a space in the corner opposite the stage and sat down. Rain trickled down the outside of his neck, lager down the inside.

He looked around, saw no familiar faces, no long-lost fathers skulking around the tables, sneaking up on long-lost sons and scaring them to death.

Okay, if he didn't want to see his old man, what was he doing here now? Come to watch the girlies take their knickers down, show their scars and sagging tits? Was that why? Was he turning all pervy at the edges or something?

No way.

A month ago – was it really that? – anyway, before the killing started, before he met Craig Watson and took him to the noose, he had come in here for the first time. There was no rain that day, the city sweltered in a prickly heat hot enough to bubble brains. So nobody's fool had walked in and ordered a pint of something cool.

He had been there a couple of minutes, time to sink half his lager and think about – shit, it was hard trying to remember the kind of things he thought about before he killed the Watson kid. Suddenly, someone put him in shadow. He looked up to see an old dosser staring at him as though he had just stepped out of a coffin.

Dominic had sneered, already reaching for the change in his pocket to get rid of the old sod. But the dosser stood there with his mouth open. Then a name came out in a dry croak.

'Nick?'

Only one person in the world ever called him Nick. But it couldn't be him, no chance, case of mistaken identity. His father was locked away in some institution or cell or wherever it is they put the criminally insane. Or was he?

'Nick?' The dosser said again, and slid into the chair opposite. Dominic could not look at him. Too much, too soon.

'Sod off, eh?'

'You ashamed to greet your father, Nick?'

He was forced to look up now. 'You're not my father, never were.'

'You've a poor memory, Nick.'

'Twenty-five, six, seven years and you expect me to remember every fucking little detail? Christ!'

'How's your mother, Nick?'

'Better now she's dead. Anything else you want to know while I'm still here?'

'Dead?' His eyes suddenly looked lost behind the black-rimmed spectacles.

'That's what I said. Don't they tell you nothing when they lock you away?'

'Oh God.'

'Yeah, that's the idea. Now sod off, leave me in peace.'

'Nick . . .'

'What now?' Christ it was getting hot.

'When did she die?' his father asked.

'Three, four year ago, I don't know. In her sleep, like she went to bed and forgot to wake up. You know?'

Old John McBean nods, his eyes now dead in his head. After a long pause, he said, 'What about you, son? How've you been keeping?'

'I'm okay, right? Just fine and dandy'

'You married? Got a girl?'

'Yeah, yeah. What about you?'

His father looked at him, a sadness taking over his face, relaxing all the muscles.

Dominic climbed to his feet. 'Did you know, I read it somewhere, you've got more muscles in your face than the rest of your body? Makes you wonder, eh?'

'Does it, Nick?'

'Anyway, I've got to go. Can't hang around all day, you know. Things to do, right?'

'Nick, please——'

'Don't touch me!'

'Tell me where you live! We must talk. Dominic!'

Nobody's fool had to throw off the clutching paw and almost break his ankle running down the street trying to ignore the old man's voice, calling, 'Nick, son, come back, after all I ever did for you!'

Now, sitting across the room from the window seat as the lights dimmed and a girl stepped out onto the stage, he was thinking all the things that had happened since that day were down to the old man. Did he regret the lies he had told about Mother-dear being dead? Did he hell. If something's working, don't mess it about. He didn't want the old man coming in, spoiling the whole cosy set-up. That would never do. Better to believe she was dead, then he wouldn't come looking.

Spotlights came on, fixing the girl to the stage.

She sat cross-legged on the floor, hands in her lap, leaning forward with her head dipped and limp like a puppet on a nursery floor. A black cape covered her whole body and her hair was a curtain across her face. The music from the juke-box died. And then started again, this time a slow South American beat accompanied by the whistles and catcalls of the audience. The girl began to move.

Dominic was struck by something he could not immediately define. Something in the way she moved, perhaps. Or the way she held her head. He had to squint harder through the bank of smoke to see her.

She was sheathed in gossamer – or so it appeared. Her body-stocking as thin and transparent as a membrane and when the lights caught it, she was scaled in soft greens and blues.

*Like a snake.*

She danced with closed eyes and bare feet, writhing to the beat as the tempo increased. Coiled and uncoiled, the soft pressure of her breasts, surge of hips and thrust of her thighs moulding the material to her body like a new skin. She was in a different league from other dancers he had seen. He edged closer to the stage.

Now, with her back to the audience, she flicked at invisible buttons with long tapered fingers. Hips swaying hypnotically, like the dance of a cobra. He saw that she was tall, maybe five foot nine, with taut skin, flesh firm and luxuriant. She turned, and he saw her face clearly. Lines and angles but soft and subtle. Shadows playing a bewitching role, diffusing light, confusing the eye. An elfin face, expressing innocence and experience all in a single look.

She shrugged her body-stocking off her shoulders, down her arms . . .

*The snake sheds her skin.*

Dominic was spellbound.

Her face remained impassive. Only the shadows moved. But Dominic wasn't watching her face anymore, he was watching her peel the body-stocking slowly down the curve of her thighs. Released now to reveal the sweep of pelvis, dive of crutch, G-string.

Bain gasped involuntarily – the G-string concealed nothing but the kiss of petalled lips.

*She was shaved!*

The music climaxed in a crescendo of congas and brass, Dominic higher than he should have been on Valium and booze. Through clouded eyes, he watched her gather up her props and leave the stage to raucous cheers. He returned to his seat, dazed and finished his pint, waiting for the mad rush for the door to subside. He leant over to a man near him, 'What's her name, the girl just been on?'

The guy leered and breathed beer in Dominic's face, saying, 'Natasha. Why? Getting knobbly, are you, cock?' The guy stumbled off, laughing and shaking his head.

Dominic waited around, maybe catch her when she comes out, the idea growing familiar as the minutes stretched. Eventually he walked out into the rain, floundering like a fish on the shore of anti-climax.

He felt suddenly cold and uncomfortable, needing a shower, change of clothes, time to think. He flagged down a taxi and returned home, thoughts simmering on the heat of desire.

# Chapter Seven

Self-pity is a disease which pulls all that is positive into a spiralling spin to nowhere. In an interview like this, with a subject like Moxton, it must be gently nurtured and encouraged to grow. It needs delicate technique. Used too fast or ruthlessly, it provokes two general reactions: either the prisoner throws himself into his deepening pit of despair by confessing all; or he becomes stubborn through shame and anger – and closes like a clam. When Moxton's sobs had subsided to snivels and he eventually raised his head to look at me, I knew we had blown it.

'Do what you like,' he said, wiping his eyes with the back of his hand, 'but I'm not saying another word until I see my solicitor.'

I tried to stare him down but failed. His defiance was impenetrable. Perhaps I'd been mistaken – he was stronger than he appeared.

I stood up, nodded to Harry and without another word we left the room. The PC outside was dozing on his chair. I kicked him gently and he sprang to life, stammering apologies all over the place. I told him to put the prisoner to bed, or hand him over to Kettle or do what the hell he liked, then led Harry up to the canteen.

There were three other people there, one of them a sergeant in uniform with his legs up on a stool, snoring loudly. The other two, detectives I recognised from 'C' Division, were talking quietly at a table in the corner. We sat near the window, sipping sweet black coffee.

'What are you going to do about Moxton?' Harry asked.

'Nothing. Let someone else waste their time. I've had enough.' I rubbed my irritated eyes. 'What did Kettle want with you?' I asked casually.

Too casually. Harry missed nothing. He cocked his head and frowned. 'Nothing much,' he answered, vaguely enough to let me know I was out of order. 'It concerned some reports I asked him to get for me.'

'What reports, Harry?'

His frown deepened, eyes clouded. 'What's up, Frank? You don't believe me?'

'What reports, Harry?'

'The ones you asked me to get,' he snapped. 'All the cases of death by hanging. Remember?'

'Sure, I do. But why so secretive? Why the cosy wee chat round the corner?

'Christ, Frank! You're beginning to sound like a jealous husband. What the hell's the matter with you? Why suddenly all these questions?'

'There's something going on, Harry. You know it, I know it. So tell me what it is. We're partners, aren't we?'

His hesitation hurt.

'Well, maybe,' he muttered.

'What the hell does that mean?'

He leant close across the table. 'It means you've got a

professional death-wish, Frank. You seem to be going out of your way to provoke everyone you come in contact with. You don't seem to care anymore. I'm not the only one who's noticed. I think . . .'

'Yes, Harry? What do you think?'

He glanced across the room, then at his watch, then out the window, before replying. 'I think you ought to see a doctor.'

'That's nice, Harry – just what I like to see. Confidence in your superiors. Well, do me a favour. Either get yourself a transfer off my bloody back or turn up at my door tomorrow morning with the stuff I asked for and don't ever mention anything like that again. You understand?'

'Don't take it so personally, Frank. I'm only trying to help.'

'Don't take it personally, Harry,' I told him in a harsh mimic, 'but up yours.'

I left him there and walked home across the sleeping city.

Eight-fifteen, and Harry rang midway through my second bacon roll. I mumbled and told him to come on round. He sounded distant, almost wary. 'Maybe. We'll see,' he said, then hung up.

I had a second coffee, another roll, then fetched the two boxes of files from the hall and took them through. The sun was up and splashing the table in warm light. I opened the windows, let in the rumble of the street. Then I sat and worked my way through each box, using a red marker-pen with all the relish of a British film censor let loose on Bambi.

As I shuffled through the papers, I could almost feel the malevolent presence of the killer squirm beneath the mountain of dissembled data. His traces were there, I was sure, imprinted on the routine enquiry reports. Unnoticed perhaps, behind casual comments and incomplete observations.

By eleven o'clock, I was left with two stacks of reports: some marked with red, some without. The larger pile – the ones without – went back in the box. I made another coffee, then set to work again. Thirty minutes later, I had a list. I read through it again.

1. Craig Watson and Janice Young both lived in Morningside.
   Both went to school in Morningside (though not the same one).

2. Both went swimming at the Commonwealth Pool the day they died.

3. Both died on a Saturday.

4. Both bodies were wrapped in council bin-liners tied with string.
   Knots used were similar in both cases. (Someone checking with knot specialist?)

5. Rope (blue synthetic, 1¼" diameter) cut and left around neck of each victim. Knots similar.

6. No trace of bodily hair or tissue left by perpetrator.
   (Except semen.) Body washed, hosed down?

7. Semen found only on Janice Young. (Neither victim was sexually assaulted.) Deposited on purpose, *after* washed down? If so, why? (See below.)

8. Little attempt made to conceal bodies. Why? Perpetrator wanted bodies to be found? Again, why?

9. Drives car. Colour and make unknown.

10. No fingerprints. Wore gloves.

11. Footprint found near locus. Forensic suggest size 10, est. weight: 11½–12 stone. (Possibly work or combat boots.)

12. Path. report suggests perp. has gap between front teeth.

13. Bloodgroup – B Rhesus. Not common.

14. Psychiatric history/patient? (Royal Edinburgh Hospital in Morningside is psychiatric hosp.)

15. Janice Young possibly shaved by perp. If so, why?

16. How does perp. get victims to accompany him?

17. Where does he take victims? (Access to water?)

18. Why hang them when they are already dead?

19. Motives? Why children?

20. Trace of barbiturates in J.Y.'s blood-stream. Explains lack of defensive struggle?

I sat and stared at the list, convinced there was something I had overlooked. I could feel it, whatever it was, burrowing its way through layers of memory like an insect seeking a distant light. So I sorted through the reports for the millionth time, trying to find the something I had missed. I missed whatever it was again.

I switched on the television and sat down in the armchair, a brown swivel job left me by Angus McPheep, an ex-colleague-turned-PI, who had died of apathy one typical February afternoon. I wondered . . .

I wondered about motive.

Motives never change. There are six of them which account for ninety-nine percent of all known murders: greed, lust, envy, jealousy, rejection and revenge. All powerful emotions which can explode into sudden murderous violence. All to be found quietly simmering in any decent, civilised family.

It is the remaining one per cent that constitutes the detective's nightmare. The elusive one per cent in which the killer has no direct relation to his victim, in which both parties are complete strangers until the moment they are brought together by some quirk of fate. In such cases, the usual motives cannot be relied upon to point the finger of accusation, and searching for a plausible motive is like struggling through a hostile swamp shrouded in mist. Quicksands lurk treacherously at every turn, eager to suck in the desperate, straw-clutching detective. Red herrings swim invitingly close, their beady eyes like beacons offering an illusion of safety. A place where logic and reason are as tangible as smoke.

Logic and reason.

Even in the mind of a twisted pervert, there is logic. It is only the detective's inability to understand that logic which gives life to the fear of policeman around the world – 'apparently random behaviour'. Such behaviour, we were told repeatedly at Training College, can only be understood when all the circumstances are known.

And what did we know? We knew everything except who he was, where he lived, what he looked like, why and where he killed, when he was going to kill again – and a thousand other relevant details. We knew there was a Morningside connection: that maybe he lived there or worked there – or perhaps just dumped the bodies there. We knew he probably picked his first two victims at the Commonwealth Pool. Short of genetically fingerprinting the whole of Morningside, I could see little else that could be done except wait and hope. I had reached that point when my confidence was pulled out of an earthbound spin by the ring of the doorbell.

Harry stood at the door replete in raincoat, hat, and briefcase. He gave me a curt nod and pushed into the hall. His eyes were tired orbs peering from deep shadows.

'Long night, Harry?' I led him through to the front room. He collapsed into an armchair and cuddled his briefcase like a child on his lap.

'Coffee,' he gasped.

As I went through to the kitchen the lunchtime news

97

flashed from the television. '. . . *the Prime Minister called an emergency meeting of the Cabinet this morning, to discuss the implications of last night's inner-city disturbances. Political observers believe . . .*'

When I returned with the coffee, Harry had removed his hat, and, '. . . *A man was brought before the High Court in Edinburgh this morning, charged with the murders of two local children. He appeared, briefly, handcuffed to two detectives and after a hearing that lasted only two minutes was remanded in custody pending further enquiries.*

'*Outside the court, Chief Inspector Kettle who is leading the investigation into the Hangman murders, would not be drawn on speculation that the charged man is indeed The Hangman. From our northern correspondent, a more detailed report . . .*

'*Security was tight here in the High Street of the Capital this afternoon as crowds gathered outside the court, straining to catch a glimpse of the man now widely speculated to be The Hangman. Extra police were called in when missiles were thrown by an angry crowd of women, enraged after weeks of terror as The Hangman stalked the streets of the Festival City. The prisoner was led in through the rear of the courthouse, handcuffed to two detectives, with a blanket over his head. He is charged with . . .*'

I switched off the set with an angry punch at the button.

'So Kettle's opted for the easy way out,' I said.

Harry stared at me blankly. 'How are you feeling today?'

'Never better.'

He studied me for a moment longer and when he saw I was going to say nothing more about yesterday's scene opened his briefcase, pulling out a wad of papers.

'Developments?' I asked.

He shook his head. 'These are the files you asked for. Precedents of murder by hanging. I've managed to whittle them down to four – '

'Out of how many?'

'Twenty-six, going back thirty years. You're lucky to get them. Most records don't stay around that long. If it wasn't that Archie was so – '

I cut him off. 'And these four?'

'I've noted down all the relevant information, but even so . . .'

'You think it's a waste of time?'

'See for yourself.' He offered me the papers but I waved them away. Harry's handwriting is as comprehensible to me as Sanskrit.

'Tell me about them,' I said.

He put on his reading-glasses and in a stilted court-room fashion began to recite.

'Julian Swan, born 15 march 1951, Glasgow. Sentenced to eleven years in 1974 for the murder of his eighteen year old wife, Sheila, found hanging from a clothes-line in her kitchen on 3 January 1974. One of her neighbours bringing in washing from the tenement green, happened to look up and see Sheila hanging, and called the police. They arrived and, getting no answer, broke down the door. They found Julian Swan asleep in bed. He protested his innocence, claiming it was suicide, but there was no note. Furthermore, a postmortem examination revealed bruises on the side of the neck and body. He was subsequently charged, appeared in court and the jury's verdict was unanimous. He served eight of his eleven year sentence in Barlinnie, and was released in November 1982.'

'A domestic dispute?'

'Mmm. It appeared his wife had been flirting with a guy in their local, Swan got jealous and started a fight. They were asked to leave. Later on that night a neighbour heard shouting.

'No indications of psychopathy?'

'Not according to the psychiatrist's report. Minor schizophrenia, though nothing more than most of us.' He tossed me a meaningful look. I chose to ignore it.

'How did he plead?' I asked.

'Not guilty. Insisted throughout he was framed, that someone else must've killed her while he slept.'

'Was that possible?'

'Sure. It was always possible. But the evidence was there. Bruises on her neck suggested she was strangled by a left-handed man. He was left-handed and the span of his hands matched the bruises exactly. He had motive. The postmortem examination estimated death had occurred between midnight and two o'clock, which coincided with the time the neighbour heard the argument.'

'Do we know where he is now?'

'Not yet. I wanted you to see these first.'

'Okay. Read on.'

'Next is Richard Wallace, born 30 September 1927 in Aberdeen. On 2 October 1972, he was charged with the murder of John David Preston, a partner in his law firm.

Preston was found hanging from a beam in his garage by his son, Donald. There was no note, and no apparent reason for the lawyer to take his own life. No clues were found at the locus to suggest foul play, but further investigation uncovered the fact that Preston's wife was having an affair with Wallace, that there had existed a strong difference of opinion between the two partners concerning a proposed merger, and that the two people who benefited most from Preston's timely demise, were his wife, and partner Wallace. They both pleaded "alibi", with each other as witnesses. Evidence was purely circumstantial, and when Wallace appeared in court, it took the jury three hours to find the case against him Not Proven. He subsequently married Preston's widow, sold up his practice and moved down south. They now live in Surrey.'

'Too old,' I observed. 'Move on.'

'Alfred Thompson, born 24 May 1957 in Dorking. In 1976, he was found guilty of the murder of Sonja Treeops, fifteen-year-old daughter of a wealthy Norwegian businessman. This was a copy-cat murder, a year after the Black Panther abducted and killed Lesley Whittle. If you remember, she was found hanging sixty feet down an inspection shaft.

'In the case of Sonja Treeops, she was discovered down a similar shaft on the outskirts of Carlisle, where she had been dead for more than three days. Crude demands had been made to the girl's father for ransom, though in each arrangement made to collect the money, Thompson failed to appear. Due to the abundance of clues left at the scene of abduction, he was soon apprehended and led police to the body. It was obvious from the outset that Thompson had intended to kill the girl, and had done so after continued sexual assault. He was sentenced to life imprisonment but escaped from Peterhead in 1979 and is still on the loose.'

I remembered the case. It had been used as an object lesson during Training College. 'Psychiatrist's report?' I asked.

'Definite psychopathic traits. Schizophrenic, with a liking for violence and a record to prove it. He had three previous convictions, two for assaulting minors, one for GBH. Of the four, I'd say he's our man.'

'Where is he now?'

'A lot of people would like to know.'

'Okay . . . Who's next?'

'John MacBean, born 7 January 1926 in Ballaig, Perthshire. Not much on file about this one. On 17 July 1958, police were called to a house in Ballaig where they discovered the body of a young boy. He'd been hanged from a rafter in a carpenter's workshop and the man who discovered the body had cut him down and then searched the house. He found the carpenter's son locked in the bathroom but John MacBean, the carpenter, was missing. His wife, Margaret MacBean, who worked in the village shop, had no idea where he was. The dead boy turned out to be the son of a neighbour. A massive search was organised, and it took police and army nine days to find MacBean who had taken to the hills. He confessed to the murder and was sentenced to death. His subsequent appeal was upheld, and the sentence commuted to a period of imprisonment of not less than twenty-five years. He was released in August 1986.'

'Again, too old,' I said when he'd finished. As an afterthought I asked, 'How old was the boy?'

'Who, victim or son?'

'Victim.'

Harry looked down at the file. 'Eleven.'

'What did MacBean's wife have to say?'

'Very little, it would appear. She cooked her husband lunch, then went to work in the shop. Next thing she knows her husband is gone, suddenly turned killer. She never said more than that, not even at the trial.'

'Doesn't leave us with much.'

'Nothing at all,' Harry said, glumly. 'So what now?'

'First, find out where they all are, then interview them, check alibis for the dates of the murder. If we get nothing, we'll try CRO at Hendon, begin on the English precedents. Whoever this killer is, he has form. I'm sure of it. His traces must be on record somewhere. Craig Watson might not have been the first victim.'

'Kettle's already onto that.'

'No luck?'

'What do you think?'

For a while we sat and nursed our thoughts. Mine needed more than nursing, they needed intensive care. In that state of mind, I need to do something – anything to stop the jackals of doubt tearing away at my confidence.

So I said, 'Come on, Harry. Let's see if we can find them.'

We drove down to the Squad HQ in Tollcross, where everything got off to a good start when I walked in to find my desk cleared out and all my belongings thrown into a couple of carrier bags. That was to be expected: space is scarce in any police station. But what raised my hackles was the smug expression on the face of the man behind my desk, Kettle's new lapdog from Central Vice, DI Pitts. I felt like the guy returning home early to find someone humping his wife.

'It's the man himself,' Pitts smirked. 'Come to collect his valuables.'

Blood rushed to my head. 'You don't waste much time,' I sneered.

'You're dead right I don't – not when I'm going places, McMorran.'

'Yeah? How about like out the window if you don't move your arse from behind my desk?'

Harry laid a hand on my arm. 'Frank, I'm sorry. I forgot to tell you. Look, no problem, we'll find a desk downstairs.'

'But that wouldn't give me an excuse to punch this creep through the wall, Harry.'

Pitts leaned back in my chair and said, 'You so scared you need an excuse, McMorran?'

It was touch and go after that. I think I might have hit him a couple of times, but I can't be sure. People jumped between us and there was a lot of pushing and shouting, threats and curses. Eventually Harry ushered me out of the room, down the stairs and out into the courtyard, mumbling the whole way.

'Christ, Frank, I might as well retire, forget my bloody pension. Just spend the rest of my life wet-nursing you, stop you from getting bloody killed. Why me, eh? Why bloody me?'

'Thanks, Harry,' I said, some time later.

'Huh,' was all he would say.

We went back inside and spent the rest of the afternoon trying to track down Wallace, Thompson, Swan and MacBean. By the time we called it a day, we had come up with the following:

Julian Swan was living in Shrewsbury and was known by the local Drug Squad to be a small-time dealer in hash, speed, acid and downers. He had been busted twice, had served a total of seven months, was released from the second term three days after the murder of Craig Watson.

We found Richard Wallace in Bournemouth. A quick word with the local CID and they sent someone round to see him. We got the call two hours later. His wife had died two years ago. He lived on his own, was a member of a local golf club and played regularly every Saturday. A further check at the club confirmed Wallace's presence there on the days Watson and Young had died. End of story.

Alfred Thompson was still a free man. No trace of him anywhere.

That left John MacBean, released three years previously. For the first eighteen months he had reported regularly to his Parole Officer, as required. He had stayed in one of the hostels on the Grassmarket and had received Social Security for that period. But then, four months ago he had dropped from sight. No record of him signing on since, or paying tax. He wasn't back inside and, as far as we could determine, he wasn't dead.

So where was John MacBean?

'What do you think, Harry?' I asked as we pulled up outside my flat.

'I admit it's strange, MacBean disappearing like that and then the murders starting, but . . .'

'But what?'

'I mean, you said it yourself – he's too old. Another thing: if he's not working or on the dole, how come he's got a car all of a sudden? And where is he living?'

I climbed out and said, before closing the door, 'You know, I've got a feeling about this guy, Harry. I think tomorrow we should check him out some more. What do you say?'

He said, 'Goodnight, Frank,' and drove off.

# Chapter Eight

Walking. And thinking, where is John MacBean? The question there since the moment I opened my eyes this morning. You wake up sometimes with a tune in your head you haven't heard in years and then can't stop singing. Driving you mad because it is the only song you ever hated. 'Don't cry for me Argentina' or something like that.

Where the hell was John MacBean?

The morning was warm, with a sluggish breeze shunting heavy clouds across a sea-blue sky in straggly procession. Jacket over shoulder I strolled through The Meadows, remembering a game we had played as kids called 'Spot the summer, win a prize!'. No-one ever won and no-one ever will, yet we keep on playing. Still, it wasn't grey or foggy, it wasn't drizzling or raining, sleeting or snowing, it wasn't blowing a Force Ten gale. Small mercies . . .

Harry was down at Force HQ, hanging around the Operations Room to pick up whatever had come in over the last twenty-four hours, glad I think to be far enough away from me not to get contaminated. I could understand, I kept telling myself. Harry was nervous, near the end of his career, not wanting to blow his precious pension and waste, how many years? Twenty-five? Thirty? Thirty-five?

A few brave folk were already stripped down and sprawled on the grass, the kind of people who see a glimpse of sun in April and the mirrored shades are never off their face till someone tells them it is Christmas. Any excuse.

Walking and thinking about Harry, scared to take his own life in his hands because all he can think of is the next two more years – better not mess it up now. You have a cop like that at your side and you start to wonder – can you trust him? With your life, with anybody's?

Stopping for a while, no hurry, to watch the endless parade of people walking dogs, throwing sticks for dogs or peeling the horny little yappy ones off the legs of strangers passing by. Thinking. Somewhere, there should be a record of John MacBean's blood-group. Prison records, for one. Harry could find out.

Now ambling past young kids playing football, pensioners basking like sea-lions on the benches in front of the council tennis-courts. Up Middle Meadow Walk onto Forest Road. Down onto George IV Bridge, and into the cool depths of the Central Library.

Before leaving the house, I'd thought of getting hold of Jimmy Slater at *The Scotsman* and asking him to find out what he could about the MacBean trial in 1958. Second thoughts forced me to abandon the idea: Slater wasn't exactly the world's greatest keeper of secrets; and if he sniffed the slightest scent of a story connected to the Hangman enquiry, it wouldn't be long before it was splattered across the front pages of the nation's press. Still, there was more than one way to skin a cat – or whatever else was on the menu.

The Edinburgh Room is not exactly a room, but a wide gallery overlooking The Scottish Room. If you are bored or tired of living, you can spit on the people using the microfiche-readers below. If not, you can fill out a form, hand it to the librarian and watch her scamper off to wherever they keep the microfiche records. Then you can wait. After ten minutes, I didn't have long to wait.

The librarian returned with two spools: back-issues of *The Scotsman*, July 1958 and October 1958. I went downstairs.

Downstairs, the Scottish Room was a pool of hush. Almost. A couple of old men sat rustling the morning papers with concentrated boredom, a student scribbled furiously in a loose-leaf pad at one of the desks, while a grey-haired woman with a straight back and hawkish nose replaced books on shelves.

I sat at the machine, threaded the spool into the reader, switched on, turned the knob until I came to the front page of the 17 July edition. Headlines reported 'US Troop landings in Turkey . . .' and 'Macmillan calls unexpected midnight meeting of Cabinet . . .' But no murder.

The next pages covered agricultural and financial news. I skimmed through them and suddenly there it was, squeezed between an advert for wigs and a report headed: 'Loch Ness Monster broke surface, claim women'.

'The body of an eleven-year-old boy was discovered hanging in a carpenter's workshop in Ballaig, late yesterday afternoon. He has been identified as James Robertson, son of local doctor Finlay Robertson.

The body was found by Mr Alec Lawrie, a Forestry Official who lives in the village and had called at the workshop on business. Although Mr Lawrie would not comment yesterday, it is believed that he is a close friend of John MacBean, the carpenter in whose workshop the body was found.

Mystery at present surrounds the events that led to the discovery of the body, and a police spokesman admitted yesterday that "... under the circumstances, foul play has not been ruled out, and we are now anxious to trace the whereabouts of John MacBean, whom we believe may be able to help us in our enquiries".

John MacBean has been missing since yesterday afternoon.'

I moved on to Friday 18 July 1958, where the murder had become front page news among such headlines as 'Revolt imminent in Jordan' and 'Premier ignores Bevan, polite to Gaitskell'.

'Events surrounding the death of eleven-year-old Jamie Robertson, found hanging in a carpenter's workshop two days ago, became

110

clearer last night when police confirmed that the army had been asked to help in the search for thirty-two-year-old John MacBean, who is believed to be hiding out in the hills and forest surrounding the small village of Ballaig.

Although Chief Inspector Eaves, who is leading the investigation, refused to add any-thing to the fact that they wish to question MacBean on events leading up to the discovery of the body by local forester, Alec Lawrie, it is widely speculated that police are now treating the case as one of murder.'

I wrote in my notebook: Chief Inspector Eaves? Then wound the pages on – until I came to 26 July.

'Murder suspect in custody.'

The report was brief. It stated that the man, believed to be local carpenter, John MacBean, had been taken into custody and was now 'helping police with their enquiries'. There was continued speculation by the reporter, several ambiguous and anonymous quotes from so-called 'villagers', and a blurred photo of the suspect.

On 28 July, it was reported that MacBean had appeared briefly in court, charged with the murder of James Robertson. He was remanded in custody pending psychiatric reports, and a date set for a preliminary hearing.

I rewound the spool, replaced it in its box and threaded October 1958.

The trial began on the 2nd. Aneurin Bevan would

launch a General Election Fund the next day. A week later, Pope Pius XII died. The trial continued, relegated to pages five and six. I made notes. John MacBean was sentenced to death.

Half an hour later, I rewound the spool and sat there awhile, staring at the blank screen, thoughts staggering past my mind's eye like drunks caught in a searchlight.

There had been an appeal, MacBean's death sentence commuted to twenty-five years minimum. Now he was out and free and the killings had started. Coincidence?

Jamie Robertson – like Craig Watson and Janice Young – had been killed for no apparent reason. Coincidence?

They'd all been hanged – coincidence?

In the press accounts of the trial, MacBean's motives had never been explained satisfactorily. Neither by prosecution or defence. Although this was partly due to the conflicting evidence of psychiatrists, it was also down to MacBean's stubbornly maintained silence since the moment of his arrest.

Why the absolute silence? Did it automatically signify guilt? Perhaps not, but the jury had thought so. Was there something he had been trying to hide? Several journalists had hinted that there was, but had failed to come up with anything more than vague speculation, none of which had been validated.

Why then, was I researching a murder nearly thirty years old? Desperation? A mad clutching at straws? Exactly – if there is nothing else to go on, go for what you've got. Maybe soon something else would come up, lead me off on another red herring. But until then . . .

I handed in the spools and climbed the stairs, cursing the futility of my deliberations, the sudden overwhelming sense of helplessness. Only too aware that tomorrow was Saturday, the day The Hangman liked to pick children off the street, hang them up to dry. Would he kill again so soon?

I came out of the library and turned down the High Street. I heard the shouting first, then saw the small crowd on Parliament Square outside the entrance to the High Court where seven uniformed policemen were being jostled by the angry mob.

I approached a sergeant speaking to a traffic cop at the back of the crowd.

'DI McMorran,' I said. 'What's going on?'

'Lynch mob, seems like, sir,' the burly, silver-haired sergeant said, pushing his cap back in what might have been some form of salute. 'That Hangman's been in all the papers, killed the kids? He's up for a second hearing in the High Court.'

'Expecting trouble?'

'Trouble? Far's I'm concerned they can let the crowd have the bastard, save us all the bother. There's a unit standing by but I don't reckon it'll come to that, punters just out for a little fun, let off steam, scream a bit, you know?'

'Hang the bastard, right?'

'That's what they're saying, aye. Can't say I'd disagree, if you know what I mean.'

'Yeah,' I said. 'Okay, thanks.' I made to leave.

'Are you the McMorran solved the Maxwell case?' the sergeant asked.

'So?'

'It was a good piece of work, if you don't mind me saying.' The sergeant repositioned the cap on his head, squinted at the crowds. 'I knew Maxwell. Had reason to pick him up once, a few years ago when I got called to a domestic at his house – the one he burned down – and found his mother in some hell of a sorry state. I tried to get her to press charges but I think she was scared of what her son might do to her after I left. I didn't like it, but I had to leave it like that. There was nothing I could do, save giving the lad a kicking he wouldn't forget.'

'You did that?'

He shook his huge head. 'It would have given me the greatest pleasure, but I reckoned if I did, he'd just take it out on his mother anyway.'

'Maybe you should have,' I suggested.

'Maybe you're right.'

The sergeant wandered off and I hung around the back of the crowd, thinking it must have been something like this those hundreds of years ago when the gibbet still stood at the head of Liberton Wynd and the Old Tolbooth was the Heart of Midlothian. All we needed now was the slow tolling of the bell in St Giles to complete the morbid atmosphere.

Punters out just for a little fun, the sergeant had said. Maybe. Maybe there were a few, here and there, people like myself attracted by the noise, the happening. But the underlying current was ugly, a malevolence in the air. Voices were angry, bitter, cheated. Near the front of the crowd a man stood silently bearing a placard with the words 'Suffer the little children'.

114

'Innocent little children,' a woman next to me said to no-one in particular. 'What's he got against innocent little children? That's what I want to know. Where's he get off doing things like that?'

A man in a flat cap turned his head. 'There's only one thing for the likes of him,' he said, looking at anyone who would catch his eye. 'An' we all know what that is.'

I told him, 'We do that and we're no better than him.'

He thrust out his chin, turned square-on to give me all his attention. 'You the police or what? I mean, what's the bloody law got to do with it? He gets life, he's out on the streets in five, ten years an' starts all over again. Only one thing for the likes of him an' that's give him what he gave the poor wee bairns.'

He looked at the woman by my side. '*You* know what I'm saying, right, doll?'

'Aye, too right,' she said. Her attention was drawn away by shouts and jeers. She stood on tiptoe, said, 'They're bringing him out.'

I thought of Horace Moxton and tried really hard to imagine him as the Hangman, with his cringing eyes and pale delicate hands but it just didn't work.

I walked home across the Southside, pushing through the steady stream of tourists, thinking about Ruben Maxwell, unable to stop myself now the sergeant had unlocked the memory.

After torching his family in their house, dear sweet Ruben had played the grief-stricken son. The media had loved him. Scenes at the Fatal Accident Inquiry – bitter irony there, I felt – and the funeral made him into some kind of local hero. Although police and insurance

115

investigators had failed to come up with any evidence of arson, or anything else to link Maxwell to the tragedy, suspicions were rife. Then one day his alibi collapsed. The girl who claimed he had been with her all night suddenly changed her mind. A lover's tiff or something. Now she claimed she hadn't seen him for weeks. Half an hour later we arrived at his door with a warrant for his arrest. Too late, he was already gone. It took us three weeks to find him and when we did it was in the twelfth floor flat belonging to another ex-girlfriend. He was a greasy little bastard. He escaped onto the roof. I got to him first. We had a little chat. Then he tried to throw me over the side.

I don't know how I survived. He had the strength of desperation. I had to use every dirty trick in the book just to stay alive. At some point I lost my temper and things went a little hazy after that. I remember him screaming. I remember liking the sound of his screams. I remember the rain and the look on his face as he toppled over the edge. I remember the silence as he fell, the dull thud as he landed. But I remember nothing else. Did I push him or did he stumble? I don't know. Did I regret his untimely death? I'd have to wait and see.

As I walked, I thought also of Horace Moxton and how unlike Maxwell he was. Where Maxwell was big and strong, Moxton was small and wimpy. Where Maxwell had a ruthless streak, Moxton had a yellow one. Where Maxwell was insane, Moxton was merely perverted. I could find no similarity between the two.

But what if I was wrong? What if Moxton really was the killer? What if, what if, the paranoiac's refrain.

Even the doubts could not dispel the feeling – the instinctive intuition that every good copper recognises and acts upon – that Moxton, although guilty of something, was innocent of murder. Feeling? No, it was more than that. Conviction.

What could I do? The planned operation and reconstruction of the crime at the Commonwealth Pool tomorrow would be cancelled now that Kettle had his man. And if the Hangman read the papers or watched the news, what would he think? Would he stop killing, now he had the chance? Call it a day and hang up his rope?

Not a chance in hell, I thought. Once in the blood, to kill and get away with it is an addiction stronger than smack. The power of life and death over an individual a greater high than any self-induced. Confidence growing with every unsolved crime . . .

He'd be out there, tomorrow, I felt sure.

And so would I.

# Chapter Nine

Bain rose, wicked.

In a world not of his making, not of his choice. He could feel the meanness burning through his veins, sense its cruel contortions in his head. So took a cold shower to cool the brain down, take the edge off his mood. But he only felt worse.

He dried and slipped on his bathrobe. Slicked back his hair and studied his face in the mirror. Something about the eyes, tension perhaps. So he dropped a couple of Valium – supplies getting low – and washed them down with a swig of gin. Pressures of madness, he thought, but could not bring himself to smile. He was mean even to himself. One of those days.

He took the bottle through and sat in the black leather armchair waiting for the tranquillisers to hit the mark. Outside, the afternoon was well on its way, the sun high, the clouds high, everything high.

The wall over his desk was no longer bare. Glossy black-and-white prints were now blue-tacked to the surface in a kaleidoscopic array that made it look like a cracked mirror. The prints were of children, mostly Craig and Janice. Curly-haired Craig and sulky Janice. In life and in death.

He flipped over a print, read the name on the back and pulled a stack of folders from a drawer. He shuffled through them until he found a matching name, then replaced the others.

*Order . . .*

There were three sheets of paper in the folder and an envelope of negatives. He scanned the papers, absorbing the details of his research. Conviction gelled as he read; he felt close to her already. It was only a matter of time.

*Precision . . .*

He put the print and sheets of paper in the folder, left it on the desk and returned to his chair.

He could feel the Valium moving in his blood now, was beginning to mellow-out. A week's frustration not easily swept from mind.

Since – yesterday afternoon, was it? – he'd been able to think of little else but Natasha. Even now, images of her face and body pecked and tore at his brain. He had never experienced such desire before, was confused by the force of his emotions.

*Direction . . .*

In the Yellow Pages he found agencies for dancers, for models, for entertainment. He noted down the numbers. Then added those of massage parlours – you never know. Monday, it was back to work, holiday over. Monday, and someone would put him on the trail of Natasha.

But today was Saturday and swimming was out. The Commonwealth Pool would be swarming with cops. He wasn't stupid and didn't think the police were either. They would have found the connection by now but too late. Too late for them, too late for Heather.

Thinking now of Heather. Heather Munro, the name on the third dossier. An outgoing girl, popular among her friends, vivacious with dark unruly hair, large brown eyes and a mischievous smile. He loved her. She attended Boroughmuir High. She liked sport, especially swimming. Her parents had a dog, a labrador called Victor. She took it for a walk every evening through the Hermitage. Seven o'clock, on the dot. For over a month he had watched her and waited. Like he had done with Craig and Janice. Till the time was right.

Like today.

Anticipation coursed his veins and drove him from the chair. He dressed in shorts and sandals and walked down to the little barn to check on Boris, Vincent and Monty, his pets. He took them out of their aquariums one by one, let them coil around his body for a while, loving the slither of their dry skin against his. He had always admired snakes, even as a kid, smooth and hairless.

After a while he tired. He replaced them in their tanks, locked the door and returned to the house.

No Mother-dear in the house today. She was out on a trip with a bus-load of seniles, wouldn't be back till late.

He carried a sun-bed and some gin out onto the lawn. Settled to a little relaxation, the calm before the storm. The sun was warm between banks of shifting cloud, a soft breeze blowing and a brain full of Valium; smoothing away the rough edges of his waking-mood, instilling instead a growing sense of excitement as evening approached.

Watching the sky, thinking.

He had always been good at thinking. Talking was for

the insecure, the lonely – people who did not want to recognise their fears, their inner foes. In lucid thought there was power and beauty. Ideas dovetailed invisibly, logic flowing in an effortless stream. Order. Precision. The natural passage of events.

He mused over the events of the last few days. He had done well, outwitted them all. The police now claimed they had him, The Hangman. Some civil servant or something, wimpy little guy with a blanket over his head as they led him into court. Demonstrations outside the High Court, mass-media indignation and so forth. Well, he'd give them indignation. He would show them fear.

He wondered about Mother-dear. This morning at breakfast, she had had a surprise for him. The police, she said, had called round yesterday, something about wanting to interview Dominic, no special reason, just routine enquiries. He hadn't done anything wrong, had he? She wanted to know, because they had said they might return, she added. Luckily, she didn't see the expression on his face. He shrugged it all off with a laugh and changed the subject. Didn't want to question her in case she became suspicious. That would never do. He was lucky enough she never read the papers or watched the news.

Then there was Cathy: he'd handled her well, too. They would get married once the old sod was dead and live in the guest house. He would leave the city for good and become a carpenter. They would have children and go to church and walk the hills and fish the rivers and fuck in front of the coalfire. No more working in the hospital, no more cooking limp meals for geriatrics or listening to the inane chatter of the monkeys he worked with.

Drinking, dozing, drinking.

He awoke, the sun gone, his flesh cool, his head throbbing. Feeling a bit weird, like someone was dancing on his grave. Or watching.

He went inside, fetched his binoculars. From his bedroom window he surveyed the top floor of the block of flats beyond the railway, the only windows overlooking his house and garden. They would be there, he thought, on the roof or in one of the flats. But nothing moved. No glint of binoculars, no twitching curtains or drawn blinds. Nothing.

So he went outside and spent the next half an hour searching the grounds. Probing bushes and shrubs, peering round trees, checking the locks on the barn doors, walking to the end of the drive, studying the parked cars, noting make, colour, registration. He saw no-one.

5.30pm.

Dropped a couple more Valium, then showered. Scrubbed his skin pink beneath the steaming jets but could not expunge the vague sense of unease growing in his mind.

He shaved in front of the full-length mirror. Face, neck, chest, stubble of pubes, arsehole, armpits. He cut himself seven times. Unheard of. He *never* cut himself shaving. Never. Omen.

6.00pm.

He dressed slowly. Battledress. Khaki canvas trousers, khaki cotton shirt, camouflage jacket. All new, bought yesterday. He took the black rubber swimming-cap from its hook on the wall, slipped it over his cropped dome. Then he fetched the woollen khaki hat and fitted it on top. He looked good. Slick and cool, nobody's fool.

Downstairs he collected together gloves, rope, camera, bone-handled razor. Wound the rope around his waist, secured it. Donned gloves, checked the camera, dropped it in his jacket pocket. Slid the razor into his right sock.

6.20pm.

He was ready.

He stepped softly from the house, and pushed his bicycle up the drive. It took him four minutes against the breeze to reach the Hermitage.

6.25pm.

The Hermitage of Braid is a narrow wooded valley squeezed between the Braid Hills to the south and Blackford Hill to the north. The Braid Burn cuts through the Hermitage on its journey to Portobello and the Firth of Forth, accompanied for a while by a walkway that provides access to the Hermitage of Braid House before continuing on past Blackford Quarry. There is a gate-house at the Morningside end, and a sign that says *Cycling Prohibited*.

Dominic Bain cycled past the sign, dismounted fifty yards on and chained his bike to the back of a bench.

There were people. Three bikers in denims and leather jackets, a middle-aged woman dragging a reluctant poodle. Ahead of Bain, a couple in their twenties walked arm in arm, taking it slow.

6.28pm.

No-one paid him any attention as he climbed the slope, following the path that clings to the southern ridge. He was soon out of sight. He went slowly, scouting. Not many people used this path: at certain times of the year it could be treacherous. As it would be tonight.

6.38pm.

He came to the dell, a wide hollow whose northern lip was rock and boulder and overlooked the burn seventy feet below. Birds called and sang in evening chorus as splintered sunlight filtered through the canopy of leaves. Shadows flickered and danced. This was the place, the killing ground.

At the back of the dell, shielded by shrubs and bushes, stood an ancient oak. Names and slogans and hearts crudely carved in its broad, twisted trunk.

Dominic unwound the rope and slung it over a bough, anchoring one end in a loop around the trunk, the noose at the other, six feet off the ground. He returned to the rocky ledge. It was 6.45pm and the sun retreated behind a cloud.

Below on the road the bikers continued their barrage of laughter and horseplay. An old man walked stiffly by, followed by shouts and howls of derision.

The bikers would be remembered, come tomorrow.

He lay waiting, anticipation burning as his body screamed for action. Heart hammering at the walls of his chest.

6.52pm.

The doubts had just begun, when . . .

He heard the dog first, barking, crashing through the undergrowth. Sunbeams burst through the lattice of leaves. A hundred, maybe a thousand spotlights waiting for the star.

6.54pm, and there she was.

Thin summer dress, white with floral patterns. Yellow cotton jacket with dinky little hood. Hair wild, as usual, out of breath as she climbed into the dell. The dog was out of sight, somewhere behind her. She didn't see Dominic, poised to spring. She didn't see him at all. Until too late.

He was the last thing she ever saw.

'Come, my love,' Dominic crooned, hands about her neck. 'Embrace me.'

She gouged at his face, drew blood. She kicked and struggled, tried to scream. No sound passed her throat. The struggles ceased.

'Let us share our love,' Dominic told her. But she was already gone, limp in his hands.

He carried her to the oak and slipped her head through the noose lowering her gently. He looked over his shoulder – where was that damn dog? He cut away her clothes, all except socks, then took out his camera and shot off a few exposures. He was so absorbed he never saw or even heard the dog.

It came out of the bushes like a silenced bullet aimed at his throat. He jumped back, dropped the camera and held up his arms to ward off the attack. Teeth sank deep in his left forearm, drawing blood. He hit it, a rabbit-punch to the nose. It whimpered and let go. He threw a kick, missed, and the labrador came in low. He met it in mid air. Brought his knee up into its throat. It dropped, howling, stunned. He grabbed the slack at the back of its neck and running, dragged it to the rocky outcrop. It twisted in his grip, kicking and snapping at his wrist and face. In vain. He lifted it high and sent it arching through the air.

A woman screamed.

He retreated hurriedly from view. Then peered cautiously over the edge. The young couple he had seen earlier now approached the twitching dog, their voices rising on the warm air.

'It didn't fall, Derek,' the woman insisted. 'It was thrown. I saw it.'

'Don't be silly, Mags. It must've fallen. Who'd throw——'

'I told you. There was a man up there. I saw him throw the dog over. He's still there now.'

'Are you sure, Mags? I don't want to——'

'Hurry up, Derek! You can climb up there.'

'It doesn't look very safe.'

'Are you going up or do I have to?'

Dominic panicked and ran, crashing through the undergrowth, branches and briars whipping at his face, tearing at his clothes. His thoughts were chaotic, his left arm numb and warm. He stumbled and picked himself up, cursing as he ran.

An omen. He should have recognised the signs.

He broke from the trees. As he hurtled down the slope he heard shouting, the word 'police'.

He skidded and fell, rolling down the incline until a sapling brought him to a sudden halt. He picked himself up and ran for his bike, fumbling for the lock, with fingers more like raw sausages than delicate killing machines. What was the combination? He couldn't think, panic clamouring at his brain. The number! He could hear the woman's heels on the road, running for a phone.

She rounded the corner as the lock snapped open, saw

him, stopped and screamed. He took a step towards her and she turned and ran, soon lost around the bend. He whipped off the chain, thrust it in his pocket. Then he was astride the bike and moving.

He made for the gates, pedalling furiously, blood pounding in his ears, breath rasping from his lungs. Travelling fast now, tears in his eyes, the woman's screams in his ears, so when he burst out onto the road he never clearly saw, never really heard the growl and surge of the car until it was too late.

By then, there was nothing he could do.

# Chapter Ten

I was mackerel, gutted. My skin wrinkled as a whore's tits. I stank of chlorine. It was all I could taste or smell. My temper was frayed beyond repair. I'd been in the Commonwealth Pool almost ten hours, from the moment it opened till the moment it closed and I knew it would be a long, long time before I ever went again.

I'd only been back in the flat ten minutes when the doorbell rang. I opened it on George Barrie.

His face was grim, unsmiling. Mouth set, eyes hard and direct. He made no move to enter.

'Get your jacket,' he said, glancing contemptuously at the whisky in my hand. 'Hurry!'

I didn't need telling twice. I knew the score, could see it in his eyes. I locked the flat and two minutes later we were in his car, jumping in and out of the traffic streaming into town. Ours wasn't the only flashing light to shred the twilight sky.

'Where the hell have you been?' Barrie demanded.

I told him. 'The Pool.'

'Looks like he outsmarted both of you.'

'Eh?' I said.

'You and Kettle both. You in the pool all day, Kettle

129

working on Moxton, and The Hangman, the real one, he's out having the day of his life. Brilliant. The press will have a field day.'

'Yeah? Seems like you're more concerned with what the press think than actually finding the killer.'

'And up yours too, pal,' Barrie said, throwing me an angry glance. 'We're all in the same tree, McMorran. Someone starts shaking the tree and . . . see what I mean? People will fall. Especially those on a limb.'

'Is that a promise or a threat?'

'It's the truth.'

I gave it some thought, about a second's worth.

'Where we going?' I asked.

'The Hermitage,' he said through his teeth. 'Morningside.'

We touched seventy going up Grange Road.

'Boy or girl?' I asked.

We took a corner on two wheels, ignoring the red lights.

'Girl,' he said. 'That's all I know.'

We did the rest of the journey in silence.

The road to the Hermitage was already sealed off, a crowd gathered. A WPC waved us through and we turned into the gates. What with the trees and all the natural stuff around, it was dark here, almost night. There was a confusion of cars, ten or maybe more, parked inside the gates and people standing round in small groups. A PC came over, told us Chief Inspector Kettle was up by the Braid House. We drove on.

I had come here a few times as a child. Never since. It was still the way I remembered. Stream, road, bushes,

trees – and the house, square, squat and ugly. We had
smashed one of the windows once, I can't remember
why, maybe just because it was an ugly building. We were
chased off the grounds, never to return.

More cars, more men, and a mobile command unit.
Chief Inspector Kettle stomped across as we got out,
ignored me, spoke to Barrie.

'She's up there.' He nodded towards the slope where
ropes had been secured to facilitate access. 'Parrish is
there now.'

Barrie pointed at the sheeted object by the side of the
stream. 'Who's that then?'

'Not a who – a labrador. Belonged to the girl, we
think.'

'Any ID on her yet?'

'We found a purse nearby, but no name, no clue as to
who she might be. We're checking Missing Persons.'

'Anything else?'

'A camera. Looks like it could be his. We won't know
till——'

'Witnesses?'

'A young couple. Seems they disturbed him and he ran
off. We're interviewing them now.'

Barrie sucked at his teeth, frowned. 'Sure it's The
Hangman?' he asked.

Kettle squirmed, looked away, said in a drained voice,
'No doubt about it. Different MO, the bastard's getting
clever – but like I said, no doubt about it.'

'Different? How?'

'She's still hanging there – no bin-liners, that kind of
thing. This might be where he killed the other two but

was disturbed tonight, not enough time to cut her down and dump the body. We're working on that possibility now, men combing the woods. You want to see her?'

Barrie nodded like he had a million better things he wanted to do and we headed for the slope.

I said to Kettle, 'I s'pose you'll have to release Moxton now?' He didn't seem to hear.

We gained the ridge, crossed a shallow dell and like Kettle had said, there was no doubt about it. The girl was still hanging, swinging gently. A shudder rippled through my body and I had to swallow a couple of times just to get the taste of bile from my throat. Even the chlorine was better than that.

I could see immediately it was the same kind of rope. And like the last girl, she was naked but for her socks. Plastic sheeting had already been laid, and a couple from the audio-visual unit were setting up lights for the video, taking stills of the body and surrounding area. Parrish greeted us with a tired smile, but there was little warmth in his eyes. It seems to get to us all, one way or another.

We had to wait a while for the photographers. Barrie gestured towards the pathologist, 'Get going, Jack. Let's not waste any more time.'

I held the rope, taking the weight as Parrish cut it. She didn't weigh much. Four, five stone. We laid her carefully down on the sheeting. She was still warm, but very dead. There was little more to do without getting in someone's way, so I made my way back down the slope with Barrie following.

We crammed into the command unit. I recognised most of the faces. A smartly-dressed young couple sat at

132

the table opposite Kettle. They looked uncomfortable. Perhaps it was the heat, it was stuffy as hell in the cramped space. Or maybe Kettle facing them.

Barrie tilted his head in the direction of the couple, raised an eyebrow at Kettle. 'What's the story?'

The Chief Inspector made the introductions, then said, 'Derek and Mags live up on Corennie Gardens. They check out so far. They say they come here most evenings, were walking along about seven o'clock, when splat, the dog hits the road just in front of them. Mags screams, says she saw a man throwing the dog over the edge. Derek here goes up the same way you went up. There's no sign of anyone, but he hears the sound of someone – or something – crashing through the trees. Then he spots the girl, runs over, takes her pulse – clever boy – realises she's dead and shouts to his lady here to call us up. She goes running, turns the corner in the road, and sees this guy struggling with the lock on a bike. She gives a little scream – right, hen? – and then turns back the way she came.'

'I wasn't going anywhere near that man!' Mags said, hotly. 'He was *evil*. He sort of looked at me, and . . .' She shivered, clasped hold of Derek's hand, moved closer to him.

'Can you describe him?' I asked.

'She's agreed to do a Photofit,' Kettle commented.

'Please,' I persisted.

'Well, he was dressed in green. You know, combat jacket, that sort of thing. Like a commando. With a black cap like the terrorists use.'

'What did he do when he saw you?'

133

She put a hand to her throat, widened her eyes, made a small oh of her mouth.

'I told you. He looked at me all queer. Sent shivers down my spine, he did. I was rooted to the spot. If he'd . . .' She shuddered for effect, went on. 'Anyhow, I wasn't going to stick around. To tell the truth, I turned and ran. I——'

'So you didn't see which way he went?'

She shook her head.

'You phoned from where?'

'The big house,' she replied.

'Could you describe the bicycle?'

'One of them old, heavy ones. You know, with the old-fashioned handlebars.'

'Any accessories?'

'It had a saddlebag,' she said in rush. 'And one of those, you know, old-fashioned lights that you put on the wheel and it——'

'A dynamo?'

'Yes, one of them. And . . . well, no, I don't think there was anything else.'

'What colour was the bike?'

'Black. Definitely black,' she said, then after a moment added, 'Or dark green. It was . . . well, you see, I wasn't exactly looking at the bike. It was him I saw mostly. And then only for a second, maybe two.'

'Did you see anyone else while all this was going on?'

'No', she answered. 'Though I did see some, you know, bikers. They were hanging round down by the gatehouse when we came in. Drinking and that. And there was an old man, too. I remember him.'

134

I wanted to know. 'These bikers, did they have their bikes with them?'

'I didn't see any, and they didn't have any helmets, did they, Derek?' She turned to her man, who agreed with her, patting her hand.

'They just looked like bikers,' Derek said. 'You know, long hair, jeans, leather jackets, that kinda thing. They had a bottle of whisky or something they were passing around but they weren't drunk or aggressive, like.'

'Were they still there when the man was unlocking his bike?' I asked Mags.

'No. No-one else. Just . . . *him*.'

Kettle shifted his bulk on the chair, said to Barrie: 'We're checking the bench for prints. If he panicked, he might have left something.'

'Better get a description of the bikers and the old man and put out an appeal,' I suggested, watching the frown deepen on Kettle's face. 'The old man will probably be local, maybe the bikers too if they were on foot.'

'Don't teach your granny, McMorran,' Kettle said through a sneer, getting to his feet. He thanked the couple, said someone would take their statements and reminded them not to talk to the press. 'Now, if you don't mind, I've matters to discuss with the Procurator.'

Barrie gave me a fleeting flash of his teeth as he followed the Chief Inspector outside. I didn't hang around either.

They were bringing the body down the slope now, Parrish in attendance, looking more like a mad professor than a leading forensic pathologist. I caught his arm as the stretcher slid into the back of the mortuary van.

'Find anything else?' I asked him.

He ran long, bony fingers through his hair, regarded me coolly for a moment before shaking his head. 'Maybe the autopsy will bring something to light,' he said, 'But I wouldn't put your hopes on it. You'll get more from Forensic, I reckon.'

I thanked him and climbed the slope again. ID Branch had moved in, making the most of what little light there was. I didn't envy them their task. Most likely, they would have to wait until daylight before they could really begin a proper search. Meanwhile . . .

I stuck to the path, going slowly, not really expecting to find anything, merely retracing the killer's exit from the locus. I avoided footprints in the dried mud. It had not rained for a couple of days and the mud was hard enough to withstand the pressure of my weight without leaving an impression, but a running man, a desperate man, might leave some trace. We all hoped.

The path shallowed out into broad steps cut irregularly into the side of the valley. I came out among a cluster of cars. A group of men were gathered round two ID men examining the bench where the bicycle had been chained. There was intermittent laughter, good-natured banter – anything to stop the real emotions coming out – everyone waiting for orders. They all knew it would be a long night, an even longer tomorrow.

I saw Harry's car turn in the gates. He climbed out and walked back. I caught up with him on the road outside.

'What took you?' I asked. He was dressed in his usual grey mackintosh and hat, his eyes uneasy in his florid face.

'Trying to find *you*,' he snorted, angrily. 'You could

have let me know.' Sometimes Harry forgets I'm his superior. But then, I suppose, I seldom act like one. I filled him in on the details.

'On a bicycle?' he exclaimed when I had finished. 'The bastard's getting cockier all the time.' He scuffed at the ground, the way he usually does when trying to put things in perspective.

'The cockier he gets, fine. Then we'll have him,' I said.

Harry stopped scuffing, picked a piece of glass from the sole of his boot and studied it abstractedly. Without looking up he said, 'How many more kids have to die till then?' He made a motion as if to discard the fragment of glass, stopped suddenly and stiffened. 'Wait a minute . . .' he said.

We squatted, began picking at the fragments on the road. There were quite a few. 'What are you thinking, Harry?' I asked.

'Headlights,' he said. 'Not a windscreen. Maybe side-lights. But recent – you can tell the way it's still lying, fresh.'

'Say it's The Hangman, right? And he's coming out that gate – fast, you know, panicking – and there's a car coming down the road here. What do you think? Smacko right here?'

'Where's the bike then?' Harry stopped rummaging through his pockets. 'Got any bags?'

I found a couple and gave him one. He took a few samples of the glass, resealed it. I said, 'The guy in the car stops, picks up The Hangman, no-one around, takes him to a hospital or home, or maybe let's hope he's saved us a lot of trouble and killed the fucker. Whichever way, you wouldn't just leave the bike lying around; put it in the car, that's what I'd do.'

'Okay. But if The Hangman's not hurt? He dusts himself down, gets on——'

'His bike hits the car, it's not going to work too well after. What's he do? He wants to get away fast, not let the driver of the car see his face, right?'

'What about the girl?' Harry said. 'The witness? Did she say anything about a crash?'

I shook my head. 'Too busy screaming, running, trying not to get murdered.'

'Okay. So what do we do?'

'Check Accident and Emergency at the Royal Infirmary. Then put out an appeal for the driver of the car and witnesses, anyone who might've seen someone pushing or carrying a bike in the area. Release a description of the bike. Try and find the three bikers who were here earlier. Have I forgotten anything?'

Harry was scuffing the ground again, looking up to where a small knot of people had gathered by the cordon. 'There's always the possibility the driver didn't stop. Or the broken glass was the result of an earlier accident.'

'In that case, we check all Accident Reports.'

'And search the immediate area. If the driver didn't stop, The Hangman might've dumped his bike, you know, if it was a write-off.'

'In fact,' I said, 'we better shift our arses.'

Shift them we did.

# Chapter Eleven

Cooper:   I never seen 'em, honest! If I had, I would have rung you, right?

Kettle:   They were in all the bloody papers, son. On every news broadcast since Sunday. You must've been the only person in Scotland who never seen them.

Cooper:   I'm here, aren't I? I'm answerin' your questions, aren't I?

Kettle:   If you'd come in Sunday, we might have had him. If he kills another kid you can tell yourself it's down to you.

Cooper:   It's not my fault. I never done nothin'.

Kettle:   What were you doing in the car?

Cooper:   Drivin'.

Kettle:   Don't get sassy, son. I can get you for driving without a licence, failing to report an accident, withholding information . . .

Cooper:   I was on my way to pick up a mate, right?

Kettle:   Whose car is it?

Cooper:   My Dad's.

Kettle:   He let you use it? Knowing you didn't have a licence?

| | |
|---|---|
| Cooper: | He was away the weekend. He hid the keys but I known where he hides 'em for yonks. |
| Kettle: | So you went out for a little joyriding . . . |
| Cooper: | Yeah. |
| Kettle: | Tell me about . . . how come you hit the man in the first place? Were you drunk? Is that why you didn't stop or report the accident? |
| Cooper: | No! I never touched a drop. I was scared is all. If my dad found out, he'd fuckin' kill me. |
| Kettle: | Say your prayers, son. How old are you? |
| Cooper: | Fifteen. |
| Kettle: | Why did you hit the man on the bike? |
| Cooper: | He came straight at me! I wasn't goin' fast. He just came flyin' out a nowhere like a madman. I didn't have time to do nothing. No brakes, no swerve, nothing. He just bounces off the bonnet. |
| Kettle: | What then? |
| Copper: | I haul on the anchors, right. I look back an' he's gettin' up off the ground an' lookin' at me like he wants to kill me. I bottled out. I don't care what you say. He starts running at me, so I takes off, ain't no way I'm stayin' aroun' get my head caved in, right? |
| Kettle: | What state was the bike in? |
| Cooper: | Write-off, I'd say. All twisted, like no way he could have rode it after. |
| Kettle: | How badly was he hurt? |

Cooper:     He was limpin', sort of. Bit of blood on his hands, right? But nothin' bad.
Kettle:     Describe him.
Cooper:     I only seen him a couple a seconds.
Kettle:     You've studied the Photofit. Do you think it's accurate?
Cooper:     Not bad, yeah. Like I said . . . I only seen him a couple a seconds.
Kettle:     Book him.

I finally got hold of the transcript Tuesday morning, along with a pile of other reports Harry brought round to my flat. Kettle was being as obstructive as possible.

The bike turned out to be an old post-war dinosaur, black and heavy, with a dynamo, three gears and a saddlebag. In the saddlebag were big-liners and a ball of string. The bike had been dumped over the wall by the gatehouse and was discovered early Sunday morning by a young PC on search detail. Chief Inspector Kettle, doubtful of our theory until that point, had then been forced to act through the media.

Precious hours lost, the way I looked at it.

I tossed the transcript aside in frustration. We had had high expectations of the driver being able to help us. No such luck. All we get is a fifteen-year-old joyrider who sits on his brain.

I picked up a Forensic report. They had analysed the blood and tissue found beneath the nails of Heather Munro, had grouped it. Big deal. We already knew that. It wasn't going to help us find The Hangman, only convict him if we did. I tossed that aside, too.

The next reports dealt with enquiries at the bank where Janice Young's father worked, the dance studio where Janice went once a week, and her so-called boyfriend, Philip. They all came up with nothing. No further enquiry necessary. Into the bin.

Ditto the search for the retailer or wholesaler of the blue rope used for the hangings. No-one interviewed remembered a man buying a large quantity. Mountaineering clubs and associations had also drawn a blank. Into the bin.

ID Branch had found a couple of footprints near where the bike was discovered. Only partials, but they matched the one found at the locus on Greenbank Drive. Confirmation – but no revelation.

I wondered what to do next.

George Barrie was out of town. Who was going to tell me where he was, how I could contact him? Nobody. I wasn't going to miss him, but I did sort of wonder what was going on.

And where was Harry? He should have been back by now. He was out trying to track down the movements and whereabouts of John MacBean since he had broken parole and dropped out of sight. At the time he had been living in one of the men's hostels down on the Grassmarket. I had an old photo of him and sent Harry down to try his luck. I didn't have much hope. Harry had none. He considered the whole thing an obsession on my part.

I took a slip of paper from my wallet, pulled the phone across and dialled the number. A man answered on the seventh ring. I asked for Chief Inspector Eaves and was told it was he. 'Retired,' he added. I introduced myself and he said he'd heard of me. What could he do to help me, he wanted to know. So I told him.

It had been a long time ago, he said. His memory wasn't what it always had been. I said I'd like to talk to him anyway. He told me to drop around any time, he didn't get out much.

I paced around the flat for a while. I felt hyped up with my nerves on edge. My thoughts were like flies in a bottle. I swallowed one of the new pills the doctor had given me, then paced some more. Then I stuck a note on the door for Harry and paced down to the pub. I sat and ate a plate of something called 'Sweet and Sour', downed a couple of pints, held back on the third. Then Harry came in.

'Any luck?' I asked when he had brought his poison over.

'There's a guy named Paterson who owns one of those big houses down on Comely Bank Avenue,' he said. 'I got the address. He specialises in accommodation for parolees, that kind a thing. Rents are high, but he knows the DHSS will pay anyway. I met this guy down in one of the hostels, one of the workers, who said MacBean left the hostel to go live out at Paterson's. I asked him what else MacBean had told him and he said nothing much but the old man was always going on about going home, back where he came from, somewhere up north. I said Ballaig? The guy said yeah, that's the one. Looks like maybe the old man went home. They always do, you know, go back to the scene of the crime.'

'You think?'

'Why not?'

'He's hardly going to be welcomed back with open arms.'

'Maybe he hopes they've all forgotten, or he's changed so much they won't recognise him. I don't know why we're wasting our time on this guy. He's got nothing to do with The Hangman, he's just got under your skin, that's all. I've seen it happen to you before, you know, getting sidetracked by something that strokes your curiosity so much you got to scratch.'

I thought about that, but not for long. 'Maybe. But we've got nothing else to do. Kettle's got all the angles covered, it's only a matter of time. I've not been brought into this to solve the case, I'm sure of that. So if we don't follow up on MacBean, what d'you suggest?'

'Resign.'

'Great, Harry. Thanks for the vote of confidence.'

He made a big thing of draining his pint, wiping his mouth with the back of his hand.

'Okay,' I went on. 'I'm being set up. So what? I've done nothing wrong. I'm not about to jack it in. No way. I'll do what I enjoy doing, scratch my bloody itches and the hell with them.'

'What do you mean, you're being set up?'

'Are you blind? Can't you see what's happening.'

'I know Kettle wants you off the squad.'

'He wants more than that. He wants Commander Aitken's job. If I get disciplined after the FAI, then that's a black mark for Aitken, because he was the one who gave me the okay to move in. His responsibility.'

'But that on its own won't help Kettle get the Commander's job.'

144

'You're right. So what happens? The Chairman on the Committee of Chief Constables suddenly changes his lifetime opinion of me and wants me back on The Hangman investigation. Not as part of the Squad, but out on a limb, under some dubious title of Advisory Investigative Officer, or some such crap. I'm a suspended officer and still working on the case alongside the Procurator-fiscal. If the press get hold of that——'

'Who's going to tell them?'

'Kettle, for one. He pretends he doesn't like the whole set-up at all, but it suits him fine. Inside he's laughing. He can pull the plug any time he likes and watch me flow down the drain.'

'Why doesn't he do it now then?'

'It all comes down to timing, Harry. The only thing I can do is find The Hangman before he does. That way, I might just salvage something of my career.'

Harry frowned. 'Okay,' he said slowly. 'Just don't forget I've got a pension to work out.'

'How could I forget, Harry?'

He offered me a nervous smile, said, 'What next, then?'

'First, we pay Paterson a visit, then up to Callander, home of Chief Inspector Eaves, retired, the man who put MacBean behind bars. Coming?'

'Is the Pope a Catholic?'

Paterson lived halfway down Comely Bank Avenue, behind a door of blue flaking paint. We rang and waited.

The guy who opened the door was a slob in clothes. None of the clothes fitted and were all several sizes too small. He was somewhere in his late twenties, with hanging cheeks, hanging chins and a hangdog expression that made you want to throw him a stick to fetch. He blinked at us through vacant brown eyes.

'Paterson?' I said. He blinked again. I let Harry do the introductions.

'Better come in,' he growled, and led the way into a dark hallway. We followed him down some stairs to a dingy room at the back of the house where a television offered the only source of light this side of the drawn curtains. The room stank the way a burrow would after years of hibernation.

Paterson shovelled a pile of newspapers and magazines off the sofa onto the floor, kicked them out of sight and motioned us to sit. We sat and Paterson fell into an armchair which fitted him better than his clothes.

He waved a hand at the curtains. 'Sensitive eyes,' he said in explanation. He leant forward and turned the television down. 'What is it?' he asked. 'Looking for one of my lodgers?'

'You get a lot of that?'

'Now and then. Nothing to do with me, see?' He pulled a packet of cigarettes from his cardigan pocket, nudged one out and lit it. 'Who is it this time?'

'John MacBean.'

'What kept you? He skipped at least a couple months ago.'

'Yeah? Where'd he go?'

'Think he'd tell me?' he said, talking through his cigarette. 'He owed a month's rent, he ain't going to come up and say, hey, Mr Paterson, I'm skipping out tonight without paying my rent, here's my forwarding address in case any coppers come looking for me. Eh?'

'So you don't know?'

'Not for sure, no.'

'But you've got an idea, right?'

'Yeah.'

'Why don't we share it?'

He appeared to consider the idea for a moment, stubbing out his cigarette with exaggerated concentration.

'Okay. Why not. He was always babbling about some-place he called home. Up in the Highlands somewhere. That's all he ever talked about, how he was saving the money to get up there, maybe set up another workshop or something like that. I got sick listening. The guy was cracked for sure. The lady from the parole board, she told me he killed a wee laddie, had been away twenty-five years, was a changed man now. I didn't like the idea of him staying here, I don't take the violent ones, see. But this MacBean, he didn't look like he could harm a fly, see, so I took him in. He was okay, paid his rent regular, till he done a bunk.'

'Did he drink? Go out? Have people come to visit? Get any letters?'

'Nothing. Most of the time kept to himself 'cept Saturday nights, he'd buy in a bottle an' sit in front of the telly till he fell over. Only post he ever got were Giros.'

'Did he speak to anyone living here? Form any relationships?'

'Like I said, kept to himself. He only spoke when you spoke first, asked him a question or something. A couple of drinks in him and yeah, he'd babble. Always the same thing, right, like I told you. Going home and that.'

'He leave anything behind?'

'A few bits and pieces. Newspaper cuttings, stuff like that. He didn't have many clothes, must've walked out wearing 'em all, the sod.'

'What did you do with the stuff?'

'Threw it out.

'What kind of cuttings were they?'

'Don't ask me, I never looked. Old, yeah, the paper was old, I could see that. But I never bothered to read the stuff.'

'What else was there?'

'Books, magazines mostly. He read a lot, always had his face buried in something. Know what I mean?'

'What kind of books?'

'Serious, you know? No fiction, mostly fact. Documentary books, glossy pictures, diagrams, that sort a thing. Nature books.'

'Is that the impression he put across? Serious?'

'Yeah. Like . . .' he stopped to light another cigarette, continued through a pillar of smoke. 'Like some professor – the way he dressed, his hair, glasses and that. Always looked like he had some great problem on his mind he just had to get sorted out, like no-one else could solve – if you know what I mean?'

I nodded. I glanced sideways at Harry. Our eyes met, held, both saying the same thing: nothing more here, let's hit the road, Jack, don't come back. We stood in unison, thanked him and left.

The M9 and roads north were quiet. We left the cloud-cover behind us and broke out under a blue sky. Windows down, good to be out of the city. It had been a while, missed. I think Harry felt the same, though he didn't speak, most of the hour-long journey done in silence.

We had to stop, ask directions twice and double back. Chief Inspector Eaves lived in one of the modern estates we had passed coming into Callander. We found the house and parked behind a silver Datsun. The front door opened before we got there.

Eaves wasn't as big as Harry but they would have had difficulty going through the same door together. He was in his late sixties, early seventies, but his body looked well-preserved in dark-grey trousers, white shirt, fawn cardigan and shiny-brown leather slippers. He still had a few wisps of whitish hair. I could see a couple of purplish birthmarks on his scalp, and his ears were thick and large, close to his skull. His expression was alert behind round steel-rimmed spectacles that made him look nothing like John Lennon, except maybe the nose which was a bit hawkish.

He peeled off his glasses and squinted at me. 'You must be McMorran,' he said, though I don't know how he worked that one out. He slipped his glasses into the breast pocket of his cardigan, offered his hand.

We shook, and I introduced Harry. They shook, and Eaves invited us in.

Inside was almost the way I had imagined it. Living-room spotlessly tidy, framed photos of family on the mantelpiece over the gas-fire.

'Sit, gentlemen, please,' he indicated the two arm-chairs, side of the fire. 'Don't give me any nonsense about duty, what will you drink?'

149

I settled for a whisky, Harry for a can of shandy. Eaves left the room on stiff legs and returned a few minutes later with the drinks on a small silver tray. He laid it on a lacquered coffee-table and sank onto the settee, massaging his knees.

'Help yourselves.'

For the next five minutes we small-talked while Eaves asked questions. So I told him the lot, the way I saw it, how the investigation was progressing or regressing, depending on your frame of mind. He listened, appreciative I think. Old coppers never die, not until they are dead.

'I don't see the connection,' Eaves said. 'Between The Hangman and – whatsisname – MacBean.'

Harry nodded in agreement.

I told the truth. 'I don't really know, sir. It's just a feeling I can't explain. It's got something to do with the way MacBean killed the Robertson boy, apparently motiveless, like The Hangman killings now.'

Eaves laughed, a rumble in his belly. 'That famous copper's hunch,' he said. 'Don't get me wrong. I'm not saying it's a fairy-story. I relied on it often enough myself. You get a feeling and you know you're right. Whether you are or not doesn't matter, just that you act on it anyway.'

I told him that was what I was doing.

Eaves placed his empty glass on the tray. 'And you want me to tell you . . . what, exactly?'

'About MacBean. I don't know, his motives never seemed to come across properly at the trial or in the press reports . . .' I trailed off, unable to phrase exactly what I wanted.

'Motives, yes. Never really substantiated, you're right.

None of the usual motives – elimination, gain, lust, conviction, jealously or revenge – none of them fully explained why MacBean murdered the boy. I didn't believe the defence plea of diminished responsibility one bit. Hell, I thought MacBean one of the sanest killer I've met. But he had a good lawyer, young and eager, out for a big score.'

'Looks like he got it.'

'Sure. He got MacBean out of a death sentence. But twenty-five years . . . I know which I'd choose.'

'So he struck you as sane?'

Eaves nodded, folded his arms across his chest. 'He knew what he was doing, aye.'

'No doubt of his guilt?'

'None. But he *was* hiding something. I was certain of it, though I could never pin him down. He wasn't stupid, never slipped up, not once, but——'

I smiled. 'You had a feeling?'

'Ballaig, have you ever been there?' I shook my head and he went on. 'Well, it's a small village, a closely-knit community, they don't like people coming in, raking up their personal lives, asking a lot of questions. So they closed up, made it hard for us to get anything on MacBean at all. A conspiracy of silence. They knew something but they weren't telling. I never found out what it was.'

'Why, then,' I asked, 'if he was sane, did he kill the boy?'

Eaves shrugged. 'I'll tell you this and you see what you can make of it. It was about the only piece of gossip I managed to get from the villagers, and then only by

151

accident. Rumour had it that MacBean's wife, Margaret, was having an affair with Dr Robertson, the father of the dead boy. It seemed everybody in the village knew except MacBean. I faced him with it soon after his arrest but he denied it vehemently. I confronted both his wife and Dr Robertson and they denied it too. In fact, I could find no-one prepared to admit that it was anything more than a rumour. Eventually, I had to let it go.'

'The press never found out?'

'I was the only one who knew. I felt both families had suffered enough.'

'So what you're saying is that MacBean came home that afternoon, found his wife in bed with the good doctor and went downstairs and murdered the doctor's kid. Is that right?'

'That's what I thought at the time.'

'And now?'

'Now it sounds pretty lame. You come home and find your wife in bed with another man, you don't go out and kill his offspring, you kill him. Or your wife. Or both.'

'Or you ask if they'd like a bite to eat when they've finished. No, you're right. It doesn't make sense.'

'Though it was the nearest thing to a motive that I could hang on MacBean.'

'You mentioned a conspiracy of silence. Do you think it was to conceal the affair?'

'Possibly. But I wasn't convinced. I still think there was something else they were trying to hide. A darker secret.'

'MacBean himself never gave any hint?'

'He hardly spoke at all. He was more composed, I

think, than any criminal I've ever met. Throughout the whole interrogation and trial he maintained an almost stolid silence. He merely confessed and then nothing, not a word more.'

'In the newspaper report of the case, it claimed that Margaret MacBean spent the afternoon working in the village shop. Did you substantiate that?'

'We found several witnesses who visited the shop that afternoon who said they didn't see her there . . . and the same amount of people who said they *did* see her there.'

'Could she have been with Dr Robertson that afternoon?'

'It's possible. I certainly thought so. I interviewed everyone who lived between the MacBean's house and the shop but no-one saw her either going to or coming from the shop.'

'Convenient. Any of these witnesses still around?'

'Could be. I'd have to do a bit of asking around.'

'I'd like to talk to the man who found the body – Lawrie, I think his name is. And whoever ran the shop then.'

'It's a long time ago,' Eaves said. 'I hope you're not expecting too much.'

'I don't expect anything. By the way, where was Mrs Robertson that afternoon?'

'Here, in Callander, getting her hair done. She had about ten witnesses and arrived back at the village some-time around six, I think.'

'You've a good memory.'

'I use it a lot these days.'

'I hope I'm not putting you to too much trouble,' I said.

'No, no,' he replied, shaking his head. 'No trouble at all. It'll give me something to do. I've still got friends on the force. I'll see what I can dig up. How can I contact you?'

I told him and thanked him. Then we took our leave.

In the car Harry said, 'There's the kind of cop I always thought I wanted to be. You know, small-town, respected, a little pride in your job, that kind of thing.'

'You still think that?'

'Aye,' Harry said, with a wistful sigh.

It seemed a shame to have to return to the city.

# Chapter Twelve

In the days when Morningside was little more than a village, Drummond Hall had been the home of a prominent city banker. Built in the grand Georgian style typical in Edinburgh at the time, the house was much the same then as now, except for the low annexe built onto the east wing in 1926, when the Hall had been turned into a private hospital catering for psychiatric patients with very rich relatives. In 1952 the hospital passed into the hands of the Health Board, and the extended kitchen buildings were added later that year. Dominic Bain had been working there almost eleven years now, the first and only job he had ever had.

He hated it, seldom spoke to his colleagues and never socialised. At lunch or tea-breaks, he remained in the kitchen. He despised the triviality of their lives expressed in their banal conversations. Plastic people with television minds.

He tossed aside the newspaper and poured another cup of thick black tea. The kitchen was low-ceilinged, long and cluttered, with white-tiled walls and a red-tiled floor. Around him, the comforting sound of the slumbering workplace. The hissing of steamers, the creaking of pipes, the hum of the electric fan-ovens, the simmering pots and boilers.

He sat in the head chef's small office – large enough for a desk, a chair and a stack of overstocked shelves and nothing more. Menus and order-sheets papered the wall, the ashtray was full, and two empty bottles of Pils stood on the desk next to the telephone. The head chef liked his Pils.

Dominic was pleased – he had hit the headlines. Hangman kills again, that kind of stuff. But the story told him nothing. He wanted to know how close the police were, what they had on him. But they were admitting nothing and he didn't like it. There was no mention of the camera he had left behind, or the bike, or the guy in the car. What were they up to? Perhaps they hadn't found them, didn't know about the bike or the crash; silence meaning ignorance.

Then there was the Photofit thing. Not me, he thought. Not even in the mirror. There was a likeness, but it was a stretch of the imagination. The hair was fair and too long and showed under the woollen hat. The eyes were too large, the mouth too small, the nose an insult. No-one would recognise him from it. Thank you, witnesses.

Arnie knocked and came into the office. 'Oh, it's you,' he said. Arnie was twenty, emaciated and pale. Like a dried-up husk of the punk he once was, and still tried to be. He wore white overalls that were too large, and heavy workboots he could hardly lift. His hair was black; spiked in some places, shaved in others.

'Who did you expect?' Bain said. Arnie was a patient

they let work in the kitchens. He was cheap and it kept him out the way. He took these fits sometimes, would cut off bits of his body and mail them to his father. That kind of guy.

'Where's everyone else?' Arnie asked.

'Upstairs.'

Arnie shrugged, sat on the edge of the desk. Picked up the paper, glanced at the front page. 'Looks a bit like you,' he said. 'Don't you think?'

'Bollocks. Looks like a hundred people you see every day.'

'Yeah?'

'Sod off, Arnie.'

The punk stared at him with eyes as empty as his own.

'I just wanted to tell you the trollies are back,' he said.

'Right. You told me. Now I know.'

'What's for breakfast?'

'Why don't you find out?'

Arnie grunted and left the office. Bain heard him sliding doors, rattling containers, making as much noise as possible. Did he suspect? He was by nature a nosy little bastard, always prying, always spying. Being a loony didn't make him stupid, Dominic thought. And we know what happens to spies, don't we?

Jamie Robertson was a spy – and they found *him* hanging from a beam in old MacBean's workshop.

Ho-hum.

A few minutes later the remaining kitchen staff came downstairs and commenced work. The morning passed like a thousand other mornings had. The food was the same, the banter the same. People he had spent years working with, despising every breath that left their bodies.

At lunchtime, he went down to the telephone in the front hall. He had a list of agency numbers, a pile of coins. He dialled the numbers, pumped in the coins. On the fifth call he struck the jackpot.

Natasha.

He returned to the kitchen with new blood flowing through his veins. Wednesday, she would be dancing in Willie's down on Tollcross. He had been there once, way back, a grotty wee dive, dark and dingy, full of hard men with unfriendly eyes. Maybe it had changed. Most likely it hadn't.

He sweated a while at the canteen servery, doling out food to arrogant doctors, harassed nurses. Then had his lunch and signed out. Upstairs, he stripped off his whites and climbed into fresh clothes. No-one around to see the bruises and cuts that mottled and crossed his skin.

He walked home. It hurt to walk, but the painkillers helped though his body was still a museum of bruised bone and torn skin. So he walked slowly, sauntering almost. The air was warm and muggy, the sky heavy, threatening to fall. As he let himself into the house, it began to rain.

There was a note from Mother-dear by the telephone on the hall table. It said she was out having her hair done but she would be back in time for tea. How nice.

He went upstairs and showered. He stepped from the shower and dried himself gingerly, then dressed in a navy-blue tracksuit. As he descended the stairs the door-bell rang.

Two men in raincoats stood on the step getting wet. They had hard faces and cold, flat eyes. The nearest one presented a card for Dominic's inspection.

'Police,' he said. 'Could we have a word?'

# Chapter Thirteen

'Sorry?'

'Police,' said the man again. 'We'd like to ask you a few questions. May we come in?'

Dominic did not answer, found himself closing the door behind them. He wondered if they could hear his heart hammering as the adrenalin hit his bloodstream. He led them along the hall into Motherdear's sitting-room, told them to sit. They remained standing.

Dominic managed a puzzled frown.

'What's the problem?'

The cop who had done all the talking studied him for a moment with the flat, unblinking eyes all policemen seem to have at birth.

'A few questions, if you don't mind, sir.'

Bain had a fixed smile now, he was getting into the game. He watched Flat-eyes take out a notebook, lick the tip of his pencil and ask, 'Your full name, please.'

'Dominic Bain.'

'Do you own this house?'

'Yes.'

'You live alone?'

'With my mother. She's out getting her hair done.'

Flat-eyes' lips moved as he wrote. He looked up with each question. 'Occupation?'

'Cook. At Drummond House Hospital.'

'Been there long?'

'Almost eleven years.'

'Were you working there on Saturday?'

'No. I just got back from holiday.'

'When did you return from holiday?'

'Last week. Wednesday.'

'And Saturday? Where were you Saturday?'

'Hey, what's this all about?' He lost his cool for a second. 'You're supposed to tell me why the questions, right?'

'Purely routine, sir. You'll have heard about the murder, no doubt?'

'What, you mean The Hangman?' The cop became impatient. 'That's right, routine. So *if* you'll answer my question, sir.'

'Didn't my mother tell you? You were round the other day, right?'

'Someone else, sir. We're just following up. Now, Saturday . . .'

'I spent most of the day in the garden. You know, relaxing. Sunbathing. Then in the evening I sat and watched television with my mother.'

'Do you have anyone who could vouch for you?'

'Apart from my mother, no. We're very close, spend a lot of time together.'

'I see.' Pause. Dragging it out. Thinking of more smart-arse questions, trying to be a tricky-dicky.

'Ever been in trouble, sir?' he asked.

Bain shook his head.

'No previous convictions?'

'None.'

The other cop, the faceless one who watched and said nothing was looking out of the window onto the garden. A radio crackled in his pocket. He took it out and mumbled. Dominic couldn't understand a word. Maybe checking him out. No sweat. He was slick and cool. Nobody's fool.

Flat-eyes wanted to know if he had ever owned a bicycle? Dominic shook his head, said no, he had never learned to ride and anyway he had a car.

The Faceless One pocketed his radio and spoke to Dominic for the first time. He had a high-pitched nasal whine instead of a voice. 'What's in those buildings at the end of your garden?' he asked.

'I keep my snakes in the small one,' Dominic said, 'and the other one's just full of junk. My mother-dear keeps getting on at me to have them demolished but I——'

'Snakes, sir?'

'South African Pythons. Three of them. They're pets.'

Flat-eyes shuddered. The Faceless One said, 'Do you mind if I have a look round?'

Which meant he was going to look round whether Dominic liked it or not.

So he said, 'No problem. But I'll need to get the keys.'

As they followed him down the garden path, Flat-eyes asked, 'Did you see or hear anything suspicious on Saturday night?'

'Like what?'

'Anything out of the ordinary.'

'Like I said, all I did was watch television then go to bed.'

The Faceless One whined, 'You don't go out Saturday nights? Have a drink or something?'

'Depends how my girlfriend feels.'

'Girlfriend? Was she here on Saturday night?'

'Nah. She works weekends.'

They came to the barn and Dominic fumbled with the lock.

Flat-eyes asked, 'This where you keep the snakes?'

Dominic nodded.

Flat-eyes told the Faceless One, 'You can go in there if you like. I'm staying out here.'

'Don't tell me you're scared of snakes?'

Dominic was trying hard to remember if he'd left anything lying about. Incriminating evidence, they called it. He was pretty sure he hadn't. Only the bin-bags, and the rope. They couldn't convict him on that. But it would make them think. Not a good idea.

He opened the door, waved the two men inside. Flat-eyes tried to smile. The Faceless One walked across the sand floor, studied each of the glass aquariums in turn. Then he called to his colleague.

'Like he said, Royal African Pythons.'

'Hey,' Dominic said, 'you know your snakes.'

The Faceless One shrugged modestly and gave an impression of a smile. It was a poor impression.

'My son has a python,' was his only comment.

'Let's take a look in the other shed,' Flat-eyes said to Dominic, his eyes fixed to the aquariums where glistening skin was coiled.

164

Dominic locked the door with shaking hands. He was wondering if he could overpower them both, whether they'd be missed, if anyone knew they were here, when suddenly the Faceless One's radio crackled back to life.

They became instantly alert. They listened. Still Dominic could not make out a word. They looked at each other. Glanced at Dominic. Flat-eyes nodded. The Faceless One spoke something into the radio.

'Okay,' Flat-eyes said to Dominic. 'Show us the other one.'

The Faceless One objected. 'We've no got time. We'd better go.'

Dominic unlocked the padlock, pushed open the door. His heart was racing.

Flat-eyes stood at the door and let his eyes graze across the dark interior. 'Junk is right,' he said, and turned away. 'Okay. That's it. Thanks for your time.'

'No problem, officer.' Dominic closed the door, and accompanied them up the path. 'We'll be setting up a Fingerprint Unit by the Morningside Clock. We'd appreciate your co-operation if you came down and had your prints taken, sir,' Flat-eyes said.

'I've done nothing wrong,' Dominic complained.

'In that case, sir, once your prints have been taken and checked you can have them back or destroy them.'

'Yeah? All right, officer, I'll do as you say.'

He watched them walk away up the drive.

The shakes hit him a minute later. He pounded up the stairs, threw off his tracksuit, gulped down another Valium – on ration now – then buried himself beneath his duvet. He free-fell into a deep, bottomless sleep for fifteen solid hours.

When he awoke, suddenly, he was propelled into a life he didn't know, didn't want.

Where was he, who was he, where had he been?

The answers came to him, like filling in a crossword; but there were gaps where some of the clues were missing. He found his feet at the end of his legs, used them to get across to where the mirror was fixed to the wall. Studied his reflection.

Stared into his eyes, struggling for recognition. No go.

Whose eyes?

Had it always been that way? Body, a mass of bruises, ripening. He ran sweaty hands over his naked torso and his skin cringed beneath his touch. What the fuck was going on?

He spent twenty minutes under the shower, scrubbing, scrubbing, the stink of the city, so deep. Dried and dressed. Breakfast was a coffee and two valium.

Then it came back to him. The bastards had his camera. Probably his prints, too, he couldn't remember if he wore gloves or not. And the bicycle? He could not return, not now, too much risk. He would have to think this out. But no problem, not really, they knew nothing, couldn't pin him down on any one thing, even the prints – someone stole the camera and the bike. What is this, harassment? Slick, yeah, they would have to be pretty damn smart to catch him out like that.

At eight-thirty he set out for the hospital, heedless of the soft rain, trundling traffic, oppressive sky.

Morning tea break. Bain and Arnie sat alone. Arnie was in a strange mood; restless, curious and sullen. He sat on a drum of vegetable-oil, nibbling at his cuticles and staring at the floor while Bain doodled on the back of a menu sheet.

'You live on your own?' Arnie now asked. 'In that old house down by the railway?'

Dominic turned slowly, fixed Arnie to the wall with his eyes, kept his voice deceptively soft. 'You been spying on me?'

'Happened to see you down there, so what? I'm allowed to walk where I like, ain't I?'

'When was this?'

'Saturday. Week ago, maybe two. What you getting so mad about?'

'Who's mad? I'm not shouting.'

'It's in your eyes,' Arnie mumbled. 'Okay, I'm sorry, right? Sorry I ever saw you. I ain't spying, Nick.'

'No?' Dominic said, listening for something behind the words, but finding nothing. He said again, 'Like I said, better not catch you, Arnie.'

The punk looked as though he might start something, it lit his eyes for a second but blew away under Bain's direct gaze. He went out and slammed the door, muttering his way down to the kitchen.

Arnie had suddenly become a problem. Dangerous, perhaps. He'd have to think about Arnie, decide soon. Decide and act, then act fast and clean.

He left the office, unlocked the cold-room, carried out three boxes of macedoine, another three of carrots. Turned on two of the boilers, partially filled them with water, added salt, then sat on the boxes waiting for the water to boil.

The rest of the staff returned from their break and the quiet throb and hiss of the kitchen turned to cacophony.

Arnie forgotten, Dominic thought of Natasha. Tomorrow, he would see her. This time he wouldn't lose her. Maybe open up a file, follow her, get to know her better before he made his move.

First he would have to do something about her name. He couldn't go round calling her Natasha: it was too posey, far too theatrical. He would have to think up something shorter, more to the point. Like . . . Tash. That sounded okay, not over the top, not too much.

Why not?

Tash.

# Chapter Fourteen

We were making good time back up the motorway; Harry the reluctant driver, heading for the village of Ballaig. The retired Chief Inspector Eaves had come through this morning with the names and addresses of the two witnesses at MacBean's trial I had asked him for. Both still alive, both still living in the village. We had a day of inactivity stretched out before us, so I had spent a hard half-hour persuading Harry that we sign out, take a trip north and make a day of it.

It was a balmy sort of day, close, with a wind high up, hustling clouds along, never giving them much chance to stay in the way of the sun. Harry was in shirtsleeves, me with shades, laid back, letting the warm air push at my hair as the green of the countryside slipped by. I felt relaxed.

Out of Callander, we followed the Ballaig signs west, the road narrowing, trees closing in. There was a river to our left, moving fast over shallows, the first river that wasn't a sewer I'd seen in years. We dipped in and out of shadow, the effect hypnotic. I felt even more at ease, it seemed, the further we left the city behind. Strange thoughts for a city man. Maybe I had been one too long.

Ballaig jumped at us out of nothing; a one street village with low stone cottages, a few hotels, a garage, something being built in a piece of space, and a small shop.

'Try the shop first.'

I left Harry in the car and entered the low doorway. It was dark inside, only a few rays of light managing to squeeze through the small display window. I heard a bell tinkle somewhere in the back of the building as I closed the door.

There were lots of things in the shop, everything you would expect and a little bit more, but no-one at the glass-topped counter. Voices came from the back, though. Then a door opened and a woman in her forties came out.

'Good afternoon,' she said. She was a solid woman, dressed plainly, no make-up, no fuss, dark hair short and simply cut. No rings on her fingers.

'I'm looking for Mrs Bovellie,' I said. 'I was told I could find her here.'

She sized me up, looked me down, came to a conclusion. 'My mother is asleep,' she said. 'Perhaps I can help?'

'Does she usually talk in her sleep?'

She blushed, shrugged, began knitting her fingers while she let the welcome slip from her eyes. 'She's in bed; she always retires for the afternoon.'

'I've come all the way from Edinburgh to see her,' I said, then added, 'I'm a police officer.'

She regarded me shrewdly. 'Aren't you out of your jurisdiction?'

I gave her a disarming kind of smile. 'It's nothing serious,' I said. 'Just a few questions about something that happened a long time ago. I won't keep her long.'

170

'I'm afraid——' she began, but was cut off by a shrill voice from the back, saying, 'Who is it, Hazel?'

Hazel glared at me, turned and went through the door. I could hear the voices, but not what they were saying. Then the daughter came back, raised the flap in the counter.

'My mother will see you now.'

She led me through into a room that was light and warm and stuffy. Two large windows looked out over a field where a couple of horses grazed. Beyond the field, two men in waders fished the river where it lazed in shadow below the squat bulk of a heather-clad hill, or mountain, depending on how you look at a thousand or so feet. Mrs Bovellie sat with a tray in her lap, one hand at her throat, the other playing with a piece of jigsaw. She waited till I came into her line of vision before raising her eyes.

I introduced myself, told her my business; she didn't seem surprised, merely nodded, smiled and showed me a chair.

'If you'll excuse me just a moment' she said, waving the piece of jigsaw at me. 'I must find where this goes. Hazel, a pot of tea, perhaps?'

I took the opportunity to look around. The floor was varnished oak, covered here and there in mohair carpets, mostly deep red, patterned. There was a gas-fire; framed photos, souvenirs and ornaments on a mantelpiece; a highly-polished table against one wall with a lace centre-piece on which sat a silver candlestick-holder; there were also two overstuffed armchairs; a television, an ancient radio and a silent grandfather clock; a door through which Hazel had gone, from which came sounds of tea-making.

Mrs Bovellie was a tiny woman who looked as though she would blow away if I breathed too hard. She had white Will-o'-the-wisp hair, recently permed, youthful eyes and a small, tight-lipped mouth. Her frail bones protruded from the heavy tan tweed skirt and jacket which she wore over a white lace blouse with intricate cuffs and high neck. Her feet were buried in fluffy suede slippers.

Hazel brought in the tea, placed it on a low mahogany occasional table and was about to pour when the bell tinkled. She went through to the shop and after a moment I heard voices.

'Do you ever do jigsaw puzzles, young man?' Mrs Bovellie asked, without looking up.

I shook my head. 'Too impatient,' I replied.

'Ah, there we are,' she said eventually, triumphantly slotting the piece in position. 'Now, young man, first the tea, then we can talk.'

I ended up being Mum and put her cup and saucer on the window-ledge beside her.

'Now,' I began, but she didn't let me finish.

'I'm intrigued, Inspector,' she said. 'Tell me, what's this all about? You're not going to arrest me, are you?'

I felt maybe she needed a jolt, something to show her I wasn't only wood between the ears. But I settled on kid-gloves.

'John MacBean,' I said. 'Remember him?'

Her polite smile faded like sun behind a cloud. She settled on a puzzled frown, finger to lower lip, head cocked to one side. 'John . . . MacBean, you say?' I nodded. 'Mmm. I don't seem to——'

'1958. You were a witness at his trial. He lived here in Ballaig, was imprisoned for murder. Not a small matter, something you might forget.'

'Of course! How silly of me. John MacBean. Yes, I remember now.'

'I'd like to go over the events that occurred on the day of the murder, the events about which you testified.'

'Surely you could find all that in your records, Inspector?'

'I prefer first-hand accounts,' I told her, not quite honestly. 'I'm not good at reading between the lines.'

'My memory is not what it used to be.'

'Can you remember how long you had known MacBean, before he appeared in court?'

'There's nothing wrong with my memory, young man,' she scolded. Then pursed her lips to help her think. 'Since just after the war, 1947 or 1948, I think. He came up alone first, I recall. Bought the house and workshop, then spent several months doing it up before sending for his wife and child, who must have been two or three at the time.'

'How well did you know him?'

She regarded me over her cup, her expression guarded.

'You must understand, Inspector, that in a community this size it is virtually impossible to keep any secrets. However, it is also essential to respect another man's privacy. John MacBean was a private man. He lived quietly, worked hard and didn't go out much. He attended the service on Sundays, and spent a lot of his spare time in the hills with his son or out in his boat, fishing on the loch. I knew him well, but no more or less than anyone else in the village.'

'You knew him well, even though he kept to himself?'

'That is what I am saying, yes.'

'So when he killed the son of his next-door neighbour, you were not surprised?'

She looked at me with something close to contempt. 'Surprised?' she said, her brittle voice rising. 'I couldn't believe it. No-one could. We all thought it must be some mistake, an accident perhaps. He loved children, you see.'

Perhaps too much, I thought. 'He never exhibited any violent traits in the ten years he lived here before the murder?'

'No. Never.'

'Then what made him change?'

'I'm not a psychoanalyst, Inspector. I was as dumb-founded as everyone else.'

I tried another angle. 'His motives were never satis-factorily explained during the trial. Why do you think he killed the boy?'

'I've no idea. No-one really knew. You see, he was such a secretive man. I doubt even his wife knew.'

'I understand his wife was supposed to be working here that afternoon.'

'She *was* working here that afternoon.'

'From when to when?'

'From midday till half-past four.'

'She didn't leave the shop at all?'

'No.'

'Not even for, say, half-an-hour?'

'What exactly are you driving at, Inspector?'

'I understand that Margaret and Dr Robertson were,

shall we say, on intimate terms?'

Mrs Bovellie snorted. 'Pah! Nothing but malicious gossip. There is not a word of truth in it.'

'However, it's strange that several customers who came to the shop that afternoon couldn't remember seeing her here.'

'It's not strange at all. She was working back here in the storeroom. I didn't live here then and this room was used for stores.'

'So you were both here when' – I struggled for the name – 'Mr Lawrie arrived with MacBean's son?'

'Yes. I was through in the front and he came in looking like death. I could see immediately something was wrong and Alec – Mr Lawrie – took me aside and told me. I then had to break the news to Margaret.'

'How did she take it?

'Badly, how do you think?'

'And her son?'

'He was in shock. He never spoke for ages after that. Who knows what that poor child was forced to witness.'

'Mr Lawrie found the boy in the bathroom?'

'Aye, that's right. He'd gone there to deliver some wood and discovered poor Jamie hanging in the workshop. So he looked around the house and found Dominic.'

'MacBean's son?'

'Yes. But there was no sign of John.'

'What happened then?'

'We phoned the police.'

'You didn't see the body yourself?'

'No, Lordy-not!'

'Did you see John MacBean?'

She shook her head wistfully. 'No. I didn't see him again till . . .'

'How long before the police arrived?'

'Twenty, twenty-five minutes.'

'And no-one touched the body in between?'

'Alec went back, you know, to make sure no-one touched the body.'

'What about the boy's mother or father, the doctor and his wife?'

'Dr Robertson was out on a call. I think Mrs Robertson was in Callander. She didn't get back till evening, I think.'

'It was quite normal then, that Jamie was left on his own?'

'Not normal, no. It happened sometimes, yes, but Mrs Robertson would usually leave him with one of us, or he'd play with Dominic or Cathy.'

'Cathy?'

'She lived next door at the time. Runs the guest house now.'

'Was he playing with them that afternoon?'

Mrs Bovellie let her eyes become vague. 'I've no idea,' she said. 'I really don't understand what you're doing, going over all this, after all these years. I would have imagined the case was closed, settled by now?'

I let the lie go by, ignored the evasion. 'What happened to the Robertsons?'

She sighed impatiently. 'You really are quite persistent, aren't you, Inspector?' she said with a near smile. 'They moved away. I don't blame them, all the memories and . . .' Again she trailed off into what was supposed to be retrospective silence.

176

'Moved where?'

'Australia, I believe.'

Which explained why Chief Inspector Eaves had been unable to trace them – but didn't explain away the impression I had that Mrs Bovellie was lying through her teeth. I tried to shake her tree.

'John MacBean is on his way back,' I said, watching her eyes. 'Either that, or he's here already. Did you know that?'

I could see she didn't in the way her jaw dropped, how she jerked herself upright in the chair. 'He can't! Can't come back, no. It was . . .'

'Part of the deal?' I suggested.

She looked away, shaking her head, but there was little conviction in her action. 'You say he might be here already?' she said, staring through the window. 'How do you know this? Who told you?'

'We have our sources, Mrs Bovellie.'

She brought her crooked hand up to massage her eyes, lowered her voice to a weary croak. 'I think you'd better leave now, Inspector,' she intoned. 'I'm feeling rather tired.'

Of course. Stupid of me not to have thought.

As I went through the motions of thanking her very much for answering my questions, I wondered why she was still lying after all these years, what she knew that was still worth hiding. I was also wishing I had a tap on her phone. See who she called now.

Harry was there in the front shop, almost filling it, taking up most of the little light there'd been, talking with Hazel, Hazel smiling. They dragged the conversation to a halt as I entered. I wished them both a good afternoon and emerged onto the street.

I walked out of the village, took a track to the left which led to a wooden bridge over the river I'd seen from Mrs Bovellie's windows. I stood there a while, watching the two fishermen, listening to the birds and the slow, sliding water. Tasting the clean air as though it were a fine wine. I let my thoughts slide, too.

I must have got carried away by the timeless quality, the natural flow of the life around me for it took me several minutes to realise the sound of the horn was probably Harry wondering where the hell I'd got to. Reluctantly, I walked back to the main road where he was waiting in the car.

'What's the hurry?' I said, climbing in.

'I'm hungry.'

'When aren't you?'

'We could probably get a meal at the hotel there,' he said. 'Then I could tell you what Hazel told me.'

We managed to persuade the barman to give us lunch, which we ate by the bay-windows overlooking the main street. As Harry wolfed down his steak pie, I picked distractedly at my haggis.

'So, what did Hazel tell you?' I asked.

'Nothing,' Harry mumbled through a mouthful of mush.

I called him something obscene but he merely smiled.

'She was away at the time. Boarding school, down south. She only heard about it when she came back a few weeks later. She never knew MacBean except when he came in the shop; said he was quiet, the way she remembered him, and polite, sometimes bought her sweets.'

'I've been thinking, if we could find out where MacBean's wife is now, have a word with her. Or her son. He might remember something.'

'Why bother?' Harry said, putting down his knife and fork, looking me in the eye. 'This whole business looks more and more like a wild goose chase. The proverbial red herring. I can't see how anything that happened here twenty-odd years ago has any bearing on the Hangman enquiry at all. I respect your itches, sir, your hunches or whatever you like to call them, but this . . .'

'Yeah?'

'It's become an obsession. You can't, or won't, justify your reasons for continuing. I mean, we could be doing something more constructive than raking around the ashes of a case that was closed when MacBean got put away for life.'

'MacBean is out, Harry. He's been out quite a while and suddenly kids are getting strung up the same way he strung up the Robertson boy. Okay, he's maybe sixty now and you're thinking he's nothing like the guy the witnesses saw running from the locus at the Hermitage. Fair enough, I'll buy that. But the modus operandi is the same and there is still no apparent motive.'

'Bollocks, sir,' Harry said. 'The Robertson boy wasn't strangled first, then hanged. Nor was he stripped, or tied in bin-liners, or dumped somewhere away from the scene of the crime. There's no record of MacBean taking pictures of his victims, or——'

'Okay, Harry. Maybe, just maybe, you're right. But

I'm not going to admit to anything until I've talked to MacBean and have found out why Mrs Bovellie is lying.' I went on to fill Harry in on the conversation I'd had with the old woman.

'So what are you going to do next?' he asked, when I had finished.

'Have a talk with Lawrie, try and get a line on MacBean. He's here, he must be here by now.'

'What makes you so certain?'

'What makes you such a pain in the arse?' I got up and went to the bar to ask the barman if he knew where I would find Alec Lawrie.

'Out on the loch, most likely. He spends most days there and doesn't usually come back till late.'

I asked him about vacancies.

'Aye, the hotel's full of them,' he said.

Harry has good ears. 'So you're thinking of staying?' he said.

'What about you?'

'I've got to get back. I promised my wife I'd take her out, you know, to make up for all these recent late nights. Anyway, Kettle'll be after me tomorrow morning. I'd better be there, see what he's been up to. What if he asks where you are?'

'You don't know,' I told him. 'Same for Barrie. You haven't seen me since yesterday.'

'You're not up to something you're not telling me about?'

'You know me, Harry. Pure as the——'

'Aye,' he broke in, heavily. 'I know you.'

# Chapter Fifteen

After Harry had gone, I took a walk down to the main street, looking for the house where MacBean had lived. I found it had been swallowed by a guest house with a 'Vacancies' sign in the window. So I checked in.

The woman who ran the place was called Cath. She was about my age, polite and efficient, with a harassed expression. She wore baggy jeans and a loose red sweatshirt, her long hair whipped into a scraggly bun, her face long and bony. She told me how she was on her own, her husband not being very well. Luckily she wasn't very busy, the weather not being too good. Not merely polite, I thought later, but pleasant. A little lonely perhaps, but who wouldn't be in a place this size? She was also rather attractive.

I spent the afternoon exploring the village (Alec Lawrie was not at home) and following a few of the nature trails into the forest but not too far. I returned in time for dinner, then spent the evening in the bar of the hotel, hoping to meet Alec Lawrie but learning only where I might find him today. Eaves was right: it seemed the word was out and the ranks had closed.

In the morning, I found myself breakfasting alone in

181

the dining-room. Cath seemed a little subdued when she brought in the mixed grill.

'Did you sleep well?' she asked.

'Yes, thank you. I hope I didn't disturb you, coming in late like that.'

'Well . . .' she smiled. 'Was it the hat-stand?'

I nodded, my mouth full.

'It usually is. I keep forgetting to move it. You're not the first, you know.'

'Who was that shouting?' I asked. 'Perhaps I ought to apologise?'

'I'm sorry. That was my husband. He didn't mean what he said. He's not well, you understand. In fact, he's only got a few months to live.'

'I met him, I think. In the lounge.'

'Yes.' She drifted off to clear two of the tables. I watched her, relishing my first cooked breakfast in months, thinking that I'd met the old man in the lounge, sitting by the roaring fire, wrapped in rugs, reading the *Daily Telegraph*, complaining about everything. I'd met a thousand like him, people so old, so wise, and yet so stupid they still hadn't learned that things have to change if they're going to get better.

I took my surly mood upstairs and shaved, feeling that perhaps Harry was right and I was wasting my time here. But then, I reasoned, now I was here, I might as well accompany my curiosity to the end. So I went down-stairs, told Cath I wouldn't be back for lunch (she seemed pleased) and started hoofing my way down the road.

It was a day for walking. The sky was clear, clear blue with a fringe of wispy cloud on the horizon, the sun warm

182

and hazy, burnishing the heathered hills, and glinting off the river that snaked along beside the road. There was very little traffic and I could smell, actually *smell* the scent of the forest, the fallen leaves, the flowers, and taste the air coming fresh to my lungs.

The old boy in the hotel bar had told me I'd find Alec down by the loch, either working on his flies or out in his boat.

'You'll not miss it, the stones of the wall are all away where someone took the corner too fast and ended up in the loch, God rest their souls. Just beyond that, there's a piece of land sticking out into the loch with a path down to it from the road. That's where he keeps his boat, that's where you'll find him. Care for another, son?'

The old boy was right. I passed the hole in the wall twenty minutes later, saw the jut of land beyond, the boat, and a man on a fisherman's stool working at something on his lap. I made my way down.

He didn't hear me till I was within five paces. Either he was deaf or I was getting better at sneaking up on people. He didn't seem surprised but merely raised bland, curious eyes.

I greeted him and sat on the edge of the boat, shielding my eyes as I looked out over the mirror-like surface of the loch.

'Lovely morning,' I remarked.

'You'll be that policeman staying in the village, will you not?'

So much for a subtle opening. 'News travels fast,' I said.

'There's little goes on up here.' Lawrie's voice was soft

and husky and whistled through his teeth. 'We get to know everything, you understand.'

'I'm beginning to.'

I reckoned Alec Lawrie to be somewhere in his early sixties. The heavy bones of his face wore a weatherbeaten skin, deeply lined, tanned like leather. His features were large and rubbery beneath a high forehead topped by thin white hair brushed back. His eyebrows white and sparse over eyes that matched the colour of the sky, his cheeks and chin, stubbled grey.

'You do any fishing?' he asked, his bony fingers winding twine around the shaft of a small three-barbed hook.

I shook my head.

'You should. It's the most relaxing sport there is. Gives a man time to think, to contemplate. You look like you need to relax, man. You're all tensed up, I can see it.'

'Pressures of city life,' I told him.

'All the more reason.'

I couldn't agree more. So I wandered along the water's edge, skimming stones across the surface of the loch, trying to arrange my thoughts. Thinking about murder on a day like this seemed a sacrilege of sorts and my mind must have thought so too because I spent a long time sitting on a grassy knoll just staring out across the water. Eventually, though, I gave up wishing my life away and returned to where the old man was working.

'What's your name, son?'

'Frank.'

'A good, solid name, that. You can call me Alec.'

I said I would.

'You see, Frank,' he said, 'I've lived here all my life.

184

My world begins and ends at each end of this glen. It's like that for most of us. We've seen changes since I was a lad, more of them in the last few years than in the fifty before, that's true. I'm not saying change is a bad thing, you understand. It's life. But life moves at different speeds. City life changes every day, progresses, you might say. Out here, things take their time. There's no rush, no immediate hurry, life just ambles on, following its own inexorable course.'

'What exactly are you saying?'

'I'm saying that here we don't welcome the changes brought up here from the cities. We don't like things forced on us by people who don't understand what it's like living the way we live. We're happy in our so-called ignorance. So when someone comes and starts digging up memories that would better remain buried, we feel threatened. We start thinking, you see what I mean?'

'You're saying, sod off back where you came from,' I said.

'Not in those words, no.'

'But the gist is correct?'

Alec held my gaze for a moment, then tucked his completed fly away in a plastic-bound book and stood up.

'If you don't need to rush back to the city,' he said, 'you can help me push the boat out.'

Ten minutes later, I was facing the shore, rowing out to the centre of the loch as Lawrie watched me from behind hooded eyes. He was sizing me up.

'I'm curious,' he said, smiling as I shipped oars and peeled off my shirt, 'as to why you're looking for John

MacBean. After all, the case was closed long ago. And he's served his sentence. Unless, of course . . .'

'Yes?' I prompted.

'Unless he's committed some other crime . . .'

I dipped the oars back in the water, began pulling again. 'What do *you* think?' I asked.

'I think only about things I know.'

Words of wisdom perhaps, but they fell on impatient and comparatively youthful ears.

'Then tell me what you know about John MacBean,' I suggested mildly.

'I know he was my friend, son.'

'You haven't seen him since he was released?'

'No,' he said, meeting my eyes with his guileless stare.

'When did you last see him?'

'The final day of the trial as they led him away.'

'Did you agree with the verdict?'

'He confessed,' Lawrie said, 'and the jury decided. He got what justice he deserved.'

I was just getting into a good rhythm with the strokes when he signalled me to stop. I shipped oars again, wiped sweat off my forehead, smeared back my hair.

'This will do,' he said. While he unpacked rod, reel and flies and began to assemble the pieces, I reclined as much as was comfortable and watched. About thirty minutes later, I reclined even more.

It must have been the soft lapping of water or the gentle rocking of the boat that sent me to sleep. Or the warm sun on my body or the remains of the hangover. Whatever, I slept deep and awoke beneath a fastly clouding sky and Alec Lawrie prodding me with his foot.

'Better make our way back,' he said, then grinned. 'How do you feel?'

'Relaxed.'

'I like a man can relax. Maybe I was wrong about you.'

'No,' I said, 'I think you got me right.' I put my shirt back on and returned to the oars. 'Catch anything?'

He shook his head. 'Your snoring scared them off.'

I pulled for the shore.

I helped him unload, turn his boat over and carry his gear up to the road. We headed toward the village, walking against a cool breeze that was now chopping the loch.

'Did you know MacBean was coming back here?' I asked after we had been walking for a while.

'No, I didn't. Who told you that?'

'It came up in the course of our enquiries. He told a lot of people he intended to return. A few months back, that was.'

'Really?'

'He could be here now.'

Lawrie shook his head vehemently. 'If he were here now, I would know about it.'

'That's what I thought.'

He shot me a quick glance.

'Why should he return here?' he asked.

'Why indeed? It's a well-known fact that criminals often return to the scene of their crimes. But to come back here to live? I find that hard to believe. After all the shame and pain and bad publicity he brought on the village, he now thinks he can play the prodigal, return to welcoming arms? I find that impossible to believe. Unless . . .'

He regarded me quizzically, his eyes once more clear and guileless.

'Unless,' I continued, 'things are not the way they seem.'

'It must be terrible, being a policeman,' Lawrie said. 'Always questioning, yet never believing. Never knowing what the truth is or when to stop looking for it. How do you solve your innermost problems, son? By sneering at yourself?'

I didn't reply, and we entered the village in silence some ten minutes later. I made to leave at the guest-house but he laid a hand on my arm and offered me a drink. There are some things in life I can't refuse, so I went with him down to the far end of the village and up a wide track to a small white cottage set in the crutch of a hill.

Inside the cottage it was dark and cool and smelled of damp. He led me along a corridor into a kitchen at the back, told me to sit while he stowed away his gear. I stood and looked out the window onto the heath, then sat and looked round the kitchen.

'A bowl of stew, perhaps?' Lawrie asked, coming back into the room. 'I have some that only needs warming up.'

Sometime in the last few minutes I had lost one hell of an appetite. 'A dram would be sufficient,' I told him.

He came out with a bottle, found two clean glasses in a cupboard and gave us equal measures.

'Cheers, son,' he said, and after a sip, began getting his stew together.

'You live alone?' I asked as he lit a ring on his cooker, adjusting the flame.

'Does it look like a woman lives here?' he cackled, screwing his eyes up at me.

188

I shrugged, tried to look stupid. 'No, I suppose not.'

Lawrie cleared the table, dumped the plates and glasses on top of the others in the sink, stirred his stew a while.

'MacBean was your friend, right?' I said. 'You knew him well. So how did you react when you found out he was a killer?'

'Like most people would, I imagine. I was shocked, couldn't believe it had happened.'

'I understand you discovered the body.'

'Yes, I found the boy. He was in John's workshop, hanging from one of the rafters.'

'Did you touch him?'

'I cut him down, tried his pulse but he was already dead.'

'Cold?'

'Not particularly. I don't think he'd been dead very long.'

'What did you do then?'

'I searched the house and found Dominic locked in the bathroom, the key on the outside. I didn't know what to think. So I took the poor wee mite along the road to the shop where his mother was working and told Mrs Bovellie. Then we had to break the news to Margaret.'

'Did you suspect that MacBean had killed the boy? And if so, why?'

'John wasn't around. He should have been. Yes, I suspected then, I suppose.'

'What did you do next?'

'We called the police. I then went back to the workshop, to wait around there, make sure no-one came or disturbed the body.'

'You didn't do anything else?'

189

'I went to break the news to the Robertsons but neither of them was in. So I waited for the police.'

'And by the time they arrived everyone had their story ready?'

Lawrie stopped spooning stew in his bowl, looked across at me and smiled ruefully.

'If you're looking for a conspiracy, son, then you'll be disappointed. Everything happened the way you've been told, the way it came out in court. It's all settled, so why not stop banging your head on the wall and forget it?'

I nodded in an understanding kind of way, tossed back what was left of my whisky and stood up.

'Maybe I'll do that,' I told him. 'Relax a bit, eh?'

'Come and look me up again, son. Anytime you want to go out on the boat, you let me know. I don't get much company.'

I said I would, and he accompanied me to the door, shook my hand, and wished me luck. I thanked him and walked back down into the village.

Before dinner, I phoned Harry at home. He had nothing to report except that Barrie had been trying to contact me. So I filled him in on my day's progress and he urged me to return, to remember his pension. I rang off. When people start telling me to lay off, I get stubborn. I react against such pressure.

I ate my dinner, trying half-heartedly to forget about the whole thing, to see it from Harry's point of view. The more I tried to reason away the two plates and glasses I'd seen on Lawrie's kitchen table this afternoon, the more I succeeded in convincing myself that there was work still to be done.

Later, I left the guest-house and went along to the hotel. From one of the windows, I could sit and watch Lawrie's cottage. I stayed until the bar closed, bought a half-bottle, then went outside into the cold night air.

The sky was clear again, starlit. I climbed part of the way up the small hill behind the isolated white cottage and found a spot in a clump of bushes from where I could watch both front and back doors. Then I settled down to wait.

After an hour I was freezing. After three, my bottle was empty and I was still freezing. I cursed myself for my stubbornness. All this discomfort and for what? Pride? Conviction? Or plain stupidity?

My reward came at ten past five when I was dragged from my stupor by movement where there should have been none. The shadow peeled away from Lawrie's back door, crossed the garden, then made its way slowly up the hill.

At last, I thought, and prepared to follow.

# Chapter Sixteen

It was half-past nine and the world according to Dominic Bain was turning into a very strange place.

The kitchen was a quietly hissing, softly creaking graveyard of odours. It was the morning break, everyone upstairs, Bain alone in the office. No Arnie, for a change. That was good.

Maybe he did hear the small footsteps clicking across the tiled floor. He wasn't too sure. Afterwards, he wasn't sure of anything anymore.

'Anyone there?' asked a querulous young voice.

Dominic stepped out of the office and was taken back twenty-seven years to his old man's workshop with the stacks of wood, the sawdust, the smell of varnish – and his best friend Jamie.

Jamie Robertson with his curly black hair and small hooked nose, pale lips twisted in agonized lines as his dead eyes stared out across the courtyard. Tongue like flypaper, feet only inches off the ground. And Dad, shouting this, shouting that, crying all over the place, telling him not to worry, everything would soon be okay. But nothing ever was after that. Not when the police came, trying to make him talk, tell them where Dad was hiding out in the hills. Not when they had to go to court, all the fuss, the cameras, the questions. Not when they had to move away to the big city, new school, new name, Mother-dear saying, 'Please Dominic, say something, please!' It seemed like years, and still nothing was fine, not when kids came back from the dead to haunt and taunt and flaunt their bastard beauty in his face.

'Sorry. Did I startle you?'

'Jamie?' Dominic was still staring.

The kid said, 'Is my dad around?'

'Your dad?'

'Aye. Mr Wyatt. He's Assistant Head Cook.'

Pulling himself together, Dominic glanced at his watch. 'He's not around right now,' he said. 'He'll be back in five, ten minutes. Is he expecting you?'

The kid nodded.

'Well, kid, how about——'

'My name's Mark.'

'Okay, Mark, how about a can of Coke? You like that sort of thing? We can wait in the office till your father comes back, okay?'

The boy sat on the chair, swinging his skinny legs, looking around like as though he owned the place. Kids.

'Where's ma' dad? He said he'd be here.'

'Is that right? You still at school?'

'Aye.'

'Where's that?'

'St Johnstone's. You know how old I am? Go on, guess.'

'Ten?'

'No, stupid!'

'Fifteen?'

'I'm twelve next week. Dad said he'd get me a bike, one of them BMXs. You ever seen one?'

'You from here? You live around here, local I mean?'

'Aye, Comiston Road,' the kid said. 'You a cook?'

Dominic nodded.

'You live here, too?'

'Me and my snakes, all together down by the railway.'

'Snakes? Wow! You really got snakes? Live ones?'

'Sure. Used to have four, one died.'

Kid opened his eyes wide. 'They poisonous?'

'Nah, constrictors. They just squeeze you to death.'

'Yeah? How big are they?' He opened his arms wide. 'That big?'

'Bigger.'

'Big as this room?'

'Maybe bigger if you stretch them right out.'

'Wow! They dangerous?'

'Not really. Not if you treat them right, feed them.'

'Could they eat me?'

Dominic shook his head, no. 'They like rats. I give them rats.'

'I wouldn't mind seeing them eat a rat . . .'

'Maybe I'll let you come round sometime. They're due for a feeding soon.'

'You would? Let me come and see them?'

'Why not?'

'Wow! Great!'

'Your dad might not like it, though.'

'Why not?'

'They're dangerous. He might not let you.'

'You can handle them though, can't you?'

'Sure. So could you. But your dad wouldn't understand.'

The kid's eyes became shrewd.

'If I didn't tell him, he wouldn't know.'

Dominic shook his head. 'I don't know,' he said.

'Go on. I won't tell him. I won't tell anyone. I can keep a secret, mister, honest!'

Dominic pretended to think about it.

'Well, if you promise not to tell anyone.'

'It's a deal. I promise.' The kid was triumphant now. 'When? When can I come and see them?'

There was a big red book in the drawer of the desk. Bain slid it out, turned to the back. Listed were names of staff and their telephone numbers. He pointed at one.

'That yours, kid?'

'Uh-huh.'

He looked at the duty-roster to check the shifts. Bingo.

'I'll phone you Saturday. Your old man's working back-shift. It'll give you the whole afternoon to look at snakes. What d'you say?'

'Wow, thanks, mister . . .'

'Call me John.'

'Thanks, John. I won't tell anyone, right? Like I promised, okay?'

'You're a smart kid. Like your mum, I bet.'

'Mum doesn't live with us anymore. She and dad got divorced.'

'Pity.' He glanced at his watch. 'Hey, could be your dad's back. Let's go check upstairs.'

Then Arnie walked in.

'Cosy, man,' he said, with a grin. 'I like it.'

Bain ignored him, put a hand on the boy's neck. 'C'mon, let's go.'

Easy as that.

Back home he cooked tea for Mother-dear.

'Going out tonight, dear?' she asked as he laid the tray on her lap.

'Mothers, lock up your daughters,' he grinned.

'Dominic!'

'All work and no play – you know what that makes Jack.'

'You're always out these days. Where do you go? You never tell me anything anymore.'

'You always forget. I tell you something one minute, I have to tell you again the next. Okay, I'm going to see a friend.'

'You never bring your friends back. Are you ashamed of me, Dominic?'

'You know I love you.'

'I wish you meant it.'

'Sleep well, Mother-dear. Don't wait up.'

Willie's was the type of place you could pass a million times and never look at, jammed between a laundrette and a second-hand bookstore. A bouncer in the doorway gave Bain the up-and-down with sleepy-looking eyes, then stepped back to let him through.

The bar was packed, hot and sweaty. On a dais in the corner a woman with long black hair and sagging tits gyrated mechanically to a lilting beat from the juke-box. Dominic was served immediately and found a spare piece of wall at the back of the room to lean on. The dancer finished, picked up her clothes and pushed through a sea of groping hands. Nothing happened for ten, fifteen minutes, and then she was there.

She came out the door to his left. A cheer went up, shouts and laughter. She wore a relaxed smile, in control. He liked that. She moved through the crowd, no hands trying to feel her arse or squeeze her tits – she commanded respect. He liked that even more. She carried herself to the dais, climbed up and stood there casually looking over the crowd. Her eyes flicked over his, once, once again, moved on. Then the music began.

Her ten minute spot passed like a shot in the dark. Amidst a crescendo of cheers, she left the dais and made her way back through the crowd. Entering the dressing-room, she glanced at Dominic, no, *looked* at him, for a whole couple of seconds. Then was gone.

He held an empty glass. His throat was suddenly dry, he needed a drink. He had hardly had a sip when some-one pushed past, spilling his drink. A young guy, well-built, with a cropped brush of jet-black hair and mean, angry eyes. He pushed into the dressing-room without knocking, nothing, leaving the door slightly open.

Dominic listened. He heard the raised voices, the slap, the muffled scream. He stepped inside.

The man had her wrist twisted up behind her back while his other hand clamped her mouth. Just the three of them in the room and they hadn't even noticed him yet.

198

Natasha threw a slap but the man ducked and, yanking her arm, pushed her into the wall.

'Think you can go roun' doin' what you like, do yer? You'll come wi' me if I've to break yer friggin' arm. You unnerstan'?'

She sank her teeth in the man's hand to show how much she understood. He cursed loudly but did not hear Dominic close the door softly and walk across the room.

'You friggin' whore! I'll show——'

Bain caught him on the side of the neck with a rabbit-punch. There was a flat crack as Bain whirled the guy round, rammed him into the wall. Then, turning quickly, he slammed his elbow into his undefended kidneys. The man groaned and slumped to the floor. Natasha stood with wide eyes and knuckles in her mouth. He grabbed her hand.

'Let's go, okay?'

Bain moved to kick the man again when Natasha stopped him.

'No, leave him,' she said. 'Please, let's go.'

'Yeah?'

'Come on.'

He made for the door.

'No, not that way,' she said, and led him to a curtain on the back wall which she pulled aside to reveal another exit. 'This way, we don't get hassled.'

They found themselves on a dark close where several cars were parked. Five minutes later, they were in her car, moving down Lothian Road, towards the West End.

'Thanks,' she said eventually, when her breathing was back to normal. 'I owe you.'

He watched the way she stroked the gears, handled the wheel, all her movements smooth, confident, easy. He liked that.

'So what d'you fancy?' she asked.

He liked that even more.

They ended up in a small Indian restaurant, eating spicy food Dominic had never even heard of, talking small-talk the way he had never learnt how. He spent most of the meal wanting to lean across, taste that mouth, see how far he could get his tongue down her throat.

'I was looking for you,' he said, after the waiter had brought coffee and she had lit up a cigarette.

Her eyes clouded. 'You were?'

'I phoned all the agencies, asked around the bars. You're not easy to find.'

'That's how I like it.' She sipped her coffee. 'What did you want?'

'You.'

She stubbed out her cigarette, taking her time. He could see she was thinking.

'Now you've found me, what happens next?'

'I don't know. I hadn't thought it out this far.'

She laughed. 'At least you're honest,' she said. 'Are you married?'

'No.'

'Girlfriend?'

'No.'

'Gay, then?'

'No.'

'That's got that out the way. You live alone?'

He shook his head. 'With my mother.'

'Where?'

'Morningside. You know, down by the railway?'

There were two other couples in the restaurant, at the far end, both Indian, laughing and talking with a waiter. Piped sitar music played from speakers on the wall. Dominic felt at ease, totally relaxed, a feeling he had seldom known.

He said, 'You're what? Twenty-four, five?'

'Something like that. You?'

'Thirty.'

'You look older.'

'I am.'

Later on, he talked of his life in Ballaig. She, of her life in Aberdeen. He learned how she had just finished college, that she wasn't married and didn't have a boyfriend anymore, not after tonight.

'Dominic,' she said, reaching across to squeeze his hand as they waited for the bill. 'I can't go back to my place tonight.'

'Okay,' he said.

And that was that.

He had given her his room. She made no remark about its sparseness, the single mattress on the varnished floor, the bare white walls. She stood on tip-toe to kiss his mouth.

'You're a strange man, Dominic,' she said softly. 'I like you.' Then she went to bed.

Dominic took his sleeping-bag through to his study, but was unable to sleep. The Valium had worn off now, and his mind jerked and twitched like something dying on the end of a rope.

It had all been so easy. Too easy. The way he had ended up with Tash in his bed, everything going the way he wanted but out of his control, too fast. As though he were being manipulated by some unknown force. He was not sure he liked the feeling. He wanted to slow down, think it out, make plans, bring a little order into his life.

So he took down all the photos on the wall, stashed them away in the bottom drawer of his desk. Not that he was paranoid, no – just being careful. There was a new picture, a cutting he had taken from a recent *Evening News*. It showed the fat slob who was trying to hunt him down; had his name, Kettle, on the caption. He left the cutting on the desk, put on a pair of surgical gloves he'd stolen from the hospital, and pulled out some paper. He would write a little poem for the Chief Inspector. Yes, communication, that's what it was all about.

It took him two hours till he was satisfied. No literary masterpiece, but shit, he was no literary master. He folded the poem carefully, slipped it in an envelope and addressed it to, 'The fat bastard Kettle, with love from The Hangman'.

He smiled.

That envelope went inside another, which he addressed to the editor of *The Scotsman*. Then he got out his car and drove down to the North Bridge to deposit the letter. On the way home, he couldn't stop giggling. Like a fucking wee lassie.

Some time later, as the first light of dawn diluted the sky, he fell asleep.

He came awake with sun streaming through the windows. Instinctively knew he was late for work. His head was thick, throbbing with the beginnings of a headache. He would have to see the doctor, maybe sleep all afternoon.

He rolled over, stared at the ceiling, wondered what he was doing in a sleeping-bag on the floor of his study. After a while, he went through to the bedroom where he found a note on the floor by the bed.

Tash. Of course, he had brought her back to stay the night. He wondered why she had slept alone, why he hadn't gone in and fucked her stupid. She was begging for it, he remembered, squirming in her knickers. He had to show her who was in control.

'Thanks,' the note said. 'Why don't you phone me tonight?' There was a number underneath. Bugger that. He would sort her out. Ring her bell and tell her he didn't play around with whores. What kind of guy did she think he was?

He crumpled up the note and threw it in the bin in the bathroom, then showered and shaved and hunted around the cabinet for Valium, but couldn't find the bottle anywhere. He was dressing when the phone cut into his headache like a hammer-and-chisel. He picked it up, and shouted, 'What?' impatiently.

It was Wyatt, Assistant Head Chef. Was Dominic coming in or was he off sick? What did it bloody look like? Did he look well enough to come in to work? No he did not, he was going to the doctor and would be in later. He was breathing hard when he came off the phone.

Mother-dear was pottering around the kitchen, burning toast, spilling milk, dropping eggs on the floor. She wore a scowl on her face and her eyes were puffy dark bags.

'Morning, Mother-dear,' he said, and mopped up the milk, tossed the toast in the bucket, scraped the egg off the floor.

'You're late.'

'What if I am? Who's to tell me what I can do and what I can't? I'm my own man, Mother-dear. I just had to remind that idiot at work. Who does he think he is, phoning me like that, checking up?'

'You should have called in sick, Dominic. It's only fair.'

'Whose side you on, anyway?' He put another two slices of bread under the grill, dropped two eggs into the pan of boiling water, switched the kettle on.

'Who was that . . . girl?' Mother-dear asked slyly.

'What girl?'

'The one who stayed last night.'

'Just a girl, Mother-dear. Don't get jealous.'

'Your girlfriend?'

'I'm forty-one, Mother-dear. I don't have girlfriends anymore.'

'You know what I mean.'

'She's just someone I met, okay?'

'She's very pretty.'

'How do you want your eggs, three or four minutes?'

'Much younger than you. How old is she?'

'Christ, how many times do I have to ask, how do you want your eggs done?'

'Four minutes.'

'Four minutes it is.' He scooped out the eggs, bashed their fragile heads in, put them in egg-cups. Then he buttered the toast, cutting it diagonally. When the kettle boiled he made the coffee, added milk and three sugars for Mother-dear, a saccharin tablet for himself.

'Is she going to move in?'

'I only met her yesterday. Gimme a chance, okay?'

'Where did you meet her?'

'Down in some strip-club. She's a whore.'

'Don't be silly, Dominic. I'm only curious.'

A goods train clattered and rumbled along the track, the vibrations running up his legs, rattling the cups in their saucers. He was thinking of the boy, Jamie. No, his name was Mark. Jamie was dead. Must remember that. Jamie was dead.

Mother-dear said, 'What about Cathy?'

'What about Cathy?'

'I thought you were going to get married.'

'I said that? When?'

'When you came back from Ballaig.'

'Yeah? Well, you know, I'm allowed a little fun first, aren't I?'

Mother-dear regarded him for a few moments as she gummed her toast. 'You've changed in the last few weeks, Dominic. Has something happened I don't know about?'

Dominic avoided her penetrating stare.

'No, why should it?' What the hell was she getting at? Did she suspect?

'Mothers do notice these things, you know.'

'Good old mothers, eh?'

'You kept me up all night, what with your pacing around, going in and out. Where did you go in your car?'

'To post a letter.'

'At three in the morning?'

'I couldn't sleep, right?'

'What about your pills?'

'Someone's taken them. I had a full fucking bottle and now it's gone.'

'Don't use that language in my house, Dominic. Save it for the gutter.'

'This is my house too, Mother-dear. Remember who's paying the mortgage.'

Mother-dear glared, frowned and scowled all at the same time.

'Anyway, I've got to go.' He cleared away the dishes, wiped down the table. 'You want anything while I'm out?'

The *Radio* and *TV Times*, that was all.

He decided to walk to the surgery, it was on the way to the hospital and it looked like rain. There was something he liked about rain. It was certainly good to walk in and watch all the people scurrying about as if they would die if a single drop landed on their hair or stained their clothes. Primitives, frightened of the bloody weather.

He fell asleep in the waiting room, was woken by the receptionist. Christ, he seemed to be tired all the time now, sleeping more than ever, *needing* sleep more than ever. No matter. It took him five minutes to get what he wanted off the doctor, then another five to get down the chemist quickly. The world was going to look a lot better as soon as he could get these pills down his throat. He swallowed two, then another for luck, then made for the hospital. It was raining by the time he walked along the drive.

Arnie was sitting in the bike-shed having a sneaky fag as Dominic passed.

'Hey, Dom'nic! You not feeling too well?' he called.

Dominic ignored him.

'Hey! Where's your bike? How come you don't use it anymore?'

Something in the punk's voice made him stop, go back. Pills already taking effect, the sound ebbing and flowing like waves down on the beach.

'It's broken. So what?'

'I thought maybe I saw it the other day. On television – *Crime Desk* or something. Police were asking if anyone knew who owned it. Looked awful like yours.'

'Yeah? Well, you know, they don't just make one, they run off a whole fucking line. I told you, mine's broken, someone cut all the wires and spokes, had to put it in for repair.'

'Just a coincidence then,' Arnie said, smiling, with a conspiratorial look on his face.

'Still, it's funny, isn't it, what with the "identikit" picture an' all looking like you, and the bike, and you living in Morningside? Hey, have you had your prints taken yet? The cops are setting up a caravan down by the clock and they want everyone to go down and have their prints taken. You done that yet?'

'Mind your own business, okay? I've got nothing to hide. What you trying to say with all this shit anyway?'

'What d'you think?'

'I think you're looking for a kicking, that's what I think.'

Arnie glared and threw his cigarette away.

Dominic could see he was going to have problems. He would have to work something out. The germ of an idea was already there, had been simmering for days – but it needed elaboration, a touch of finesse. He would show Arnie a few home-truths.

'You want to do something useful instead of sitting on your arse talking crap? Take this sick-line in to the head chef. Tell him I didn't look well, I'll be back in a couple of days, that sort of stuff. Okay?'

Arnie shrugged, took the sick-line without a word, and with a parting glance over his shoulder, disappeared into the kitchens. Dominic made his way home through heavy warm rain.

Half an hour later, having showered and dried, he searched for the note Tash had left. He gave her a bell and arranged a session for later on, then he went back to bed. Before he let sleep take over his mind, he thought he would have to have a word with her. He couldn't let her do that sort of thing, not if she was going to be his girl.

*His girl.* That would be something.

The walls leered. Her nipples felt like organ-stops against the palms of his hands. She shuddered and sighed.

'Dominic?'

No reply.

'Dominic?'

'Yeah?'

'What's wrong?'

'Nothing's wrong.'

'Don't you like me?'

'I like you, okay?'

'Are you nervous, then?'

'Why should I be nervous, eh? Tell me that.'

'No need to get angry. I only asked. I thought——

'Don't think. Just lie still and shut up.'

'You want me to do something, help you get to sleep?'

'Look. It's happened before, no big deal.'

'You always get over it?'

'What d'you think?'

'I don't know. Maybe I ought to go home.'

'If you want.'

'You'd let me?'

'Why not? It's your life.'

'What's come over you? One minute you're fine, the next you're cold and nasty and . . .'

'Hey, don't start crying. Look – okay, I didn't mean it. Come here.'

'You don't like me.'

'I like you. I like you a lot.'

'So why can't you . . .?'

'Tomorrow, okay?'

'Promise?'

'Yeah. Promise.'

# Chapter Seventeen

The shadow moved slowly up the hill, only barely distinguishable in the confusing light of false dawn. It was too far away to make out features, but the shadow climbed with the measured gait of a man, hands pushing off thighs with each step. Not a young man.

I stood carefully and stretched, remaining motionless for a minute to let the blood rush back to my legs. I was cold and wet and as the pins and needles pierced my skin, I was forced to stamp my feet, albeit quietly.

Not quietly enough. A bird crashed squawking from the undergrowth twenty yards to my left and I dropped to a crouch. But the moment passed, the shadow did not look round or pause in its stride and I was able to breathe again.

I was about to break cover and follow when suddenly the man changed course and began to cut diagonally across the hillside towards the copsewood in which I crouched. If he continued in this direction, he could not fail to see me. I looked around for other cover, saw none, not within sixty or seventy yards.

Should I move or should I stay?

I stayed.

When he was twenty yards off I recognised his face. With a resigned sigh, I stood to meet him. He did not seem surprised.

'Pretty cold up here, this time in the morning,' Alec Lawrie said. 'Thought maybe you'd appreciate a cup of coffee.'

I glared at him long and hard but he didn't burst into tears or anything, so eventually I shrugged and went with him.

There was already a fire roaring in his kitchen grate when we arrived. He left me for a moment, came back with a dressing-gown and told me to get out of my clothes. I was in no mood to object.

'You're persistent,' he said, handing me a mug of steaming black coffee. 'I'll give you that.' He brought out his bottle, poured a hefty measure into the mug. I sat on a chair, not quite in the fire but as close as I could get without bursting into flames.

'All part of the job, I suppose,' he said, hanging my clothes from the mantelpiece before pulling up another chair.

'You knew I was there all the time?'

'I watched you leave the hotel.'

'Brilliant,' I said. 'Thanks for telling me.'

'I *did* tell you. I said you were wasting your time, remember? Did you listen?' He shook his head, 'Did you hell.'

I watched the leaping flames, seeing through them my own confused emotions in the light of yet one more goddamned day. They were not a pretty sight.

Lawrie regarded me, waiting, time on his side.

212

'MacBean was here,' I said eventually.

Lawrie sighed. 'You're right, of course. He was here.'

'When?'

'Last week. He turned up out of the blue on Friday night. He'd been walking, so he said. Stayed until Monday morning, then left.'

'Here?'

Lawrie nodded.

'The whole time, Friday through to Monday?'

'Never left this house. Was scared to, I think.'

'Anyone else know he was here?'

'No, he didn't want that.'

'What did he want?'

'I don't know,' Lawrie replied slowly. 'I got the impression he wanted to stay, was sounding me out. But he never came right out and said it, just asked questions.'

'What kind of questions?'

'How did people feel about him, if they still remembered, that sort of thing.'

'What did you say?'

'That it's all forgotten – but that it wouldn't be if he came back and re-opened old wounds.'

'He wanted to move back here for good?'

'I think so. Touch of the dying elephant, if you see what I mean.'

'Why did he leave then?'

'I said it was best. I told him go away and wait a while, let me ask around to see what the general feeling was.'

'He accepted that?'

'Eventually.'

'Where did he go?'

'I don't know. He just said he'd be back, that's all.'

'Why didn't you tell me all this yesterday, save me sitting out there all night?'

'You never told me why you wanted to see him.'

'So why tell me now?'

'I had time to think, put two and two together. If you really wanted him that bad, you'd not be here alone, unauthorised, sitting out in the cold – an officer like you – when a constable could be doing it while you slept in a nice warm bed. It doesn't make sense.'

'So why am I here?'

'You tell me.'

'You heard of The Hangman? It's in all the papers – or don't you get them up here?'

'Aye, son, we get the papers,' he said with a smile. 'And we know how to read them, too.' He looked off into the distance, perhaps at the dawn now washing the sky through the window over the sink. 'So you think John's The Hangman, do you?'

'It's not a bad idea,' I said.

'You need your head examined, son. From what I remember – and you'll have to correct me if I'm wrong – but what I remember is they already caught The Hangman. Is that not right?'

I nodded. 'They thought they had. Turned out he was nothing more than a child-molester and they had to drop the charges when another little girl was found on Saturday.'

'Aye,' Lawrie said. 'That's what I thought. The Hangman killed a little girl on Saturday.'

We fell into a silence, broken only by the hissing,

spitting fire, the crackle of logs. The realisation had been with me a few minutes now and eventually I had to let it out, however much I didn't want to.

'You're saying John MacBean was here, with you, on Saturday?'

'Go to the top of the class, son. He was here, like I said, Friday till Monday.'

'You'll make a statement to that effect?'

Lawrie thought for a moment, regarding me shrewdly. Then said, 'If that's what you want, son, I'll make you a statement.'

'I still want to see Macbean,' I said.

'You'll have to find him first.'

'And you don't know where he is?'

He leant forward and felt my clothes; said, 'They're dry now, son. Would you like another coffee before you go?'

Cath was hoovering the hall when I arrived back at the guest house. She gave me a searching look, then wished me a good morning and asked if I wanted breakfast. I thanked her, but said I was going to clean myself up a bit first. She laughed pleasantly, then let me look down her blouse as she bent over the hoover. I was suddenly overcome by the sense of another great void in my life. I climbed the stairs reluctantly.

I showered and climbed back into sweaty clothes, wishing I'd had the foresight to bring a change. Then went downstairs and sat out in the courtyard at one of the tables, absorbing the warm sun like a battery trying to recharge. I fell asleep to the sound of Cath working in the kitchen behind me.

I came awake with a thick, fuzzy head and she was sitting opposite, staring at me with a quizzical smile. I glanced at my watch: I'd been asleep an hour and a half.

'I didn't have the heart to disturb you,' she said. 'I can rustle up breakfast if you want, but I thought you might prefer this.' There was a bottle of beer and a glass on the table, and a schooner of something clear and fizzy in her hand. I didn't bother with the glass.

'I didn't realise how tired I was,' I said.

'What does a man do in this village,' she asked, with a flirtatious smile, 'when he stays out all night?'

'Walks in the hills and gets lost,' I told her. 'Why, what does a woman do?'

Her laugh was warm, her eyes bright. The air was getting to me. She didn't need to reply. We sat and sipped and tried not to look at each other too much.

'You're a policeman, right?' she asked after a while. When I nodded, she wanted to know more. I told her I was here for pleasure at the moment, and we had another little giggle.

'Seriously, I came to work, now I'm going home.'

'You found what you wanted?'

'Yes and no.'

'You've been asking about the murder that happened here, haven't you?'

'The case is closed,' I said.

'I was just a little girl then. I don't remember it very well.'

'No-one seems to want to.'

'You know it happened here? In this house?'

'I'd guessed.'

'Right where that storeroom is now, that's where Old MacBean had his workshop, where they found Jamie.'

'Jamie was a friend of yours?'

'My best friend,' she murmured. 'All the other kids thought he was pretty strange, used to make fun of him. But to me, he was quiet and gentle and didn't have anything to prove like all the others. We were the same age, you know, both born the same day, except he was about three hours younger than me. Maybe it was that which made us closer to each other than we were with Dominic or Billy or the rest of the gang.'

'How did you feel when you heard of his death?'

'I didn't really understand at first. It took a while. You see, I liked Dominic's father. He was good with children, always had time for us when the other grown-ups would shoo us away. So it wasn't easy to come to terms with the fact that he had killed my best friend. The faster I grew up, the more I wanted to get even with him. I used to dream of revenge – you know, what I would do to him if he ever came back. Then I grew up even more and just forgot the whole thing. I don't suppose I ought to be telling you this, you being a policeman and all that.'

'I don't know,' I said. 'Revenge is a pretty natural instinct. Someone hurts you, you want to hurt them back. I know the feeling myself. It's not easy to control.'

We went back to our drinks, Cath pretending not to notice as my eyes drank in her face, her body, her relaxed sensuality, with all the hunger and frustration of the confused and lonely man I had become.

'Funny, that,' she said, in a distant tone. 'Dominic, MacBean's son, was up here a few weeks ago. Stayed in the same room as you. Used to be his when he lived here.'

'Really?'

'He's been coming here quite regularly for years. Misses it, you know. Village life and that. He never wanted to leave, but after the . . . scandal, well, his mother couldn't bear to live here anymore, so they moved away, changed their name so the press wouldn't be able to find them.'

'Changed their name?' I said.

'They call themselves Bain now.'

'They live in Edinburgh, don't they?'

Surprise opened up her face for a moment. 'However did you know that?'

'Part of my job,' I told her with a laugh, trying to dispel any suspicion she might have that I was still at work.

It didn't work, quite.

'Why did you come up here, anyway? Seems a bit odd to be asking questions about a murder that happened all those years ago.'

'Och,' I said, with a dismissive wave. 'Just one of those things. Some guy in Saughton was overheard saying he was the one who murdered the kid. Routine, that's all. We get a lot of that, you know, inmates boasting, trying to make an impression. So we like to check up, just in case.'

'In case you got it wrong?'

'That's right.'

'Did you? I mean, did they?'

'I don't think so. Not this time.'

'So you're going back to Edinburgh?'

'Mmm.'

'You'll be coming back sometime?'

Did I detect an invitation? I wanted to, God knows.

'Yes,' I said.

I smiled at her and we both looked away. I read the label on the beer bottle.

'Maybe you should ask Dominic,' she said after a moment.

'Sorry?'

'You know, MacBean's son. He should be able to tell you what you want to know. Then you'll be able to clear the whole thing up for good.'

'Yeah,' I said. 'Could do.'

'I've got his address, if you want.'

'I suppose so.'

'You know, we would have been married probably, if it hadn't been for . . .'

'MacBean?'

'Yes. I was heartbroken when he had to go. I lost two good friends in a couple of months and nothing was really the same after that. I never saw Dominic till about two, three years ago when he just appeared and said hello as if he'd never been away.'

'Still fond of him?' I wasn't too sure about the motives behind that question.

'In a way. But he's changed. Perhaps that's what the city does to people.'

'How come you never left? Can't be very exciting for a young girl living here.'

'I don't know. I suppose, well, my father died when I was fourteen and my mother wasn't very well after that and there was no-one else so I just ended up nursing her.'

'And now you're nursing Joe.'

'It must be my face. Attracts the infirm or something.' She said it with deep irony.

'Why did you marry him, Cath? He must be what, twenty, thirty years your senior?'

'I've often asked myself the same question. And the answer is always the same – I don't know. Joe was always good to me as a kid and I suppose I looked on him as a substitute when my father died.'

'No other fanciable young men in the village?'

'They'd all left by then. They don't stay long.'

'I imagine it would be difficult to keep an affair secret in a place like this.'

'Why?' Cathy asked coolly, regarding me askance. 'Does my sex life interest you, Inspector?'

I blushed, damn it.

'I'm sorry. I didn't mean it that way,' I said. 'I was wondering about a rumour I heard, that Dr Robertson was having an affair with Mrs MacBean. But you were probably too young then to——'

'As a matter of fact, I did hear about it. Some years later, mind, when I understood such things. My mother told me. It came up in conversation – I can't remember why – but she told me they had had something going together.'

'Did John MacBean know about it?'

'My mother didn't say. But she implied that he knew what was going on.'

'Did Dominic know?'

'He's never mentioned it. We don't talk about that

220

time – no-one in the village does. It's like it never happened.'

'What does Dominic do for a living?'

'He's a photographer. Quite a well-known one, I think. Has his own studio, too.'

'Whereabouts?'

'Morningside. That's where he lives.'

'And his mother? Is she still alive? I reckon she'd be able to help me more than he would. He was only a kid at the time.'

'I suppose so, aye. They still live together . . . least they did last I heard, anyway.'

'You've never been down to visit?'

'No,' she sighed, letting her shoulders sag. 'I've had Joe to look after, and the guest-house. I hardly get out as it is, day-to-day, let alone have a holiday.'

A bell rang in the house and Cath jumped up, said angrily, 'See what I mean?'

I did, and watched her walk across the patio.

An hour and a half later, after I had eaten and paid and promised to return, I boarded the bus and watched the village disappear behind me. After a while, I pulled the piece of paper from my pocket and read the address written in Cath's tidy handwriting.

Morningside. Again and again, Morningside.

I let my thoughts run free. They went wild.

# Chapter Eighteen

Friday morning, I slept late, waking rough to the rumble of traffic and swollen grey skies. I had a headful of sighs: climbing out of bed was a challenge, getting dressed was a chore, breakfast a duty. I knew where I wanted to be and it was nowhere near here. One of those days when all you want to do is curl up in bed, dream about good times and forget the world.

Sod the good times, I thought, and phoned Harry at Squad HQ. He wasn't in, they said. I didn't want to leave a message so I hung up.

The fiscal wasn't in either. I dialled the 'Speaking Clock' and found it engaged. Like I said – one of those days.

I dug out the piece of paper on which Cath had written the address and tried to find it on the street map. I failed, so I broke from my flat on a wave of enthusiasm that carried me as far as the street then dumped me. Ten minutes wait for a taxi, then another ten while the driver told me the story of his life. He stopped by the lights at Holy Corner.

'What was that address again?' I gave him the slip of paper and he frowned at it till the lights changed.

Dropping down Morningside Road, he pulled over, called up Control. Five minutes later, the meter still clicking away, they called him back, they couldn't find it either. I left the driver staring with bewilderment at the exact fare in his hand.

I spent the next hour tramping the streets, getting sent a hundred different directions to no avail. Finally, getting tired, I collared a postman. He suggested I try the Sorting Office, then wandered off, cocky little bastard, leaving me wondering why I hadn't thought of that.

I found the address eventually, down by the railway at the end of a pot-holed drive, shielded from the road by a line of junipers and a crumbling stone wall.

It was a low, L-shaped cottage, white, with small leaded windows downstairs and wide dormer windows upstairs. At the side of the house – and in line with the drive – stood an empty garage with its doors open. At the other end of the house, there was a strip of garden, a few apple trees in long grass, and two ancient outbuildings, one large, one small. I climbed the one step to the latticed porch and rang the bell.

It took her a long time to reach the door, struggle with the locks and finally haul it open. She peered up at me through huge round eyes, one frail finger to her lips.

'Mrs Margaret Bain?' I asked.

She nodded, scowling. 'Yes?'

'I'm a police officer. I'd like to ask you a few questions.'

She cocked her head, looked concerned. 'About what?'

'About your husband.'

'I haven't seen him in years.'

'He was released from prison, three, four years ago. Have you heard from him since?'

She opened the door, stood back. 'You'd better come in.'

As she preceded me slowly down the hall to a room at the far end overlooking the garden, she explained. 'I always watch "Neighbours". It's on after the News, you see. A wonderful programme. Australian, you know. Really true to life. Have you seen it?'

I shook my head, almost guiltily.

'You should,' she said, wagging a bony finger, 'you being a policeman and all. Teach you a few things about life, and how real people live.'

'I don't want to disturb you,' I said, 'but——'

'It might do you good, sergeant.'

'You what?'

'Do you good. What with all these vicious crimes you deal with, you might learn something about decent people, ordinary people. We're not all like that, you know.'

'I haven't that much time, Mrs Bain.'

'Of course not. Always rushing here and there, no doubt, just like "The Bill".'

'Sorry?'

'Where have you been, sergeant? I'd have thought all you policemen watch it, though sometimes I think if that's what the police are really like, why have any police at all?'

'Mrs Bain?'

'Don't fret, sergeant. I can wait. There's a repeat on later this afternoon if your business is really that important. Is it?'

'Quite important, yes.'

'About John, you say?'

'I asked if you'd seen him since he was released . . .'

'I thought I told you no, sergeant.'

'Inspector.'

'Sorry?'

'Nothing. How about your son? Perhaps he has seen your husband.'

'Dominic doesn't tell me anything.' There was a sudden bitterness in her voice – a grating voice softened at the edges, like the wingeing of a spoilt brat. 'When we first came here, we used to do everything together. Now . . .'

'He *is* still living here?'

'When he deigns to honour me with his presence.'

'It's a lovely house.'

'Isn't it? You know, Dominic's very good with his hands. He did it all himself.'

I pointed at a framed photograph on the mantelpiece.

'Is that him there?'

'That's when he first qualified as a cook. He must have been, what, almost twenty-five or twenty-six then. Taller than his father, and much more handsome I always thought.'

'Where is he now?'

'Out,' she said, eyes fixed on the television. 'He's always out. I hardly ever see him. Things to do, people to meet – he's always saying that, though how they can be

226

'Why he's off work. He's never had a day off in all the time he's worked there – not before she turned up.'

'One for the ladies, is he?'

'I wouldn't say that. He used to care more about his mother. Now all he can think about is that ding-dong between his legs. If it's questions you want to ask him, you'll have no luck.'

'Just a few.'

'He was young at the time, ten or eleven. The whole thing affected him traumatically. When we moved down here, he wouldn't speak, not for months . . . and never a word about it since.'

'Perhaps you could tell me what happened . . .'

'I could not. I've told you once, do I have to tell you again?'

I shook my head. I wrote my number on the back of an envelope and gave it to her.

'Mrs Bain,' I said, 'I'd like to ask you a favour' – she nodded warily – 'I'd like you to give this to your son and ask him to give me a ring when he gets in.'

'He won't help you, sergeant. I can tell you that now.'

'I have to try.'

'Very well, but I promise nothing.'

'I'd also like you to call me should your husband turn up.'

'You think he might?'

I shrugged. 'It's possible.'

Was it a trick of the light or did I detect excitement in her eyes? I wasn't sure. In fact, I wasn't sure of anything anymore. So I thanked her for letting me waste her time and told her I'd let myself out.

'Thank you, sergeant,' she said, reaching for the remote-control.

'Inspector,' I corrected – but she was no longer listening.

'G'day, sport,' said someone on the television.

I closed the door behind me.

# Chapter Nineteen

Clocks should be seen and not heard. What was wrong with them nowadays, that they all went beep-beep-beep like some kind of life support system out of control?

The alarm by Dominic's bed went beep-beep-beep and dragged him from sleep. Not a good idea. He dressed and took it downstairs and out to the garage. He laid it carefully behind the rear wheel of his car, climbed in and reversed over it. Then he got out to inspect the damage. Satisfied, he returned to the kitchen.

The watch on his wrist was the kind that went beep-beep-beep on the hour, every hour – he couldn't stop it, not with any of the fancy little buttons. So he laid it on the kitchen floor, climbed on a chair and jumped on it. Like landing on a cockroach. Fixed the beep for good.

There was an antique grandfather-clock in the dining-room. It chimed every quarter of an hour, driving him crazy. So he took his hammer and knocked its fucking face in. Then pulled out the mechanisms as though he was gutting a chicken.

So much for time – it shouldn't play tricks on him. Hours and days, slipping by without so much as a by-your-leave. Nights slurring into one great darkness. Who

231

needed time anyway? You could look out the window and look at the sun and you knew what time it was. Your body would adapt. You don't eat because it's six o'clock, you eat because you're hungry. That kind of thing. You don't go to work because it's nine o'clock, you go because . . .

Well, he would have to work on that one. The idea, though, was there.

'Dominic!'

What did she want now?

'Yes, Mother-dear?' he said from the door.

Mother-dear had her scolding face on, the one with the harsh lines and brutal mouth which had meant a skelping once upon a time.

'What have you been doing? What was that noise?'

'Don't worry your fuzzy little head, Mother-dear,' he said. 'I was just seeing to the clocks. Putting them right, okay?'

'Don't patronise me! I'm not stupid you know, or deaf. You were having a tantrum. Just like you, if you can't get what you want you have to smash things. You've never really grown up at all, have you?'

'Your carriage-clock is wrong, Mother-dear. Perhaps I should fix it for you?'

'You stay away! I don't want you anywhere near me when you're in a mood like that. Go on! Get out of here!'

It seemed she too had moods most days now, as though on purpose, just to spoil his own good humour.

She had summoned him to her room yesterday as though she was royalty, wanting to know what 'that woman' was doing, was she 'damn well moving in?'. He had told her it was his problem not hers. Then she had knocked the feet from under him.

'The police were round this afternoon, he left a number for you to ring. He wants to ask you a few questions,' she told him.

*Again?*

'Questions? What sort of questions,' Dominic had asked.

'Something about Father,' Mother-dear said. 'It seems he's been let out, and the police are looking for him to help with some enquiry.'

'Nothing else?'

'He mentioned Cathy, told me all about her husband. Why didn't you tell me the truth, that she was married to Joe?'

'I told you the old sod was dying, didn't I?'

'You told me nothing of the sort. All you ever tell me is nothing or lies.'

'I must have forgotten, okay? This policeman, did he come alone?'

Mother-dear nodded. 'Rather a nice man, I thought. Quite considerate.'

'There was a time when you used to hate them.' Dominic was pacing up and down now.

'Did he look around, this policeman? Was he out of your sight for any length of time?'

'No. We sat and talked in here and he left as "Neighbours" came on.'

'You show him to the door?'

'No. He said he could find his own way out.'

'Jesus!' Dominic said to himself. Then to Mother-dear: 'He ask any questions about me?'

'You haven't done anything wrong, have you?'

'Don't be silly. I only want to know what sort of questions.'

'About your father, that's all.'

Dreams last night seething with coppers. Waking this morning with a sense of time running out crammed in every pore of his body. Not a good idea.

He left the house, went down the garden to the smaller of the two barns to check the snakes. As he closed the door, he tried to recall if he had mentioned them to Tash, their resemblance to her when she danced, shedding their skins the way she did, hairless and smooth the way she was. He could always tell her again.

He entered the large barn, switched on the light. Measuring out a length of rope from the coil by the wall, he cut it, slung one end over the central beam and set about fashioning a noose with the other. He wished Tash were here to watch the skill with which his hands worked the rope.

Tash had left early in the morning, kissing his cheek as if they had been married for years. No mention of the night before. Lucky she hadn't brought his impotency up – he might have got angry. In fact, he was angry now, just *thinking* about it. What did she expect? Happens all the time, you see it in the magazines, like, 'Dear Miss Poops, My husband can't get an erection, is it because I got a face like the back end of a horse?'. All they can think of is themselves. Right. He'd tell her.

He would say, 'Tash, you know what gets me going?'

'What? Tell me?'

'Murder, Tash. Feeling the power of someone's life flow from their body through your fingers, up your arms, into your own body. That's what turns me on, Tash. That's what would give me a stiffy to split your fucking sides.'

Tonight, Tash, he thought. As promised.

He finished the noose and secured the rope. All set. One little telephone call to make and life would be just dandy.

A goods train loaded with cars that looked more like sewing-machines clunked slowly along the line, the same line he had walked, wearing coveralls and flat cap, carrying the still-warm body of Craig Watson in a duffel bag. A mile along the line, hidden from view by a bridge, he had dumped the body wrapped in bin-liners on to the track. Then he had climbed the embankment, removed coveralls and cap, put them in his bag and caught a bus home. How long ago was that now? Seemed like ages. So much had changed since then. Janice, Heather and now Jamie. No. Jamie was dead. The boy's name was Mark. He must remember. His name was Mark.

Jamie was wearing jeans and trainers and an Iron Maiden T-shirt, his deep, brown eyes glittering with excitement.

'You didn't tell anyone you were coming here?' Dominic asked, manipulating Boris so that the snake coiled about his upper arm and not his neck.

Jamie shook his head vigorously. 'No way, mister,' he said.

'Not even any of your friends?'

'They're all at the match. They would've laughed if I'd told them.'

'That's all right, then. Do you want to hold Boris?'

He looked a little apprehensive. He would be looking a lot more apprehensive in a minute.

'Maybe . . . later,' said the kid. 'Where are the rats?'

'What rats?'

'You said there'd be rats, I could watch them eat the rats. You did, honest.'

'Yeah? I said that?'

Disappointedly, 'Aye.'

'Well, that's life, Jamie,' Dominic said. He eased Boris from his arm, let him slide to the sand.

'Why d'you keep calling me Jamie? My name's Mark.'

Dominic put a hand at the back of the boy's neck, a paternal pat.

'Jamie was a spy, you know. That's why he had to die.'

The boy squirmed under his hand. 'What d'you mean?'

'He was executed. I was there, I saw it happen. He was a spy, he deserved to die. I caught him spying on Mother-dear. She was upstairs with his father, doing grown up things on the bed. You know what I'm talking about, kid?'

He shook his head.

'Never mind. They were naked and Jamie was peeking through the door, watching his father doing the business on Mother-dear when he should have been downstairs playing with me. He preferred to spy. You find this interesting?'

Mark shook his head again.

'No problem. Grown-up stuff, right? Okay, try this for size. You ever hear of The Hangman, kid?'

'You mean the . . . the guy who . . .' The boy's voice faltered.

236

'Aye, him, Jamie.'

'I want to go,' he said. 'Please, let me go now . . .'

'You want to leave now? Just when the fun's about to begin?'

'You're hurting me!' His eyes filled with fear, pain too.

Dominic cuffed his head, sent him sprawling.

'Kids should be seen and not heard, Jamie. You understand that? Seen and not heard.'

Mark lay there, sobbing. 'Please, mister! Let me go, I haven't done anything. I won't tell anyone, promise!'

Dominic jerked him to his feet, hit him again. 'Never learn a lesson, do you?'

He screamed. No problem. Craig had screamed. No-one ever heard. Janice hadn't screamed, but she had been pretty damn weird, as if it hadn't meant a thing that she was about to die.

Dominic picked the boy up. He was kicking and punching and biting. Dominic squeezed his neck some.

That shut him up.


The boy was naked on the chair, a noose around his neck. His hands were taped behind his back, his knees taped together.

'Don't! Please!' he whimpered.

Dominic kissed his lips. 'I love you,' he said.

Then kicked away the chair.

The film was used up, the boy still, the barn quiet.

'How touching,' said a voice from the back of the barn, coming from a pool of shadow.

Dominic whipped round.

The shadow moved. Arnie emerged into the light.

237

'Like I said, how touching.'

Dominic came slowly to his feet, his mind racing. Slick and cool, remember.

'Come on down!' he said with a smile.

'Said the spider to the fly . . .' Arnie moved closer.

'We can weave a web together . . .'

'But which of us shall die . . .?' Arnie said, stopping ten feet off. 'Seems I was right.'

'Looks like you were. Caught with my trousers down, eh.'

'This the boy that was in the kitchen the other day? Wyatt's son?'

'Same one. How long have you been here?'

Arnie shrugged. 'An hour, maybe two. You know Wyatt's not going to be too pleased when he finds out about this.'

'I suppose not. You going to tell him?'

Arnie didn't reply. He reached out and touched the boy's skin, apprehensively, as if it were diseased or something. He closely examined the face, lifting the eyelids, studying the glazed pop-eyes. Dominic made no move.

'You going to take him down?' Arnie asked eventually.

'You didn't answer my question.'

'You're right, I didn't.'

'You could be a great help to me, Arnie.'

'No man is an island, Nick.'

'Everyone needs a friend, right?'

'You going to dump the boy, like the others?'

'That was the idea.'

'You're more a fucking nut-case than I am, Nick. You know that?'

'I'm top of the class, Arnie.'

'Yeah.'

'You want to cut the kid down?'

'Does that make me an accessory?'

'Depends what you do after. There's a pile of tools over in the corner, you'll find a Stanley knife there.'

'Where?'

'Here. Well, it was here earlier.'

'You can't cut a rope with a monkey-wrench, Nick.'

'Don't be stupid. Ah, there it is, on the floor behind you. Get it, will you?'

Arnie got it. He also got the monkey-wrench on the back of his skull. It made a sound like metal on wood. Dominic hit him again and this time the wrench slid off blood. Arnie went down and shut his eyes for a while.

For the next twenty minutes Dominic was busy. He hosed down the boy, donned gloves, cut him down, removed the tape from hands and knees, fitted him in bin-liners, tied him up. Then he bundled the clothes in the fireplace, soaked them in petrol and set them alight.

Next he stripped Arnie, bound his hands and feet and mouth. He fetched a ladder across and carried Arnie in a fireman's lift up to the small loft. Passing a rope through his arms and legs, he attached it to a ring set in the wall. Then he climbed down, removed the ladder, switched off all the lights and went back up to the house. He showered and shaved, then spent an hour developing the film in the darkroom, leaving the negatives hanging to dry.

Tash arrived back at eight and he kissed the proffered

cheek, squeezing her bum. He led her through to the dining-room.

'My, how romantic!' she exclaimed. 'Candles and all!'

He took her jacket the way a gentleman would, pulled out a chair for her. He was pleased that she was pleased. He had spent a lot of time preparing the scene and the meal.

'Drink?' he asked.

'Save a girl from dying. Gin and tonic, if you have it.'

He fixed two and joined her at the table.

'Hard day?' he asked. That's what spouses were supposed to say.

'Saturdays are the worst. I really don't know why I put myself through all this.'

'Then why do it?'

'For the money, why else?'

'Because you like it.'

'Is that so? How's your day been?'

'Boring. Killing time, mostly.'

'Yeah? What's for dinner?'

'Italian, I thought. You like that, don't you?'

'I could eat anything! What's with all this stuff, anyway? Are you going to propose to me or something?'

'I thought you'd like it.'

'I do. It's great. Really romantic. We can hold hands across the table, gaze into each other's eyes and whisper sweet nothings.'

'Then we can go upstairs and fuck,' Dominic said.

Tash laughed, crinkling her eyes at him. 'Such a way with words. How many other women have you seduced like this?'

'You're the first.'

'Sure. Where's your mother? Isn't she going to join us?'

'She ate earlier. Anyway, it would hardly be romantic with her sitting there, gumming her food and dribbling down the front of her cardigan.'

'Don't be cruel!'

They had lasagne to start – Dominic's own recipe, spiced with Valium, not too much. Then pizza with all the trimmings: mozzarella, olives, anchovies, parma ham, the works. Tash ate as if she hadn't eaten in days. Afterwards there was real coffee and brandy, and After Eight mints.

They talked about the past mostly. Summing up their lives in tidy little anecdotes that were simple to swallow because they had been rehearsed so long. Dominic paid scant attention, not even noticing the lies that slipped off his tongue with tranquillised ease. Later, they climbed the stairs and took off their clothes. Tash lit up a joint and they coughed their way through that, then lapsed into silence as they filled their mouths with their bodies.

They fucked. Tash came a couple of times and then had to tell him to stop, had to tell him it was hurting like hell, could he please be a little more considerate? She cried when he didn't slow down or ease off, and her crying made him harder still so that he came after a minute or two or three, how was he supposed to know how long it was?

She wouldn't talk to him afterwards, but turned over and snivelled herself to sleep. You just couldn't win. What was a man supposed to bloody do?

'Where you going?'

'Out for a drive.'

241

She peered at her watch. 'It's four in the morning!'

'So?'

'Can't you sleep?'

'No.'

'Come here. Have another joint. That always helps.'

'Not me, it doesn't. I like to drive.'

'You're angry with me, aren't you?'

'I can't sleep, right? Stop nagging. I'll be back soon, okay?'

'Dominic?'

'What?'

'Don't be angry. Please? Come back soon?'

'Yeah, okay. Go back to sleep. I'll wake you with a surprise.'

'Be gentle this time? Please?'

'You won't feel a thing. Promise.'

'Mmm.'

He headed for the barn.

Arnie stopped screaming when Dominic switched on the light.

'Dominic?'

'Yes, Arnie?'

'It is you, Dominic! I knew it!'

'Yes, darling. 'Tis I.'

'Have you brought some food?' Arnie whined in a tiny, tremulous, helpless little voice.

'No, Arnie. Why should I bring food?'

'I'm starving! Please, Dominic! We're friends, aren't we?'

'Maybe we were, I can't remember.'

'I've never done you any harm. I wanted to help you.'

'Play with fire, Arnie, and you risk getting burned. Did your mother never warn you?'

'No-oh.'

'Play with me, darling, and you risk getting killed. Did I not warn you?'

'No, never.'

'I must have forgotten. Pity. You might not have been here now.'

'Dominic . . .'

'You smell of shit, Arnie.'

'I couldn't help it. I can't move. Please, Dominic, let me go. I swear I won't tell anyone. I'll do anything you want . . . *anything*.'

'Good little dog. Say woof.'

'What?'

'Say woof.'

'Woof!'

'Like a dog, Arnie. You can do better than that. Like a dog, okay? With *feeling*.'

'Wroof!'

'Good boy.' Dominic let Arnie see the razor.

'Oh, Dominic! I knew it was a game. I knew you'd let me go eventually. We need each other, don't we? Here, you are going to cut me free, aren't you?'

'I'm going to cut your fucking throat, Arnie. You're making too much noise. You might disturb the neighbours. And I have a headache. Much easier to cut your throat than take an aspirin. See what I mean, Arnie?'

'You wouldn't do a thing like that,' whispered Arnie.

Climbing the ladder now.

'Wouldn't I?'

# Chapter Twenty

The Meadows hasn't always been The Meadows. Up to the middle of the seventeenth century it was known as the South Loch, or the Borough or Burgh Loch, supplying water for the city. In 1658 it was leased to John Straiton for an annual rent of one thousand pounds and became known as Straiton's Loch. Then drainage began, and further reclamation followed when the lease was taken over in 1722 by Thomas Hope of Rankeillor. Drainage was eventually completed in 1740.

Today the Meadows is a wide and flat swathe of grass bordered by elm and oak, cut into segments by tree-lined walks joining Bedsit City to the south, the Royal Infirmary and University to the north.

It is a park for lying in when the sun condescends to shine; there are cricket pitches and council tennis courts; a running track, a playground, a baseball corner, and a minefield of dogshit. Evenings and Sundays, The Meadows becomes a mass of improvised football pitches with a lot of mad bastards running about shouting, trying to hold on to their youth.

This Sunday, it was still too early for any of them to be over their hangovers, though not too early for bald-headed joggers to be indulging in their own form of masochism. It was one of these joggers who stumbled over the body of The Hangman's fourth victim.

The jogger's name was Cunningham and he wore all the right gear – black Nike tracksuit, yellow Nike sweat-shirt, white Nike running shoes, and a headband stained with designer perspiration. But he was really sweating now under Chief Inspector Kettle's flinty glare.

Kettle had this thing about people reporting bodies. He didn't like them. It meant work. Especially early on Sunday mornings when he could be home doing what the whole married world seemed to do on Sunday mornings before the kids woke and invaded the bedroom. So he was giving Cunningham a hard time. I didn't feel in the mood to watch, so I went over to where Harry was talk-ing with Jack Parrish. They stopped whatever they were saying, and I wasn't too sure whether the guilt in their eyes was real or something conjured up by my not very attractive mood.

'Frank!' Harry said, as if he hadn't seen me for years. 'How'd you get here?'

'Sorry,' I snapped. 'I didn't realise it was invitations only.'

Harry flinched, his fat neck reddening. 'The inspector's in one of his moods,' he said to Parrish.

The pathologist ignored him, asked, 'What's up, Frank?'

'You tell me. Kettle's gloating over something – he just smiled at me. No-one else will even look at me. What's going on, Jack? Am I diseased or something?'

Parrish hesitated. 'Have you seen Barrie yet?'

'He called me just now, ordered me here. Why?'

'Better wait till he arrives. Then he can tell you.'

'Tell me what, for Christ's sake?'

Parrish writhed beneath my gaze while Harry did his feet-shuffling trick. 'Frank.'

'Look, Jack, it seems everyone here knows something I don't. And it concerns me, right, or am I paranoid?'

'You're not paranoid, Frank, and that's all I'm saying. That's Barrie just arrived, so he can tell you while I do the job I'm supposed to do. I'm sorry, but . . .'

'Aye, and fuck you too, Jack,' I called after his retreating back. I saw Barrie stepping out of his car on Melville Drive, then walk towards the cordoned-off area beneath the avenue of elms. His suit was one of those shiny black modern cuts with narrow lapels and no vents. What a poser.

'Frank,' Harry said. 'It's not Jack's fault. He's just——'

'Are *you* going to tell me, sergeant?'

Harry regarded me coolly for a few moments, his face unusually devoid of expression. Reflected in his flat eyes I saw the end of a good relationship.

'Okay, forget it,' I said.

Barrie pulled away from the knot of officers by the cordon as he saw me coming.

'Morning, Frank,' he greeted, his smile as cold as yesterday's porridge. I didn't bother to reply. He searched my eyes for a moment, and when he didn't find what he was looking for, took my elbow. 'Let's go to my car. I need a drink after that.'

I let him propel me along.

'It's not easy to talk, is it, Frank?' he said as we approached his car, a black saloon. 'Not when you see it again and again, man's inhumanity to man.'

It's not easy to talk to someone who is just about to stick a knife in your back either. He went on:

'I used to think I'd get over it, you know, all the bodies, the blood, the sheer petty, senselessness of it all . . . Christ, you know what I'm trying to say. I don't need to tell you.'

He ushered me into the back and closed the door. He opened a small cabinet built into the driving seat.

'Not too early for you, is it?' He didn't wait for an answer, poured two small measures of Grouse and passed one to me. I let the back of my throat have it.

'Okay,' I said. 'Let's hear it.'

He looked at me shrewdly over the rim of the glass as he sipped, then set it down carefully.

'Look, I'm sorry, Frank. I didn't want it to come to this. I thought – well, it doesn't matter what I thought. What's done is done.'

'*What* is done, for God's sake?'

'The Lord Advocate got wind of your role in the investigation, Frank. He wasn't consulted and he doesn't like it. I don't know how he found out, but he did.'

'Kettle,' I said.

'What do you mean?'

'Kettle must have leaked. It means he's pretty confident of an arrest soon. Tell me, is he really that close?'

Barrie clamped his teeth shut, spoke through them. 'He's got a definite suspect. I can't say more than that.'

'So what are you telling me? I'm off the case?'

'That's it. I'm afraid there's nothing I can do.'

'You could have told me earlier.'

'Christ, I've been trying to get hold of you for three days. Where the hell have you been?'

'Up north. Didn't Harry tell you?'

'Aye. He told me you came back Thursday.'

'Friday I was working, following up a lead.'

'And?'

'Nothing. Then I spent the whole of yesterday at the Commonwealth Pool. You want to know what I got for my troubles? Piles.'

'Okay, Frank, take it easy, will you?'

'Is that all you wanted to tell me, I'm off the case?'

'No. There's more. I've been instructed to set a date for the Fatal Accident Inquiry.'

'So?'

'So they want Kettle to carry out the investigation on my behalf.'

'You what? It's supposed to be an independent investigation. You put Kettle on it and you know what you're doing to me? Christ!'

'Frank, there are things going on at a higher level – *politically* – over which I have no jurisdiction, no power. I'm a Civil Servant. I have a responsibility to the people of Edinburgh. It's not an easy job, I can tell you. In your case, what I'm giving you is the chance to clear your name.'

'What you're giving me is bullshit. I've heard it so many times it doesn't impress me anymore. You say you're giving me a chance on the one hand, then tell me Kettle's heading the investigation on the other. You call that a chance?'

'I just can't make you see, can I?' Barrie said. 'I stuck my neck out for you, Frank, taking you on as I did, when no-one wanted anything to do with you. I was hoping you'd show your true worth, come up with a quick result. But no, you get tied up in a murder which happened twenty-odd years ago, and I don't see you for a week on end. How do you think that makes me look? Everyone warned me, you know. Stay away from McMorran, they said. He's got problems, he's not the detective he used to be, better not be too closely associated, in case he——'

'In case he what?'

'Fucks up.'

I was halfway home when Harry pulled alongside, saying 'Get in.'

'I like it as much as you do, Frank,' he said, pulling out. 'I've been trying to find you since——'

'Forget it, Harry.'

'How did you get on in Ballaig?' Harry asked eventually.

'You winding me up, or what?'

'Asking, that's all.'

'MacBean's got an alibi,' I said, and went on to tell him about Lawrie, my night on the hill and Cath.

'So that's it, then?'

'That's it.' I had to change the subject. 'What about Kettle – has he got an ID on the boy yet?'

'You mean you haven't heard? Jesus. They had the ID before they even found him. Father reported him missing yesterday afternoon when he got home after work.'

'Who is he?'

'Mark Wyatt. Father works in one of the psychy hospitals up Morningside. Kettle jumped straight in, wasn't going to wait for someone to find the body. And you know what, he found one. A patient who helps out in the kitchens where the boy's father works has disappeared as well. His name's Arnold Metzger. He's got a history of violence. Mostly self-abusive but the doctors reckon it's not out of the question.'

'What isn't?'

'That Metzger's the Hangman.'

'You mean he's got a history of psychopathy and they let him in and out as he pleases?'

'He has to sign out, sign in. On the days of the last three murders he was signed out at the crucial times.'

'And the first?'

'Even if he was signed in, so what? One of the doctors says weekends there are pretty slack, skeleton staff. He could come and go and no-one would be any the wiser.'

'Which hospital is that?'

'Drummond House. Small place, annexed to the Royal Ed.'

Somewhere in my mind a distant bell rang, but I couldn't remember which door to open. It rang insistently, but all the doors I tried were locked.

We arrived at my flat. There was an awkward silence, then Harry offered me his hand, saying, 'Good luck, Frank. Keep in touch.'

I watched him drive away.


People in their Sunday best on their way to church and there was me, sucking on a bottle of MacAllans, trying not to think too much, trying not to think at all. The bell still rang in my mind – little voice going yap yap yap – what the hell had I overlooked?

I dragged out all my notes on the case so far, spread them on the table and painstakingly worked my way through them. From the scant beginnings of the Craig Watson killing through to my interview on Friday with Mrs Margaret Bain. And then there it was, staring at me from the last scribbled page.

Dominic Bain worked at Drummond House Hospital as a cook, alongside the dead boy's father.

Coincidence? Why not? The patient who had disappeared also worked there. But there was something else, a nagging something else. Yap yap yap, went the little voice.

I went through to the kitchen and looked through the pile of newspapers I hadn't thrown out yet. Friday's paper was near the top. The headline jumped out at me:

EXCLUSIVE: HANGMAN POEM WARNS OF
NEXT VICTIM.

This paper has received an exclusive copy of the letter sent to the editor by the man known as The Hangman. It was delivered by hand sometime after the offices closed on Wednesday night, addressed to the man leading the hunt, Detective Chief Inspector Kettle. It was signed 'with love from the Hangman'. Further details on Page 3.

I turned to page three where, alongside a photofit of the
killer, the poem was published in full. I read it once.

Then once again.

It chilled my bones.

> *you shouldn't have laughed, it wasn't a joke*
> *take a look at the last time the hangman spoke*
> *little heather, heather munro*
> *we came together at the end of a rope*
> *jamie was a spy*
> *on the other side*
> *they used to hang spies*
> *that's why he died*
> *next it's jamie, jamie again*
> *though he calls himself mark he'll hang just the same*
> *soon, jamie, soon you'll be mine*
> *let the fat bastard laugh*
> *he's running out of time*

Coincidence? The Jamie in the poem and the Jamie who
died twenty-seven years ago in MacBean's workshop in
Ballaig? Coincidence, that Mark Wyatt was dead and
MacBean's son, Dominic, worked in the same place as
the victim's father?

Coincidence? Bollocks.

Little old Morningside ladies hobbled past in ones and
twos, replete in furs and hats, handbags on arms, prayer-
books in hand, moving like zombies towards the tolling
of the bells. Otherwise the road was quiet, the houses still
asleep.

253

I'd found a good spot by a small iron footbridge over the railway, from where I could watch the house and not look too out of place. Anyone can look like a train-spotter.

In the ninety minutes I had been there, I hadn't seen any movement behind the windows and no-one had left the house. I wondered if the brown Mini in the garage belonged to Dominic's girlfriend.

As I waited, I spent a long time going over everything I had learned in my investigation so far, trying to find flaws in my reasoning and gaps in my knowledge. There were many. Doubts crowded in like vultures squabbling over a carcass. I wished I had Dave Nicholl to act as devil's advocate. I desperately needed an objective view.

Suddenly, movement.

A man and woman stepped from the house. They walked slowly up the pot-holed drive. I crossed the bridge, followed the footpath along the back of a row of gardens. I pushed through a rusted gate and came out onto a small cul-de-sac as the couple passed the end of the street. I fell in twenty yards behind them.

Dominic Bain was about the same height and build as myself, a little older, with cropped fair hair. He wore black canvas jeans, black trainers, black shirt, and carried a black leather jacket over his shoulder. His walk was confident, with a slight swagger, left hand in pocket.

His companion was about five foot nine or so, with hennaed hair and a fair complexion. I couldn't see her face but there was nothing wrong with the way she wore her tan leather mini-skirt, or the way her green cotton blouse hung off her shoulder. She had a walk that was healthy and natural and younger than his. She was swing-ing along talking to him, laughing a bit, looking up at him often. I wondered if she knew.

They turned on to Morningside Road, were momen-tarily out of sight. I quickened my pace and gained the main road twenty seconds behind them, in time to see the woman disappear through the front door of 'The Canny Man'.

I entered by the side door.

'The Canny Man' must be one of the strangest pubs in the city. Every available piece of wall-space is taken up by old clocks – only one of which works – of every shape and size. The walls are papered with old nicotine-stained racing papers. There are dummies hanging from the ceil-ing, bass drums, bugles. There are pinball-machines, bandits, trivia-games, and in one of the rooms, a glowing coal-fire. Light struggles through the windows.

They weren't in the front bar, or in the snug with the fire. They weren't playing pinball. They were through the back, sitting in a dark corner beyond the bar. I smothered a sigh of relief and ordered a pint, then sat and nursed it at a table two away from theirs, the closest I could get. Jukebox speakers over my head meant all I could do was observe. I took out my paper and started on the crossword.

8 Down – *Fierce fighting at these digs nearby (5, 8).* Second letter first word, L; first letter, second word, Q.

I could see his face now. It was almost boyish with its smooth skin. Boyish yes, but there was a meanness, per-haps in the sleek head, the flat ears, or the sharp brow. I was reminded of a school bully, a playground shark.

He had seemed about thirty-five at first glance, thirty at second, but now, adding the lines of his face to his expressions, his mannerisms, the way he watched the girl, I put his age up around late thirties, maybe forty. The woman was no more than twenty-four, and obviously infatuated.

*Close quarters*? It fit.

They finished their drinks and the girl went up for more. Bain looked around the bar and I met his eyes for a moment, looking up abstractedly before returning to my crossword. The girl came back with the drinks and sat down. I left the crossword and turned back to the centre pages.

The photofit was not perfect. It didn't fit exactly – the hair in the picture was too dark and too long, the chin too pronounced and the cheeks too hollow – but the eyes were right, the forehead a little too bony but good from the side and the mouth and lips were spot on.

10 Across – *Ease off, to enable one to gain promotion? (3,2)*.

Something Parrish, the pathologist, had said in the postmortem report came sluggishly back to mind. Something about the small bite-mark on the breast of Janice Young.

*Bear in mind you might be looking for a man who has a slight gap between his two front teeth* . . .

I spent the next ten minutes bearing it in mind. Then Bain smiled.

Gap between the teeth.

*Let up?* I wrote it in. Okay. 3 Down . . .

About an hour and two drinks later, I still hadn't

finished the crossword and I was dying for a pee, wondering if I should risk it – and maybe call Dave Nicholl at
the same time – when my deliberations were cut short by
the angry scrape of a chair and I looked up to see the girl
hiss something at Bain, then storm from the bar. Bain
leant back in his chair, smiling to himself. He made no
move to follow the girl.

Our eyes met again. Held a little longer.

I thought, why not? I got up and took my drink over to
his table, saying:

'Mind if I join you?'

# Chapter Twenty-One

Okay, so she'd left in a mood because she couldn't handle the fact that he had things to do and didn't need her hanging on his arm all afternoon. So what? She'd be back. Then maybe he'd show her a thing or two.

There was a guy standing over him, waiting for an answer, wanting to know if Dominic minded.

'Why should I mind?' he said, waving his hand magnanimously at the seat. 'It's a free world, last I heard.'

'Where've you been living?' the guy said, smiling a lopsided smile as he dropped his paper on the table and plonked himself down opposite Bain. He was dressed in loose-fitting jeans and a plain white t-shirt, drinking beer. Dominic had noticed him earlier, sitting further along, alone at a table. Maybe he'd been stood up. Or maybe he was queer. He certainly looked queer, the way he was looking at Dominic now.

'So,' the guy said, leaning back in his chair, sticking thumbs in jean pockets. 'What's new?'

What did he mean, what's new? 'You tell me,' Dominic said. He was feeling fine-fine-fine today, the pills buzzing in his system, the gin honing a nice edge.

259

'Who's the girl?' the guy wanted to know. 'Your girl-friend?'

'Aye.' Dominic frowned.

'Nice-looking girl. Did you have an argument?'

'Hey, what's all these questions? Do I know you? Have we met before or what?'

The guy laughed, stretched his hand across the table. 'Call me Francis,' he said. Bain made no move so the man withdrew his hand, shrugged and said, 'No problem, Dominic. That *is* your name, isn't it?'

Dominic nodded slowly, unsure now.

'Yeah, I somehow thought it was,' Francis went on, smiling. 'I've heard quite a bit about you, Dominic. Nothing good, of course.'

'Who's been telling tales?'

'I saw Cathy the other day. Remember her?'

This was getting weird. There was something strange going on, something about this guy.

'Cathy?' Dominic asked, his throat dry, needing lubrication.

'Yeah. You're going to get married, right? When the old man shuffles off his mortal coil. Know the Cathy I mean?'

'Who are you? What do you want?'

'Nice woman, Cathy. I was almost tempted myself. She gave me your address, you know, told me to look you up if I was ever down this way. Does she know about your girlfriend? Bet she doesn't, right?'

'No. Look, hey!'

'Don't worry, mate. Your secret's safe with me. I'm a man of the world, right. Get your pleasures where you can, all that kind of thing. No harm done. Can I get you another drink?'

Dominic hesitated, wanting to say sod off, leave me alone, but the voice at the back of his mind stopped him.

So he said, 'Gin and Tonic, with a slice of lemon', and watched the guy – Francis? – order the drinks, bring them back to the table, sit down and start talking again.

'Thing I like about you, Dominic,' he said, 'is your sense of humour. You had me cracking up when I read about your poem. Never laughed so much in all my life. A masterpiece it was, addressing it to "that fat bastard Kettle". I tell you, I almost died. Brilliant!'

Dominic reeled beneath the shock of the words.

'What?' he cried. This must be some kind of sick joke. That's why the guy was smiling so much.

'Look, no problem, Dominic,' Francis said. 'I told you, your secret's safe with me. Any friend of Cath's is a friend of mine, right?'

Warning bells clamoured in his head. The man's eyes did not smile, not when his mouth did. Now he was opening up the newspaper to the centre pages, where a picture of Dominic's face stared impassively up at him. Francis looked at the picture, looked at him, smiled and nodded, then closed the paper again.

'See what I mean, Dominic?'

Slick and cool. Say nothing, let him talk, see what he knows. Drink the rest of your gin and smile a lot, one big joke.

'Could almost be me,' he told Francis.

'It is you, Dominic. No two ways about it. Have you seen your old man lately?'

'Old man?'

'John MacBean. He's your father. I've been trying to find him the last few weeks. You see, for a while I thought *he* was The Hangman. Then I found out he was in Ballaig last weekend, staying with Alec Lawrie – remember him?'

'No.'

'Never mind. He said your father was with him all weekend and that destroyed my theory.'

'So it was you checked on my mother.'

'Good guess, Dominic. And you're right – I did. She was very helpful.'

'Helpful.' Dominic could see Mother-dear being very helpful.

The man looked off in the distance, puzzled. 'It's funny, you know,' he said, as if he were talking to himself. 'The way you wrote about Jamie in your poem. It was when I read that, that I knew for sure you were The Hangman. Until then, it was just guesswork, following a hunch. Is the girl in on it, too?'

'Tash?' he said, before he could stop himself.

'Is that her name? Nice. What's it short for?'

'Natasha.'

'Is she in on it, too? Same kind of pervert as you?'

Dominic felt his face flush, could do nothing to stop it. 'Hey, you better——'

'Okay,' Francis said, holding up his hands. 'No offence meant, right? Just a figure of speech. We don't get taught much in the way of manners in the CID. Accept my apologies.'

Dominic felt he was going to burst or cry. A mist seemed to close in as the man talked on.

'You ever hear the one about the pervert, why he crossed the road?'

All Dominic could do was grunt.

'He couldn't get his dick out the chicken. Ha-ha. You like that? Or don't perverts like to laugh at themselves?'

Nerves raw and twitching, panic forcing the word out. 'What?'

'Look, I'm sorry, Dominic. I didn't mean to upset you.' The man's voice came from a long way off. 'Are you all right? You don't look too well. Maybe a bit of fresh air . . .'

'You're CID?' Dominic rasped.

The guy made a face, nodded. 'Of course I am,' he said, belligerently. 'You didn't think I dropped in to see you by accident? No way. I've been following you for days. I just thought I'd have a wee chat, let you know what the score is, you know, Cathy being a mutual friend and all that. So don't worry, everything's under control.'

Dominic pushed himself unsteadily to his feet. 'I'm going to be sick. You got that under control?'

'You want me to hold your hand or what?'

'I can manage.' The door was a pinpoint of light in the far-off distance. Mr CID hadn't moved, seemed content to sit and wait, maybe finish off his crossword. Fair enough. Dominic wasn't going to wait around, he was getting out.

He peeked over his shoulder to see that the guy wasn't even looking at him, stepped to the left instead of the right where the toilets were, then ran through the front bar and out of the door onto the main road. Easy.

He ran the world's fastest stagger home, every few

paces checking he wasn't being followed. At one point he had to cram his knuckles in his mouth to stop from spewing over. His next course of action a refrain in his brain.

*Pack, get away, sleep. Pack, get away, sleep.*

He stumbled down the gravel drive. No coppers crouched in bushes or perched in trees, none in cars or peering from windows. Clear. Tash's Mini no longer in the garage.

*Pack, get away, sleep.*

He entered the house, found a note from Mother-dear saying she was out. Tough. Too late.

He locked all the doors and climbed the stairs. *Pack, get away, sleep.* Had to swallow a couple of Valium, cool himself down. Pack.

He threw his suitcase on the bed, saw it was made, the sheets pulled tight, the pillow plump and inviting. It looked so warm, so safe, so cosy. Maybe he should lie down first. A minute's rest was all he needed. Then hit the road.

One minute, okay?

He came awake screaming. It was night outside, a full moon. The moon pulling at his entrails, casting spindly, tree-like shadows across the walls. He could hear the distant murmur of traffic, a dog howl somewhere down near the tracks. He tried timing the trains but his body-clock must have come unwound; either that or they had changed the schedules. No matter – time was the least of his problems.

Or was it?

Someone had spent an age leaning on the doorbell. Mother-dear hadn't answered so maybe she wasn't back yet. He wondered who it could have been. Two choices, really.

Tash. Or the police. The police would have kicked the door off its hinges if they'd come for him. *You are surrounded! Come out with your hands up!* That sort of shit. Tanks and troops, dogs and snipers. None of this ringing the bell.

What had he arranged with Tash, then? She'd walked out of the pub. He remembered thinking at the time that she'd be back. Then that guy had come over, sat down cool-as-you-like and started talking.

Of course! Francis, CID.

Maybe it was him, checking up. Or . . .

Or what?

He didn't act like a cop, his hair was too long. Said he was a friend of Cath's and any friend of hers was a friend of his. *Don't worry, everything's under control*, he'd said, in that funny way of talking he had, as if everything was the greatest joke and tragedy all at the same time.

What had he meant by *everything under control*?

And what did he know? Everything was certainly not under control. For a start, he couldn't move, something to do with pressure or gravity. It came to him after a minute. Concentration, the name of the game. Concentration carried him to the window. It didn't hurt. Lucky, he hated pain.

The cool breeze from the open window washed over him and he started to choke, as though drowning in air. He struggled to stay on his feet, draped himself over the

265

windowsill. He was going to die, no he wasn't, yes he was.

After several minutes, vision returned, everything in focus. The moon stopped pulling at his body, strength of sorts crept back to aching muscles.

Outside, no troops or dogs. A wave of relief flooded through him. That Francis guy hadn't been lying. Maybe he was a friend, after all.

He dragged himself into the bathroom, propped his body in the shower and turned it on, cold. The jets seemed to pierce his brittle skin, then he went numb and the force of the water was just a dull sensation. His head cleared. Order returned, oh welcome the homecoming hero.

# Chapter Twenty-Two

The moon was yellow, the sky black. Shadows moved in the cool breeze but the shadow that was me was still as the tree I crouched behind at the end of garden. Silence, but for the distant hum of traffic and the pushing of the breeze through bushes and leaves. Light from Bain's upstairs window stretched out across the lawn like an elongated coffin. Still no movement in the curtainless oblong of light.

I glanced at my watch, saw the little-hand closing on one. Soon, I thought, I would have to enter the barn. I needed something a little more solid that the circumstantial evidence I'd built up so far. On top of that, I couldn't stand the waiting much longer.

I'd been waiting since the moment Bain rushed from the pub. I'd followed him back and had waited at the end of the drive. I'd waited and I'd waited. Nothing had happened. After a while I'd walked down to the house and peered in at the windows, checked the doors. All locked. I spent ten minutes leaning on the doorbell. No reply. Either Bain was asleep or dead or he was playing hard to get.

I wandered down to the buildings at the end of his

garden. They too were locked. I wished I'd brought my lock-pick. When the wishing did no good, I returned to the house.

I studied the upstairs windows. One of them was open. A strange sound drifted down to my ears. It took me a few minutes to work out what it was. The sound of snoring.

I risked it.

I went home and gathered a few things I would need. I slung them in a bag, then phoned Dave Nicholl. He wasn't in. I left a message, told him to wait for my call. Then I took a taxi back across to Morningside.

It was exactly the way I left it. Doors still locked, lights still off, snores still rasping through the upstairs window. The breeze had picked up and the sun had disappeared, and suddenly the air was full of churchbells as they pealed for Evensong. I was halfway down the garden when Mrs Bain returned. I scuttled into the bushes.

She unlocked the door and went inside. Lights came on and a few minutes later I could hear her calling her son. I heard no reply and eventually the television blared out. Still I waited.

No-one else called at or left the house. I ate a couple of the rolls I'd bought in the pub and washed them down with a bite of whisky from the half-bottle in my bag. The whisky tasted good. I tasted some more. I tasted half the bottle and hardly noticed the evening slip by and night crawl in. I was almost happy by the time the upstairs light came on and Bain appeared at the window.

Now in the distance, as a bell tolled one and cramp began to clutch at the muscles in my calves, I decided I would wait no longer.

The padlock on the door of the barn was heavy and thick, the same way my fingers felt as I fumbled with the picks. It had been a long time since I had tried my delicate hand at breaking and entering and, but for the element of noise, I would have felt a lot happier with a sledgehammer in my hand – the subtle approach. Ten minutes later I was eyeing the rusted iron clasp and thinking enviously of crowbars. Any kind of bar. I resolved to try one last time.

You have to caress the levers and tickle the tumblers, treat them soft as a lover on a first night – that's what I told myself when the lock snapped open. I breathed a sigh of relief and stepped inside, closed the door.

I was confronted immediately by a pungent smell of shit that almost took the lid off my nostrils. Breathing through my mouth, I switched on my torch and played the beam around the walls. No windows. I found the lightswitch, flicked it on.

The solitary bulb hanging from the central rafter added little more than a dull glow to the surroundings: it illuminated the piles of junk and furniture stacked against the walls and the wide walk-in fireplace that took up most of the far wall, but it failed to probe the deep shadowed corners or the expanse of blackness that hung above the rafters. I moved carefully across the earth floor, trying to quell the heavy sense of foreboding that was growing steadily inside me. It had something to do with the smell of shit.

I shone my torch on the fireplace, then squatted down and picked something up from the heap of ash. It was still warm. It was a sock. A child's tartan sock. I found a stick and poked deeper into the ash, succeeding only in raising a cloud of fine dust. I put the sock in my canvas shoulder-bag and flashed my torch some more.

There was a ladder propped against the edge of the loft which stretched across the width of the barn over the fireplace. I climbed the ladder and discovered the source of the smell. I retreated hastily.

As I searched through the precariously-piled stacks of junk I found something that heightened my interest – a box of glossy black bin-liners. On top was a ball of string. I cut off a length of string with my knife, folded it into one of the bin-liners and put both in my bag, then directed the beam of the torch deep into the shadows along the back wall. There were kitchen chairs piled high, a dressing-table with a cracked mirror, stacks of *National Geographic* magazines and more of the *Reader's Digest* on the floor. Next a couple of lampshades, a cricket bat, a lampstand, piles of old newspapers, an ancient television, a tennis racket, several rolls of carpet, a coil of rope, a tool-box, two crates with mildewed clothes sticking out the top and . . .

A coil of rope?

I hauled it free. It was the same kind of rope I had seen around the neck of Janice Young: blue, synthetic, with a half inch diameter. I took out my knife again, cut off three inches and added it to my collection. Evidence they wanted, evidence they would get.

I found nothing more of interest. I felt I already had enough, so I switched off my torch and headed for the door.

I almost fell over it.

It was lying deep in shadow, partially covered by a roll

of carpet. It brought back memories of Greenbank Drive and The Meadows. Fear prickled my scalp.

I dragged it out to the centre of the floor. It was big and heavy. Too big and heavy. I cut away the string and sliced carefully through the bin-liner. The face that stared out at me was youthful and hawkish, topped by spiked black hair that was shaved at the temples. I estimated his age as early twenties. He was as old as he would ever be, his eyes as dead as glass.

I cut away more bin-liner and immediately wished I hadn't. His throat was a gash that stretched from ear to ear and there was blood caked everywhere. I turned him slightly on his side. His skin was cold, but rigor mortis had come and gone, and the hypostasis on his back was red and fixed. Most likely he had died yesterday, I thought. Same time as the kid they'd found in The Meadows this morning.

Could this be the same patient Kettle was looking for? Harry had made no mention of age or distinguishing marks but he had said something about self-abuse. I cut away more of the bin-liner and found the body was a battlefield of old and new scars. Jackpot, I thought, so absorbed in my examination that I failed to hear the door open or even acknowledge the cool draught that entered behind him.

I sensed rather than saw the movement but by then it was too late. By the time I had turned, all I saw was a fast downward moving blur. I threw up an arm in defence. As my head exploded in a flash of light and pain, I caught a glimpse of smiling teeth, then spiralled into a fathomless black void.

# Chapter Twenty-Three

Mother-dear had a surprise for him at the breakfast table.

'Happy Birthday!' she chirped, sliding a small, plainly-wrapped box across the table to him. It was bound by a glossy red ribbon tied in a bow, with a fancy little card taped on top. Written in the card in a spidery scrawl were the words: 'Happy Birthday, dear, from your loving mother.' Below it, two crooked kisses.

Dominic tore off the paper and opened the box. Inside was a battery-operated alarm-clock. The kind that goes bleep-bleep-bleep.

'Do you like it?' Mother-dear asked, watching him closely. 'I spent hours choosing it. I knew you'd regret smashing your old one and you do need something to get you up if you're going to go to work in the morning.'

'I'm not going back to work. Not tomorrow, not ever.'

Mother-dear's face folded in on itself. 'What do you mean? You can't just give up like that. I spent good money on that——'

'Take it back then. Get a refund.'

Tears welled in the corners of her eyes, then overflowed down her cheeks. 'There's all the thanks I get.'

She brought a ball of pink tissue from the sleeve of her

cardigan and dabbed at her eyes as her frail shoulders heaved.

Dominic dropped his knife and fork on his plate and pushed back his chair.

Mother-dear raised her head. 'Where are you going?'

'Somewhere I can eat my food in peace,' he said. 'Without getting drowned.'

'Dominic! Come back here!'

He carried his plate out of the back door, down to the barn. The pig was lying on his side, awake. He squinted at Dominic over the edge of the loft and said:

'So what happens now?'

Dominic didn't reply. Instead, he fetched a chair, sat down and carried on eating. An alarm-clock, Christ! Whatever next. Mother-dear was obviously over the hill and far away. That was all he needed. He used cold buttered toast to mop up the egg-yolk, then wiped his lips with the back of his hand and put the plate on the floor. Mr CID watched but didn't interrupt.

Arnie was still lying in the same place, staring up at nothing very much. Flies were already buzzing on and off his face, feeding on his neck.

'Pity,' Dominic said. 'Arnie was a good friend. Sad he had to die.'

'He didn't have to.'

'I wasn't talking to you.'

'Who then? The man in the moon?'

Dominic propped the ladder against the loft, climbed till his face was level with that of the CID, letting the CID see the razor in his hand. He flicked it open, held it against the CID's neck.

'Pigs ought to be seen and not heard,' he said quietly, impressed by his own self-restraint.

'Seen and not heard,' the copper repeated.

'You learn quick. I like that. You and I could get to be friends.' Mr CID didn't seem to like the idea, his eyes flicking from Arnie back to Dominic.

'You said any friend of Cath's is a friend of yours,' Dominic continued.'But you tried to take Arnie away from me. That was a mistake. You go in my house and question my mother-dear and that was another mistake. You go through all my stuff with your prying little fingers and that was something I can't forgive. You said you were my friend, that you were going to help me. But taking Arnie away is not trying to help me. Spying on me is not trying to help me. Do you understand?'

Mr CID blinked, moved his neck a fraction. A globule of blood glistened bright on the blade. Dominic wasn't finished yet.

'Yes, a friend of Cath's, you said. I phoned her and she said she only met you once and you were going round the village asking questions about my father. About me. Friends don't do that kind of thing. So I start getting suspicious. I'm not paranoid but I like to know what's going on. What do you say to that?'

'Whatever you want,' Mr CID said. He was having trouble breathing. Dominic lowered the razor a little.

'Okay. Say oink. You're a pig, so say oink.'

'Oink.'

'Good little pig.' Dominic leant his forearms on the top rung of the ladder as if he was chatting to a neighbour over the garden wall. 'Now tell me about my father,' he said. 'You said the other day he's been living up in Ballaig. True or false?'

'Oink.'

'What's that supposed to mean?'

'Oink.'

Dominic studied the lethal lines of the razor. 'Don't get too smart, Mr CID.'

'He was up there.'

'In the cabin or what?'

'Cabin?'

'Little wooden house made from logs – know the kind I mean?'

'Yeah.'

'Good. So what was he doing there?'

'What do you usually do in cabins?'

Dominic stiffened. 'Do you want to end up like Arnie?' he yelled. 'Either give me a little respect or I cut your fucking throat. Understand?'

'Oink.'

'That's better. Now tell me what he was doing.'

'Checking out whether he can live there again, that kind of thing.'

'Live there? He must have lost his marbles. What else?'

'How do I know? I didn't even meet him.'

Dominic twisted his lips in a sneer. 'Not much of a copper, are you?'

'I found you.'

'Found me, shit. Cathy gave you my address. That makes Cathy not much of a friend. I had great things planned for her. Marriage, the works. Then she had to go and do this.'

276

'She didn't know.'

Dominic frowned. 'Okay, so I go and put her right.'

'Why, for God's sake?'

'Why people die?' He had to give it a little thought. 'Wrong time, wrong place, I suppose. Why else?'

'That's no answer.'

'Hey, who's in control here? I'm asking the questions. I haven't got the time to stand here talking to you all day. Things to do, people to meet.'

'I heard psychopaths liked to talk. Something to do with their basic insecurity. You know, a need to assert themselves, show the whole wide world how stupid they are.'

Dominic studied his razor again. 'You saying I'm stupid?'

'I meant evil.'

'Evil, eh? You think I'm evil?'

'That's what you want to hear, isn't it? You want people to fear you, to point you out as the world's most evil bastard. Okay, I admit it. You're evil. You're bad. You're very, very naughty. You deserve a damn good spanking.'

'I do, eh?'

'Ask Anderton. He'll tell you.'

'Anderton?'

'Forget it. Why don't you just loosen these ropes a bit before my hands drop off?'

'Because I'm evil. You said it.' Dominic began to descend the ladder.

'Hey! Where are you going?'

Dominic stopped, looking up at Mr CID. 'To sort out

a little problem,' he said. 'Then I'll come back and sort
*you* out. Any more questions?'

'We'll all miss you, darling . . .'

'I can kill you slow or kill you quick. Which would you
prefer?'

That shut the pig up. Put him in his trough.

'How about an elocution lesson before I go? How does
that grab you?'

'You what?'

'I said grunt for me, pig.'

'Oink-oink!'

'Are you deaf? I said grunt.'

'Grunt-grunt!'

'You can do better than that.'

'Grunt-snort, gorkle-grunt!'

'Such a good little pig.'

As he climbed toward the house, a brown Mini pulled
into the drive and drew up beside his Escort. Tash got out
and watched him walk towards her. He tried to smile but
found he couldn't.

# Chapter Twenty-Four

I heard the padlock click, Bain whistling up the garden path. Then the sound of a car on the gravel, stopping. It sounded like a Mini. His lady-friend back to kiss and make up, or call him names. I hoped it was the former.

It still hurt. Oink, indeed. I'd make him squeal before the day was over – that pleasure I promised myself. First I had to escape.

I was naked and cold, my body twitching like a fish on a hook. There were flies everywhere. My head throbbed and pulsed like a raw beating heart. The side on which I lay was numb, my hands and feet were numb. Something to do with the ropes I knew were there but could not feel. I was hungry and thirsty, and I hadn't slept for twenty-four hours. Unless you call unconsciousness sleeping.

The answer was simple.

All I had to do was roll off the edge of the loft, fall fifteen or twenty feet and survive. Then find my clothes and knife – if they were still in the barn – and cut myself free before battering through the padlocked door. Like I said, simple. I remained where I was.

I'd be lying if I said I didn't spend much time thinking about death. It's inevitable when you're bound and helpless and your only choices are to scream or think. I could see myself quite clearly lying in a ditch, wrapped in bin-liners or stretched out, limp and cold, hanging from a rope around a rafter. No more trouble to anyone. It drove me to action.

I wriggled forward until my head hung over the edge of the loft. I looked down on the hard-packed earth floor and scattered junk. It looked more like a hundred feet than fifteen. Wherever I fell, I was going to get hurt, but I had nothing left to lose.

I gave myself no time to think, dragged the rest of my body to the edge, counted ten, and rolled.

The pain was a pain forged in hell. It took my left shoulder and rammed it through my chest and out the other side. It took my head and squeezed it with white-hot tongs. It ground my hip to marrowbone dust. Dust in my mouth, my lungs, my eyes.

I drifted here and there, in and out, round and about. Nothing I wanted to do, nowhere I wanted to go. The pain, the only point of reference in a dark deserted land-scape. Nothing else was left, except the warmth. The warmth was good and good was better than dead. Waves thudded on the shores of consciousness, the tide sucking at my feet. Sand in my mouth, my lungs, my eyes.

I don't know how long it was, longer than a piece of string or shorter than eternity, it made no difference. All that mattered was the light. It was there when my eyes opened, and it hurt. I held onto that light like a man holds onto his balls.

Breath wheezed in my throat. Breath seemed like a good ides, dragging air into my lungs, oxygen for my brain and blood. Keeping the old ticker beating. Not a bad thing if you want to stay alive. I grabbed as much as I could.

I could feel the thoughts piling into the in-tray in my head, all marked 'urgent'. I handed in my notice and tossed them in the bin. Let someone else sort them out.

I tried moving, then I tried lying still. Somewhere in the distance a car door slammed and an engine started. Wheels span on the gravel drive. Dominic Bain was on his way. As I waited for the nausea to subside and my head to clear, I wondered if Natasha had also left. Would Dominic take her up to meet Cathy? Not if he was in his right mind. But he wasn't, he'd cracked. That much was obvious in what he'd done to Arnold Metzger. He'd given up throttling, was now slashing. Beware the leopard who changes his spots.

I examined my body. No broken bones, they just felt like broken bones. My shoulder hurt the most. It sent barbs of pain through my body when it moved, but it was bearable. My hip still felt a little gritty but I could move my leg without too much pain. My head throbbed but felt no worse that it had since I'd regained consciousness earlier this morning. I willed myself to move.

Gaining my feet, I stood there swaying, waiting for the ground to settle down, the world to stop spinning. Arnold lay beneath a hairy rug of flies. I couldn't see his face. I wondered how the flies had got in, whether I could get out the same way.

The dim glow of the bulb reflected off something blue and shiny by the door. The toolbox. I hopped across the floor and fell on it like a drunk on a pretty, young miss. It was the kind that opened out into layered compartments. It took several minutes of contortion before its innards lay exposed. Basking on the second layer was an orange Stanley knife.

Bringing my hands under my feet was not as difficult as I had imagined. Perhaps I have long arms or short legs. It involved a certain amount of complaint from my shoulder but, in the circumstances, was justified.

Once I could see my hands it needed only seconds to free my feet and a minute to cut away the rope at my wrists. Then slowly, as I massaged the cold, numb flesh, blood began to flow once more. Sensation returned with all the subtlety of a stampeding herd of buffalo. I had thought the cold and hunger were bad. I had thought the wound in my head was bad. The pain in my shoulder was sheer fucking agony, but the process of recirculation was nothing short of torture. I hopped and danced across the floor, slapping my hands and stomping on the floor like the famous cat on a hot tin roof. Pins and needles? I was dealing with six-inch nails.

I searched around for my clothes. They were nowhere to be seen. Next to the fireplace, however, I found a pair of slashed and crudely-patched jeans, a black Cult t-shirt and a black leather jacket full of tears and safety-pins. I searched through the pockets and found letters addressed to Mr Arnold Metzger, signed Mummy and Daddy. I found a small lump of dark Moroccan, a pack of ten Silk Cut and cigarette papers. I found three scrumpled one-pound notes, forty-seven pence in change and a bunch of keys. I left everything except the clothes on the mantelpiece and dressed. They were a perfect fit. All I needed was a safety-pin through my nose.

I walked back across the barn and tried the door. It was locked and about two inches thick. I returned to the toolbox, selected a hammer and chisel and set to work. Fifteen minutes later, I had chiselled out a one-inch groove around a one-foot square estimation of where I thought the clasp and padlock were. I stood back and attacked the square with the hammer. On the fifth attempt the wood gave and daylight streamed in through the splintered hole. I hit the door with my good shoulder and found myself suddenly outside, lying on the ground and blinking at the sun. The sun was warm, the air cool, the sky filling with cloud. I breathed in, then climbed the path to the house.

There was no sign of life at any of the windows. The Mini was still parked on the gravel. I hammered at the front door. Mrs Bain peered out through the two-inch gap.

'Sergeant!' she exclaimed, her wide eyes shocked. 'What on earth is the meaning of this?'

'I want to use your phone,' I told her harshly. 'Open the door.'

'Do you have a warrant?'

'I don't need a warrant to use your phone.'

'But why are you dressed like that?'

'Ask your beloved son,' I sneered. 'Are you going to let me in or do I have to kick the door down?'

'You only had to ask.'

She released the chain and stepped back to let me pass. 'My, my! You are in a mess! How ever did you get in such a state?'

'Do you know where your son is, Mrs Bain?'

'He went out in his car. He didn't say where he was going.' She wore a pink dressing-gown which she clutched fiercely to her body as though I'd tear it off. 'Is he in trouble again?'

'You could say that.' I picked up the phone and dialled Dave Nicholl's number. He answered on the third ring, listened without interrupting as I gave him explicit directions and said he'd be here. Reliable as always. I rang off and headed down the hall towards the sound of the television. Mrs Bain's voice rose sharply in indignation. 'Where do you think you are going?'

'Is Natasha still here?' I demanded.

She looked at me vacantly. 'Natasha?'

'Dominic's lady-friend. Her car's outside. Did she leave with him or what?'

'I suppose so. I was in the bath when they left. What are you doing?'

'Looking for my clothes.'

They weren't in her sitting-room. They weren't in any of the downstairs rooms. She shuffled along behind me, spluttering. I ignored her and climbed the stairs.

I found them on a desk in a sparse room with windows looking out over the garden. They'd been slashed into ribbons. My shoes lay on top and my watch was in the left-hand shoe. It was seventeen minutes past ten. The contents of my canvas shoulder-bag were also on the desk along with two cups of cold black coffee. Handcuffs, lockpick, half-empty half-bottle of Grouse, two stale rolls, my wallet and all the evidence I'd collected from the barn. I took a swig of whisky then replaced everything in the bag. By then Mrs Bain was getting steamed up.

284

'Sergeant! Come down here at once! You have no right!'

I stood at the head of the stairs and shouted down at her.

'Mrs Bain! Go to your room and sit down. You are under arrest. Don't move from your chair or I'll use these cuffs. Do you understand?'

'Under arrest? But whatever for? You must have made some mistake. I don't see——'

I started down the stairs.

'All right, Sergeant. I'll do as you say. But you better have a very good explanation.'

Twenty past ten. How long since I'd heard the car drive away? It felt like hours but was probably little more than thirty minutes. I would have to hurry.

There was a bedroom off the landing. It was as sparsely furnished as the other room, nothing but a mattress on the floor in the centre of the room and an old oak wardrobe against the far wall. Off the bedroom, a small bathroom with no bath, just a shower, sink and toilet. I filled the basin and tidied up my face as best I could, then searched through the mirror-fronted cabinet and found pills of all shapes, colours and sizes, though nothing I recognised, nothing that I'd want to shove down my throat unless I'd just heard the four-minute warning. I returned to the landing where there were two doors I hadn't tried. One was a cupboard full of camping gear – a tent, stove, waterproofs, rucksack, boots; the other was the jackpot – a dark-room.

I had to search for the light. It was red. I found another switch and the light was bright. There were films of negatives pegged to a piece of string stretched between the walls. On the sideboard, developer and fixer trays, and in the corner a black- and-white enlarger. Prints were piled on shelves above the small basin set into the worktop. On the floor, stuffed in the corner like a pile of dirty washing lay Natasha.

She was bound and gagged and her eyes were shut. There was blood on her temple. I knelt and checked her pulse. It was strong. I half-dragged, half-carried her into the centre of the floor then cut away the ropes with a pair of scissors I found on the worktop. Then I carried her through to the bedroom, laid her on the bed and fetched a glass of water which I poured on her face. I slapped her gently a couple of times and called her name. Her eyes flickered and opened. Her voice was a grainy croak.

'Who are you?'

'Police,' I said. 'How are you feeling?'

'He . . . he hit me.' I could see the tears gathering in her eyes. 'I was coming in here and he hit me.'

'Any reason why he hit you?'

'I was going to leave. I told him so. I said I never wanted to see him again. I came in here to get my jacket.'

'Why were you leaving? Did you have an argument?'

'He was making coffee downstairs. I was through in the other room. I was looking around, you know, the way you do when you're left alone in a room. I saw this photo, it had obviously fallen down behind the desk. So I picked it up. It was . . .'

'Go on,' I urged.

Colour seeped back as the tears slid down her cheeks. 'It was horrible. There was this girl . . . she had no clothes on, she was just sort of hanging, you know . . . dead. It was awful. And then I realised who Dominic was. I just wanted to get out of there but he was coming up the stairs. I tried to put the photo back but it got stuck and that's when he came into the room. He saw that I knew and put the coffee down on the desk. I ran in here and that's when he hit me.' She began to sob.

'Did he say anything? Like where he was going?'

Emotion – or shock – choked in her throat. 'He kept saying 'oh dear, oh dear' over and over again. Then I passed out . . .'

'Okay, Natasha. You can take it easy now. Just lie back and rest for a moment. I'll be back in a minute.'

I left her with her face buried in the pillow and returned to the dark-room where I unclipped a strip of negatives, studied them against the light. What I saw made my stomach heave. I unclipped the rest, rolled them all together and put them in a black plastic film-canister which went in my pocket. I shuffled through the prints and found more of the same. Evidence they wanted, evidence they would get. Let them bloody choke on it. I found an empty folder, put the photos inside and went back to the room where I'd found my clothes and searched through the desk. I found more photographs in folders. Most faces I recognised, though there were some who were not Craig or Heather or Janice or Mark. I replaced them before they made me vomit and went downstairs.

Mrs Bain sat in front of the television, the sound blaring out in defiance. I switched the set off and tossed the folders onto her lap.

'Take a look at those, Mrs Bain,' I sneered. 'See what a darling your son really is.'

I was watching her face very carefully. There was something I needed to know – her complicity in the actions of her son. If she even suspected, I would break her on a wheel and quarter her.

'I don't understand,' she said, her eyes reflecting her confusion. 'Please tell me what is going on. You burst in here like . . . like——'

'Just look inside those folders, Mrs Bain.'

She opened the first one tentatively, her fingers shaking. 'No!' she gasped, then, 'No!' and 'No!' again as she ploughed through the photos in manic desperation. 'It can't be. It's all lies! No! Not Dominic, never!'

Tears swept down her cheeks. She shrieked and hurled the folders across the room. The photos fluttered to the floor as her head collapsed in her hands and piteous chokes convulsed her body. 'It can't be true,' she wailed.

If she was acting, she deserved an Oscar.

'It's true, Mrs Bain.'

'I don't believe you. You made it up. It's all lies.'

'Perhaps you'd like to come down to the barn to see his latest victim.'

'Oh my God!'

'Yeah, you're going to need him.' The clock on the mantelpiece said ten thirty-five. I wished Dave Nicholl would hurry up.

'What time did your son leave?' I asked her.

'I don't know,'she said, her tone obstructive, petulant.

'How many more people have to die before you open your eyes, Mrs Bain? People will think you shielded your son from prosecution, that you knew what he was doing all the time. Unless you start cooperating now, you'll have a hard time convincing anyone of your innocence. Do you understand?'

Her head dipped and she began to cry again. Between sobs she said, 'About half-past nine, quarter to ten. He said he was going to see Cathy, that they had something to sort out.'

'He was going to Ballaig?'

She nodded, dabbing her eyes with a ball of tissue. 'He said something about the cabin, I can't remember what.'

'What cabin is this?'

'Up in the forest. John built it years ago. We used to go up there when Dominic was a child.'

'How do you get there?'

'You can drive up. There's a forestry track nearby that's hardly ever used.'

'Do you remember the way?'

'If nothing's changed . . .'

'Get dressed,' I told her.

She looked as if she was on the verge of arguing but something on my face changed her mind. She shuffled from the room. I picked up the prints, returned them to the folders then returned to the telephone. I dialled directory enquiries. It took three minutes for them to give me Cathy's number in Ballaig. I wrote it down, then dialled and listened to it ring. And ring and ring and ring. A gloomy weight settled on my heart.

Natasha was in the bathroom upstairs combing her hair in front of the mirror. She looked a little better but her hand was still shaking.

'How did you know my name?' she asked.

'Dominic told me.' I took a second look through the bathroom cabinet, found a bottle of pills that looked like painkillers and swallowed three.

'You've spoken to him?' Her accent was faint Aberdeen.

'Yesterday. In the Canny Man's, after you left.'

'How long have you known he was . . .'

'Since yesterday.'

'What happens now?'

Good question. I thought quickly. 'You wait here. Reinforcements will be here shortly and I want you here when they arrive.'

'You're not going to leave me here alone? What if he comes back?'

'He won't. He's gone. He's never coming back.'

'What do I do when they come?'

'Show them around. Especially the dark-room, the photos and the buildings at the end of the garden. Tell them there's a body down there, the ID's on the mantelpiece. Got that?'

She nodded apprehensively and followed me shakily down the stairs.

Mrs Bain was waiting in the hall, a little more composed in a heavy tweed coat, with a snakeskin handbag over her arm. The two women glared at each other. I picked up the phone and tried Cathy's number again. Still no reply. I called George Barrie.

His secretary, Martha, answered. He was out.

'Take this down, it's urgent,' I said and gabbled instructions. Two minutes later, I rang off. A car crunched down the drive.

'Ready?' I asked, taking Mrs Bain's elbow.

She straightened her shoulders, sniffed and nodded. I turned for a moment. Natasha was sitting on the stairs. 'Think you can manage?' I asked her. She offered me a weak smile and nodded. Dave was sitting patiently behind the wheel of the car with the engine running. I was never so glad to see him.

We headed north across the city.

'You look terrible, Frank. What the hell happened?' Nicholl was all smiles, dressed in denim and a thick fisherman's jersey, his dark curly hair still wet. His crutches were an armrest between our seats.

I told him briefly. When I'd finished, he looked at me steadily for a moment then motioned to the coffee and rolls on the back seat. Mrs Bain passed them forward. I took the flask gratefully and poured a cup. It was black and strong and went down my throat as sweet as a Frank Bruno jab.

'So you eventually called in Kettle?' Dave asked.

'I left a message for Barrie. It's up to him who he calls.'

'Christ, Frank, when will you stop playing games? These are people's lives we're dealing with here.'

'Barrie's instruction, Dave. That's all.'

'Aye. But you're no longer on the case . . .'

I felt myself getting angry.

'What could Kettle do? He doesn't even know what Bain looks like, nothing. He'd just slow everything down, and that's if he decided to believe me.'

'Okay, Frank. Calm down.' Nicholl half-turned to

Mrs Bain and said, 'You all right back there, dear?'

She didn't answer. She sat silently brooding, staring straight ahead, cocooned in her own private hell. I felt a little pity for her, perhaps a twinge of conscience, but not much. Love is blind, they say, and the kind of possessive love that every mother feels for her child may be the blindest love of all. I wasn't going to argue the point.

'What's in the rolls?' I asked.

'Cheese and pickle, chicken and tomato.'

I mumbled through a mouthful. 'Tell Dorothy thanks.'

'She thinks you're mad.'

'You told her?'

'So what? I agree with her.'

'You don't have a very high opinion of me this morning.'

'So? Neither do you.'

'Touché.'

'You're the one who's touched, pal. You should have called Kettle in yesterday, instead of trying to play the bloody hero.'

'Dave? Shut up, will you?'

'Yes, *sir*.'

I dozed a little then, coming awake about twenty minutes later as we passed through Callander, down the narrow twisting road I was gradually getting to know. For the next six, seven miles, we weaved through the forested slopes and then suddenly, coming out from the canopy of trees, we were there. As we passed the sign that said Ballaig, Mrs Bain spoke at last:

'Twenty-seven years and this is the first time I've ever

been back . . .' Her tone was a mixture of apprehension and regret.

'Over there on the right,' I told Dave. 'Behind the Escort.'

We pulled onto the wide pavement outside the guest-house. I turned to Mrs Bain.

'Is that your son's car?' I asked.

She nodded solemnly. 'Yes,' she said in a small voice.

I looked at Dave. 'You'd better wait out here with Mrs Bain while I check things out.'

'In case I get in the way, you mean?'

'In case you end up dead, okay?'

He smiled. 'You have a point. What happens if you don't come back?'

'You can have all my debts.'

I climbed out, went across and touched the bonnet of the Escort. It was still warm, but only just. I feared I was too late.

I tried the front door of the guest-house. It swung open. Hackles rose at the back of my neck. I stepped quietly inside and stood motionless in the dark hall for several minutes. I could hear the resonant ticking of the grandfather clock in the drawing-room off the hall and the sound of a car passing on the road outside. But that was all. I moved deeper into the house.

The guest-book was on the desk in the drawing-room. I flicked through it till I came to the last entry. No guests had arrived this morning, the last had left yesterday afternoon. Lucky guests.

I then checked all the downstairs rooms, expecting to find nothing. The kitchen showed no sign of activity, except for a tray on the sideboard with cold porridge, toast and a pot of cold tea. As I climbed the stairs I was thinking of Goldilocks.

The rooms were spotless and empty. I walked on down the hall. The door at the end of the corridor was marked 'Private'. It was unlocked. I entered and found another short corridor with two doors leading off. Behind the first was a bathroom. There was some kind of pulley contraption fixed over the bath, but nothing else of interest. I found Joe Gillespie behind the second door.

He was sprawled face down across one of the twin beds, the covers pulled back, his body twisted in the oversize pyjamas. There was a pool of blood below his head and on the carpet, more blood splattered high across the wall behind the bed. I leant over and felt the pulse at his neck. Nothing. Carefully, I turned him over, then left the room in a hurry.

A bottle of whisky stood on the sideboard in the drawing-room. I poured a double and drank it down. I could see Mrs Bain through the window, still sitting in the car, staring straight ahead. I wanted to run out and drag her from the car, haul her up the stairs and push her stupid face in the bloodstained sheets. I wanted to look in her eyes and scream, 'See what your precious son has been doing while you sat in front of that inane twittering box and let the world pass you by?'

Nicholl appeared at the door from the hall, swinging himself slowly into the room.

'You can't leave the stuff alone, can you?' he said, spotting the glass in my hand. There was untamed disgust in his voice.

'You want to take a look upstairs, feel free, I'll save you the bother and just pour you a glass,' I said. 'Cathy's husband, Joe, is lying on his bed with his throat slashed. Blood all over the shop, face cut to ribbons. You could hardly recognise him if you tried. Bain must have gone wild.'

Dave studied my face for a second, then came over.

'Sorry,' he said. 'Maybe I will join you.'

I searched through my wallet, found the slip of paper with Chief Inspector Eaves' phone number, went to the phone and dialled. He answered on the fourth ring, remembered who I was, and listened as I told him what I wanted. He said he'd get onto it right away and hung up. Nicholl looked at me, frowning.

'Who was that?' he asked.

'The man who led the original investigation up here, who put MacBean behind bars. He's still got friends on the force, says reinforcements should be here within twenty minutes.'

'So you finally stopped playing . . .'

'I can't wait twenty minutes. I'll have to go up there now, get Mrs Bain to show me the way. I only hope she still remembers.'

'The way where?'

'There's an old log cabin that MacBean built years ago. Somewhere in the forest. That's where Bain is headed with Cath, I'm sure of it.'

'And what do I do?'

I stopped at the door. 'There's a guy called Alec Lawrie, lives in a small white cottage by the church. He might know where the cabin is. Find him. If he doesn't, find out who does. A forestry official might know, or a local poacher. But do it quick. Now. Then wait here for Eaves or Kettle. Okay?'

'Aye. On your way. And Frank . . .'

'What?'

'Careful with the car. I haven't finished paying it off yet.'

# Chapter Twenty-Five

'Remember Joe Gillespie?' I asked, starting the car. 'Cathy's husband?'

'A *dear* man,' Mrs Bain replied, sounding preoccupied.

'A dead man, now he's met your son.'

That woke her up. She swivelled crumpling eyes to mine and cried, 'Oh my God! When will this ever end?' Her tears were tears of self-pity. Selfish to the core.

'How long does it take to climb to the cabin?'

'How can I know? I always went by car.'

We drove past the sign that offers welcome to Ballaig. 'Head out of the village and turn left, you said. Turn left where?'

'There, up ahead. Where the gate is.'

I turned in through the gate, on to the forestry road which climbed steeply. The surface was rough and pitted, but dry. The ditches were deep beds of pine-needles where the trees crowded the road.

'Keep to the Nature Trail. There should be signposts every quarter mile or so.'

I was doubtful. 'You sure you remember the way?'

'I remember. Nothing seems to have changed. I think there's a crossroads further up where three of the trails come together. That's where you turn off. It's an unmarked track. I don't know, but it could be overgrown by now. It was pretty overgrown then, when we used to come up this way.'

I was glad Dave's car was an automatic, the tracks twisted as they climbed. I was still suffering from the effects of the fall, but the pills I'd swallowed had blunted the edge off the pain. It was all I could do to concentrate on the road and keep the car out of the ditch. The higher we climbed, the more the trees closed in on us until only a thin grey ribbon of sky remained between the treetops. It seemed to make Mrs Bain nervous.

'What . . . what will happen to Dominic?' she asked. 'When you find him, what will you do?'

'My duty,' I lied.

'You won't hurt him, will you? He's a good boy, really.'

'What does he do when he's bad?'

She was only listening to what she wanted to hear – her own voice. She ignored the sarcasm and carried on:

'I can't understand where I went wrong. I did my best. He was always a difficult child, never really grew up. When Jamie died, it affected him deeply. Perhaps——'

'Is that the crossroads ahead?' I broke in.

She paused and squinted through the windscreen. 'I think so. Yes, I'm sure. I recognise it now. You have to take the left-hand trail for about a hundred yards, then the track to the cabin branches off that. Not far now.'

I wondered if Nicholl would find Lawrie. I wondered if Lawrie knew where the cabin was. I wondered if Bain would hear the car approaching and what he would do if he did.

I asked Mrs Bain about Lawrie.

'Of course,' she replied. 'He helped John build the place. In fact, John spent more time with Alec Lawrie than he did his own wife.' After all these years there was still a trace of bitterness in her voice. There were times I hated the pettiness of the human race.

The track we wanted was disguised as a tangle of undergrowth. 'Are you sure this is it?' I asked.

'Positive.'

No car was going to force its way through the dense screen ahead of us, so I stopped and climbed out. My hip screamed but I didn't. Just.

'Out,' I said. Margaret Bain turned up her nose and frowned and glared all in the same expression, but she got out.

'How far to the cabin?'

'Five minutes. The track comes out near the top of the gorge and you have to work your way down the side. It's quite dangerous sometimes if it's been raining or snowing.'

'What gorge are you talking about?'

'The one where the cabin is, of course. There's a cliff one side of the cabin and a river the other.'

'Okay. Are you ready?'

'But you can't expect me to go through that.'

'I can and I do. Take my arm.'

'You're a bully, that's what you are. I'm an old woman, you know. How can you expect me to——'

I brought my face down to six inches from hers. 'Mrs

Bain,' I said. 'You will come with me and not make another sound – is that understood?'

She looked up at me with wounded little girl's eyes then nodded imperceptibly before slipping her arm through mine as if we were off on a Sunday afternoon stroll.

It took us nearly five minutes to make a thirty yard headway. The track had all but disappeared, was barely discernible through the dense thickets of thorn and vine and fallen trees. Mrs Bain found a new complaint for every step of the way – and maybe she had cause: I, too, was struggling, stumbling often in desperate haste, driven on by the fear of being too late, weighed down by an ever-growing sense of hopelessness. It wasn't quite the blind leading the blind but it wasn't far removed.

The depth of the forest was full of sound. Even the silence seemed audible. Birds started from the trees, warned of our approach. Insects buzzed. Branches snapped and twigs cracked beneath our heavy-footed progress. Things moved – things without name, things unseen – rustling in the deep cushion of pine-needles. Cobwebs glistened. Somewhere ahead, through the brief snatches of silence, was the sound of water. We were on course.

Suddenly, the voice of terror split the morning air, cutting through the calm like a scalpel through flesh. It came from over to the right, a scream that stopped us in our tracks and sent shivers down my spine. A woman's scream. Cathy.

Ignoring the protests of the old woman, I broke into a lumbering run. Branches whipped across my face and chest, roots snagged at my feet. I picked myself up again and again, pushed myself on, heedless of the grinding ache in my hip, the stabbing pain in my shoulder. Blood hammered in my ears like a movie soundtrack. As another spate of screams curdled the air, I burst from the shadow of the trees.

Below me lay thirty, forty yards of open space sloping down to the edge of the cliff. I couldn't see the cabin or the river but the gorge dropped away on each side, and the tree-speckled screes looked steep but not impossible to climb. I searched for movement but saw none. Then a strangled cry gave me direction.

She was scrambling up the scree below me to the right. For every three yards she gained, she slipped back two. Her hands clawed at roots, at plants, at heavy boulders, anything to drag her up. Only ten yards from the top now. Every few paces jerking her head round, wasting precious seconds. No sign of Bain yet, but her increased anxiety told its own story, screaming from her every pore. Three yards from the top and Bain came bounding into sight. He was making good time, his long easy strides sure on the crumbling surface, gaining on her every second of his climb, his face a grim mask of determination.

Cathy staggered and slipped back down the slope, losing painful ground, Bain only twenty yards behind her, a tight smile now cracking the mask. With an effort fired by desperation, Cathy hurled herself the final few yards and gained the crest, then ran across the top of the cliff. Bain was there seconds later. She had thirty yards on him. Twenty-five. His body was swift and sure as a mountain lynx. Twenty yards. Cathy glanced behind her, a cry breaking from her lips. Ten yards. Hunter closes for

301

the kill. Then five yards. Four. Three. Two. Dominic Bain dropped her like a tiger dropping a rabbit.

I was already out from cover and running, handcuffs gripped tight in my hand. Neither of them saw me coming. Cathy struggled and kicked and scratched as Bain ripped at her clothes. Her blouse came off in his hands. She gouged at his eyes. He punched her in the mouth and she fell back, stunned. He tore at her jeans and dragged them from her passive body. She came to and kicked at his face, drawing blood from his nose. He hit her again, the blow glancing off the side of her head, sending her spinning. Throwing himself on her, he pinioned her arms with one hand, his other scrabbling at his zipper as he used his knees to force her legs apart. Still she fought. Still neither of them heard my approach.

Five yards off and Cathy saw me, her eyes opening wide. Bain must have sensed me too, for he turned as I swung the cuffs and they caught him full in the face. Cathy heaved and Bain rolled from her body, hands clutching at his torn face. I kicked at him as he rolled. In the kidney, the liver, the groin, the stomach – whatever he presented. And still he rolled, trying to block my feet as we edged closer and closer to the edge of the cliff. Then the good little pig connected with Bain's face and heard a bone go crack. I had time to smile and draw my foot back for the curtain shot – then someone screamed and blew my concentration. It was the old woman yelling as she stumbled down the slope. I turned back to Bain – but too late. He was up on his feet fast, facing me squarely, snarling obscenities between his gritted teeth. No time for pleasantries, I had to do it now . . . or never. I dropped my injured shoulder, watched him fall for it, then from somewhere down near my feet I brought up my right fist and caught him under the chin. I swear his feet left the ground. By the time he shook his dazed head back to consciousness, I had him prone and cuffed and was kneeling on his back. I twisted his arms up his back till he screamed, then put my mouth close to his ear and said:

'Say life.'

'Life,' he groaned. 'Life, life, life, life!'

'Good little pervert,' I said, and released his arms. 'Because that's what you're going to get.' I was breathing hard.

Behind me, Cathy was climbing back into her jeans, smoothing herself down. Her blouse was a waste of time, She caught my eye and forced a smile. Mrs Bain was a few yards off, hands on her knees, gasping air into her lungs. Cathy glanced at her, then at me.

'Who's that?' she asked, her voice cracking.

'His mother,' I peeled off my jacket and threw it to her. She slipped it gratefully about her shoulders and pulled it close.

Dominic Bain lay inert and silent. Since the last time I'd seen him – was it only this morning? – he'd changed his clothes from black to combat. I searched through his camouflage jacket, removed an ivory-backed cut-throat razor from one pocket, a small camera from another. I found nothing else. I tossed the camera aside and put the razor in my own pocket.

Mrs Bain hobbled the last ten yards, stood glaring down, first at me, then at her son, whose face was turned away.

'Dominic!'

'Yes, Mother-dear?'

'Look at me when I talk to you!'

Bain turned his head to look at her. 'Yes, Mother-dear?'

She sank to her knees, threw me a dirty stare, then tried to cradle his head in her arms. 'Why, Dominic? Why, for God's sake?'

'You wouldn't understand.'

'After all we did for you when Jamie died?'

Until that moment, Cathy had ignored Mrs Bain, held back perhaps by the shock of her ordeal or just plain disgust. Now, she suddenly sprang forward, her fists balled at her sides.

'What do you mean by that?' she shouted in the old woman's face. 'All you did for him when Jamie died?'

Mrs Bain cringed beneath Cathy's whiplash voice.

'Dominic killed Jamie,' I explained gently. 'He strung him up and then let his father take the blame. That's the kind of guy he is.'

'It wasn't like that at all,' Mrs Bain yelled. 'John volunteered. He gave himself up willingly. He didn't want Dominic's life wasted. He wanted to give him a chance.'

'That's probably what you've been telling yourself all these years,' I said, waving aside her spluttering objections. 'The way I see it, it was you who persuaded your husband to shoulder the blame. You made him believe he would only get a few years, and then he'd be out and free again. You told him if the truth came out, Dominic would be locked away in an asylum for the rest of his life. Am I right?'

'You're nothing but a dirty filthy liar!'

'Is it the truth?' Cathy asked me.

I shrugged. 'It's the closest you'll ever get to it now. It's the only way to figure out why John MacBean did what he did. He wasn't the only one in on it either. There were others. Mrs Bovellie and Alec Lawrie are two I know. They concocted a story and covered up for Dominic. No-one had any reason to disbelieve MacBean's confession and who would have credited the mind of an eleven-year-old being capable of such evil.'

'But why did he kill Jamie?' Cathy pleaded, then shouted. 'Dominic, why did you kill Jamie?'

Bain said nothing, so I continued:

'Mrs Bain here was having an affair with Jamie's father. They were there in the house that afternoon, doing what lovers do. Dominic must have caught Jamie watching them – he referred to it in the poem he sent the press, how Jamie was a spy. Maybe he thought it was some kind of conspiracy between Jamie and Dr Robertson or he was trying to protect his mother or his father – I don't know. But I do know he hanged Jamie in the same way he killed Craig and Janice, Heather and Mark. Then he sat back and watched his father go down for murder.'

I looked at Mrs Bain for confirmation or denial but she avoided my gaze, began rocking back and forth on her knees, and sobbing as she stroked her son's hair.

'Why?' she kept repeating. 'Why didn't you tell your mother? I could have helped you, Dominic, I really could have helped.'

'You murdered Jamie . . .' Cathy said, staring at Dominic whose eyes were now closed. Her voice was emotionless. 'You murdered my best friend. You killed my husband. All those poor children . . .'

It was time to move.

I had to shout to get their attention. 'Cathy. Take Mrs Bain. We're going to the car.'

Mrs Bain was doing the grieving widow, Cathy had to haul her from her son and lift her to her feet. When they were clear, and before Bain knew what was happening, I unlocked one of the cuffs and snapped it over my own wrist. Then I told him to stand.

Arrogance was the sneer on his lips as he smiled.

'Are you going to carry me or what?'

'I don't need to,' I said, looking off up the slope. He followed my gaze, saw the line of uniformed men advancing out of the trees. Without warning, Margaret Bain broke free from Cathy's grasp and flung herself at her son.

'Dominic!' she wailed. 'Don't let them take you away . . .'

A shout distracted my attention. I looked up to see Chief Inspector Kettle storming down towards us. I had time to recognise the stooped form of Alec Lawrie, the ugly face of DI Pitts and the vast bulk of Harry before Cathy's shouted warning fell on my ears a second too late. Suddenly my wrist with the handcuff was yanked up my back and I was looking down the blade of a knife that would have made Norman Bates seethe with envy.

Bain yelled at the line of police now thirty yards off.

'Stop where you are! One move and he dies!'

The line came to a halt. Everyone looked at Kettle. Everyone except Margaret Bain and Cathy standing between us and the cliff. Nobody moved or said a word. I didn't even breathe.

Then Kettle – the bastard – stepped forward.

'You haven't got a chance, Dominic,' he said, his voice echoing off the walls of the gorge. 'Give yourself up. You won't come to any harm.' Walking slowly forward all the while.

'Put the knife down, Dominic. It's the end of the road.'

I felt Bain's body tense. 'Do you want this man to die?' he shrieked. The blade of the knife shook against my throat.

Kettle continued to walk forward. He was fifteen yards from where we stood and I could see his eyes. He was looking at me, not at Bain, when he spoke.

'He's expendable,' he said.

'You what?' I yelled. The blade cut into my skin.

Bain was close to breaking point, his whole body shivering. 'Don't come any closer! I mean it, I'll kill him.'

'No you won't, Dominic,' Kettle was saying. 'You're not that stupid. You gave us a good run for your money, but now it's all over. So put down the knife and let's call it a day.'

It was a kitchen knife, with a long solid blade and a chunky yellow plastic handle. It had probably been in Margaret Bain's kitchen in Morningside when I'd turned for a moment earlier on. We all make mistakes.

Kettle, ten yards and closing. He gestured at Cathy to move away. She had to drag Margaret Bain with an arm around her waist, lead the broken old woman up the slope. She turned once to catch my eye and I saw concern there, deep in the powder blue kegs of her eyes. But deeper still lurked something else, something cold and dead in her mind, like the memory of a lover she now despised. The tired smile she offered was at the same time full of hope and sad regret. Then she continued up the slope.

Bain was a plane shuddering at the end of a runway. His eyes swirled like fish in a bowl. Lips drawn back in deathly grimace, erratic breath hot on my face. I felt the warmth of blood trickle down my neck, the prickle of sweat at my collar. Shoulder forgotten, hip forgotten, I was too busy watching the closing few seconds of my life.

Kettle had stopped, was standing there with his hand outstretched, saying:

'Give me the knife, Dominic.'

Anger burst like a flood inside me. Was I going to wait around for ever while these maniacs played out their game of piggy-in-the-middle?

I let my knees buckle, my body go limp, twisting as I fell. The deadweight was enough to pull Bain off balance, the twist enough to pull me away from the jerk of the knife. Vision became a kaleidoscopic flicker of images as time slowed to witness my struggle for life. I grabbed his wrist and turned it savagely. He screamed as the knife fell to the grass, his mouth a frozen rictus of agony, his eyes no longer human.

Kettle was on the move.

I lay helplessly by the edge of the cliff.

Bain looked desperately around. He saw Mother-dear climbing the slope. Head twisted round, unable to tear her eyes from his, terror screaming from her haunted eyes. He raised himself to his full height and a strangled cry broke through his snarling lips, bounced off the walls of the gorge.

'Mother-ther-ther-ther!'

Then he launched himself over the cliff.

# Chapter Twenty-Six

My arm left its socket, the weight of Bain's body dragging me towards the edge. Inch by inch, gaining
momentum. Pain so great, it wasn't pain at all. Just
warmth – gentle, cosy warmth. I looked down, saw the
cabin. Saw the river. All so peaceful, so calm. Another
world. How easy to let myself go and fall, fall, fall, till
there was nowhere left to fall.

Cathy's screaming brought me back.

'Kill the bastard! Kill him!'

Mother-dear screamed too.

'My son, my son – don't let him die!'

Bain, laughing at the end of the world, was kicking
against the face of the cliff like an abseiler.

'Come on down, come on down!'

No control. Body inching closer to the point of
imbalance. Senses ebbing. I watched my life slip slowly
from my hands.

'Come on down!'

Watched Bain swing against the wall, brace himself
and push.

My body jerked forward . . . and stopped. Kettle
dropped from the sky and landed on my back, forcing

the breath from my body. I didn't care. I couldn't breathe. Hands hauled at my feet. I didn't care, I was dead and this was hell.

I was stretched across the rack. Or maybe it was someone else. Branding irons hung on dripping dungeon walls. The devil at one end, the Lord at the other. Yelling at each other across my cracking bones, my splitting skin:

*He's mine, he's mine!*

*No, he's mine, he's mine!*

Piggy-in-the-middle for ever and ever.

Grey, grey sky, pregnant with rain. Voices near and voices far. The words meaningless. I was lying on my back, a feathery rain tickling at my face. McMorran. They were talking about me. *To* me.

'Can you walk?'

I could stand.

There was more to the world than just grey, grey sky. There was nausea and pain and vomit on my shoes. There were soothing comments and steadying hands. There was Cathy. There was Dominic Bain shackled between two uniformed officers. He was crying, howling, no longer human. There was Margaret Bain, the husk of his mother being helped up the slope by a WPC.

There was Harry, and DI Pitts. They were laughing at something. Something funny, perhaps. A joke.

And there was Chief Inspector Kettle. He had something to tell me. He nodded at Bain being led away.

'There's one at least who didn't die on you.'

I smiled. I could afford it. I was feeling benevolent.

Cathy slipped an arm around my waist. Poor me.

We walked towards the trees.

If you have enjoyed this book and would like to receive details on other Walker mystery titles, please write to:

Mystery Editor
Walker and Company
720 Fifth Avenue
New York, NY 10019